Determ... ...ile at the next turn and
what I ... learn. I headed up the street and then, in
front of ... ...rocery, a cluster of senior citizens stood as
if in conference. It reminded me of the scene across the street
from Grandy's house. Sweat prickled my scalp, from nerves
or the heat or both, and I quick-timed it to Aggie's Gifts and
Antiques and burst through the door.

"Carrie?" I called over the jingling of the bell. "Hello? Are
you here?"

Impatient, I circled the perimeter of the store, passing by
jewelry armoires, quilt racks, and an old vanity table to where
the register sat midway along the western wall. Back to me,
she was climbing down from a step stool, feather duster in
her hand, when I located her.

"Carrie," I said again.

Her eyes found me and opened wide. "Oh my gosh! Georgia, is it true? It's not true, is it? It just can't be."

"I—uh—is what true? No, wait." I squinched my eyes shut
for a moment, as if that action alone could pause the conversation. "What happened at the hardware store?" I asked, then
opened my eyes.

Carrie's eyes remained wide, and were now accompanied
by a slack jaw. "It's Andy Edgers," she said. "Bill Harper
found him yesterday, dead in the back room with . . .
with . . . " She swallowed hard, and I imagined she had a knot
in her throat as big as the one in my stomach. "With his . . .
head . . . bashed in. Murdered."

D0205321

ILL-GOTTEN PANES

Jennifer
McAndrews

BERKLEY PRIME CRIME, NEW YORK

THE BERKLEY PUBLISHING GROUP
Published by the Penguin Group
Penguin Group (USA) LLC
375 Hudson Street, New York, New York 10014

USA • Canada • UK • Ireland • Australia • New Zealand • India • South Africa • China

penguin.com

A Penguin Random House Company

ILL-GOTTEN PANES

A Berkley Prime Crime Book / published by arrangement with the author

Berkley Prime Crime Books are published by The Berkley Publishing Group.
BERKLEY® PRIME CRIME and the PRIME CRIME logo
are trademarks of Penguin Group (USA) LLC.

For information, address: The Berkley Publishing Group,
a division of Penguin Group (USA) LLC,
375 Hudson Street, New York, New York 10014.

ISBN: 978-0-425-26795-0

PUBLISHING HISTORY
Berkley Prime Crime mass-market edition / July 2014

PRINTED IN THE UNITED STATES OF AMERICA

10 9 8 7 6 5 4 3 2 1

Cover illustration by Stephen Gardner.
Cover design by George Long.
Interior text design by Kelly Lipovich.

For my sisters Judy, Laura, and Carolyn

ACKNOWLEDGMENTS

Because there is no possible way this book would exist without her, the first and biggest thanks I can extend goes to my editor, Faith Black. For years I wanted to work with her, and I'm so glad it was this book that at last made it happen. May this be the start of many good books to come. Further thanks to all the wonderful people at Berkley Prime Crime who went out of their way to welcome me into their fold and make this book the best it could be—especially Stephen Gardner, who is responsible for that gorgeous cover.

Big thanks to my family near and far, especially Judy Grant, Laura Finan, and Carolyn Hassett. When I'm down they pick me up, when the world is crumbling they stand beside me, and when a celebration is in order, together we do the Time Warp with joyous abandon. You just can't beat that.

Acknowledgments

Continous gratitude to my critique partners, creative cohorts, and all-around besties Julie O'Connell, Linda Gerber, and Ginger Calem—mercy buckets!

Finally, as ever, thanks to my husband, Bob, and my daughters, Tracy and Christine, for the brainstorming, the endless cups of tea, and the noise-cancelling headphones that make this dream possible.

For generations, my family followed a simple principle: If everything goes wrong, go back to the beginning. Every back to the beginning my mother undertook—every time her marriage tanked or her job failed to support us—she went back to the house she grew up in, with me in tow, to get back on her feet. Thus, it stood to reason that when my job fell apart in the midst of an epic investment banking scandal and my fiancé invited me to move out because he couldn't stand the heat, I had no urge to take shelter in the over-decorated apartment where my mother currently resided. The only place in my life that had enough consistency to qualify as a place to go back to was that same rambling house my mother spent her childhood in and retreated to throughout her life. I took up residence in my grandfather's spare room in the past-its-prime town of Wenwood, New York, population eighty-four hundred and me.

Make no mistake. I made a good effort to get back on my feet without leaving the city. But jobs were scarce for brokenhearted accountants caught in a scandal, and not being able to find a decent, affordable place to live on my own made the challenge of starting over seem insurmountable. And the lure of the familiarity and acceptance of my grandfather also seemed insurmountable.

So I had landed in Wenwood and there I would stay until such time as my life had direction again. Or my grandfather got sick of me turning the "hi-fi" too loud, I got sick of him sneaking cookies into the bathroom, and it was time for me to move out. For the time being, though, I was a Wenwood resident. And on a hot Monday morning in the early days of summer, I headed along the pitted, cobbled main road, admiring the weathered shops lining the village on my way to run some errands.

I steered my grandfather's Jeep into the sixteen-space parking lot behind Village Grocery and slid into a spot in the shade of a black walnut tree whose branches overhung the boundary fence. With my stash of reusable bags in one hand and my list in the other, I crossed the cracked macadam and ducked in through the back door of the grocer's. This was not the thing to do if you wanted to slip in unnoticed.

My eyes had yet to adjust to the sudden shift in light when a cheery voice called, "Good morning, Georgia!"

I stood just inside the door at the back end of the produce aisle and tried to identify the hulking shape of the man who greeted me. "Morning, Misterrr . . ." I began, hoping he would throw his name into the hole in my memory. No luck. He slowly came into focus, a half-bald gent in a white polo shirt and pale khaki trousers standing behind a fruit-strewn cart. His face was familiar, but his name remained elusive. While the awkward silence built, his smile faded.

"Harper," he said at last. "Bill Harper."

"Right. Harper. Sorry." I tried for a smile; it might have come off looking like I was about to be ill.

He returned this with a grin that might be gas. "Can I help you find anything?" he asked.

I pointed along the produce aisle stretching behind him. "This is all I need."

"That right? You're not going to pick up anything for Pete?"

I called my grandfather Grandy. Hearing him referred to by his given name would take some adjustment. "Not today, thanks. Plenty of cake and cookies in the house as it is," I joked, chuckling a little and looking to Mr. Harper as a fellow conspirator.

He scowled.

I stopped chuckling, cleared my throat, but his scowl didn't budge. "Okay, then. Well. You know I think I'll just hold off on the groceries until I've done the rest of my errands. Don't want anything to spoil in this heat." I forced a smile then scuttled past Mr. Harper. The grocery store aisles were no more than forty feet long yet I wished like mad they were shorter.

Talk about getting off on the wrong foot. Grandy had

Jennifer McAndrews

introduced me to Mr. Harper in the middle of the Sunday
after-church rush at Rozelle's Bakery. Really, was it so
unforgivable that I couldn't remember his name? I met a
lot of people that day, before I had my coffee. I'm not a
miracle worker.

The front door swung open automatically at my approach, and I left the market feeling far less assured than
when I'd entered. I kept my head down as I walked away,
reluctant to make eye contact with anyone else who might
expect me to remember their name and take offense if I
didn't.

Homesickness rushed up and blindsided me. I missed
New York City. I missed the noise and the fast pace and
the strange marriage of anonymity and camaraderie. In
the life I'd led, I knew Mr. Wang operated the produce
shop on Third Street that sold the most amazing Asian
pears. I'd shopped there every week. But it had taken more
than eight months of residency for me learn his name, and
a few months more for him to start putting some of the
juiciest pears aside for me.

I missed the life I'd left.

Stopping on the old brick sidewalk as though something more substantial than a tear had caught my eye,
I turned to face the display window of a narrow shop. I
used the moment and the illusion to take a deep breath.
Inside the shop, on the other side of AGGIE'S GIFTS AND
ANTIQUES painted on the glass, a smiling face gazed out
at me. The woman waved then motioned emphatically for
me to step inside.

Fighting the urge to look over my shoulder to see who

she was waving at nearly made me shake, but I knew there were few people on the street. Who else but the elderly and unemployed would be wandering the village mid-morning on a Monday?

With my forehead wrinkled in confusion, I sidestepped to the door—a lightweight wooden door with three-over-three windows, the kind you'd find on any home in any town where theft and vandalism were rarities. Sure enough, pushing the door open sent the little bell above it jingling. No high-tech electronic sensors for Wenwood, not when the old-fashioned methods worked just fine.

I stopped just inside the shop, angling my head to where the woman stood. "I . . ." I began, but I had no idea where to go from there.

"You're Georgia, aren't you? Pete Keene's grand-daughter?" She was older than me, but not by much, mid-thirties maybe, simply dressed in a polo shirt and jeans.

"Um . . ." I hated to ask it, I really did. "How did you know . . ."

"Oh, your hair." She nodded as if her response were perfectly obvious.

I forced a smile but I'm afraid I might have come off looking constipated. My hair is, in fact, remarkable. Not remarkable in the sense of salon-inspired conditioner commercials or studio cut and style. Not even in the wild heyday of fast finance could I afford hair like that. I had curly orange hair. And when I say that, I'm not being modest about my auburn tresses. Little Orphan Annie would laugh at my hair. Irish red, corkscrew curls, and fine as the day is long. Oh, yeah, I was a looker all right.

"Okay, so what is it that . . ." I had no idea how to ask the right question. Did she want something from me? Need something from me? Want to know when Grandy would give in already and start selling off some of the old family heirlooms? A quick scan of the shop, with its frames and old crystal, earthenware and accent tables, assured me that most of Grandy's living room would look right at home in an antiques shop.

"It's in the back," she said, and headed away from the window and to the rear of the store.

"I'm sorry. What?" Was I supposed to follow her?

She spun, hand over her heart, and laughed. "I get ahead of myself." Waving me closer, she continued, "I have a lamp in the back that needs a little restoration work. Pete was by the other day and told me you had some skill with stained glass. I was hoping you could look at it and let me know, well, you know, if you could help."

Okay, so one of the few things I took with me from my city life and carted back to my second-chance starting line was a half-dozen boxes of stained glass materials and equipment. Yes, it was technically bringing the past to the future. But the best thing I found to relax me while I was working at Washington Heritage Financial was glass. And okay, I took up stained glass because the receptionist for the company advised me to take up a craft instead of blowing money on a psychotherapist. After looking up the cost of psychotherapists in the city, I figured crafting was worth a shot. I tried a few different things, learned I was more dangerous with knitting needles than I was skilled with them, ditto for quilting needles, before I discovered the immense satisfaction of breaking glass *just so* and assembling the aftermath of destruction into something beautiful. All the scattered pieces had a very special place. I was hooked.

So there should be no surprise that I eagerly followed the shopkeep through a narrow passageway to the back of the store.

"Are you Aggie?" I asked as she led me past an employee-only washroom and a paper-strewn inlaid desk that looked precisely like a piece I'd once admired in the Metropolitan Museum of Art.

She reached for a switch plate, and the far end of the space was flooded with light. Stacked tables, tilting curio cabinets, and an old schoolhouse desk cluttered the right side of room, with smaller pieces shelved along the left. "Lord, no. Aggie was *my* grandmother. She ran the place until her Corolla was totaled in a snowplow drive-by and then she was off to Palm Beach, where it never snows and no one even owns a plow."

While she rattled on about Granny's home in Florida and her mother's disinterest in running the antiques shop, I walked to the shelving to my left, chockablock with dusty miscellanea and stacks of dishes. On the floor in front of it sat a lamp that called to me as loudly as a Godiva salted chocolate bar.

I tiptoed close and knelt beside the lamp. Resting my shopping bag on the ground, I reached to finger the edge of the shade. It was a Tiffany style, better than two feet in diameter, with delicate iron scrollwork forming the base. The shade had a classic floral motif: full-blown blossoms and trailing leaves dappled by unseen sunlight. It was also missing a large portion out of one side, as though the lamp had fallen over and the impact had shattered the side on which it landed. A hint of sorrow washed through me to see the forlorn condition of such a beautiful piece. A wilted flower needs water to restore it to beauty; this lamp needed me.

And yes, I know that sounds super-presumptuous and self-aggrandizing. But I'd just lost my job, my home, and my fiancé. I was in need of a little positive-self-talk pick-me-up. And maybe some of that Godiva.

"What do you think?" Aggie's granddaughter asked. I had no idea when she'd stopped talking about the migratory patterns of her female ancestors. The lamp held me enraptured.

I stood and wiped the dust from my palms. "All right if I take it back to Pete's to work on it?"

Her hand fluttered at her throat. "Really? Are you sure? You really think you can restore it?"

"I can try." Then I confessed, "I would be truly honored to try."

Her smile did more to start a friendship than all her chatter about Florida. "I'm Carrie, by the way," she said. She extended a hand and ducked her head a bit. "I should have started with that, huh?"

"Leading with the lamp was good."

Laughing, she shook her head. "You must think I'm crazy."

"Well, now that you mention it . . ." I grinned to show her I was kidding. There was something about Carrie—

about the way she stood close enough to be friendly but far enough to be respectful, about the way she looked straight at me when she spoke, and the way she kept her back straight and shoulders squared like she was ready to take on the world—that I instantly liked. "Just one question, though. You said you knew me by my hair, but . . ."

"Oh, that. Helen told me you'd be easy to spot." Carrie wandered to the doorway leading to the front of the shop and peered out—perhaps in case an antiques hunter with highly honed espionage skills had entered the shop without setting off the jingly bell.

"And Helen is . . ." A butcher block table huddled beside the lamp, its surface scattered with gift boxes in a variety of sizes. Spools of boldly colored curling ribbon were affixed to the side of the table, tails dangling like strings of gems in the sunlight of the high-set window at the back of the room. I tugged on a bit of bright green, the texture of the ribbon somehow soothing beneath my fingertips. "I don't remember meeting anyone named Helen."

Carrie returned her attention to me. "Helen is Grace's sister."

Not a big help. "So who's Grace?"

"Grace runs the luncheonette. See, she gets her rolls from Rozelle's Bakery. And I guess you were in there with your granddad?" Carrie's brow puckered, intimating she herself wasn't quite clear on the progression of the gossip. I couldn't blame her. That was quite a chain to go through. My arrival in town and visit to the bakery appeared to have made something of a stir. I wasn't sure whether I should be flattered or frightened.

I told Carrie I had a few things to pick up while I was in town and promised to stop back for the lamp before I headed home. Then I was back on the sidewalk still carrying my empty grocery bag. If I'd had a schedule to maintain, I would have been a full half hour behind. Since the only schedule I had to adhere to ran on the whims of my imagination, I walked slowly up the street, nodding good morning to the odd passerby, trying to match them with the vehicles lining the road. A battered pickup, a faded minivan, a late-model Buick . . . those people I felt confident in identifying. But I had no idea who on earth would have driven the Jaguar parked in front of the hardware store. Surely anyone who drove a Jaguar could afford to hire someone to do their household handiwork.

Hand on the door latch, I eyed the sleek car at the curb, dimly aware of the sounds of heated words coming from the other side of the hardware store entrance. For a moment I considered delaying my stop there for a while longer, at least until the shouting stopped. Certainly I could take the time. But I'd spent too much time in a too crowded city to be dissuaded by the bluster of arguing men. It didn't sound as though anything was being smashed or thrown, so in I went.

Like the door at the antiques shop, a jingling bell announced my entrance. Voices that were no more than disjointed sound clarified into words.

". . . need you coming in here and treating me like some country bumpkin. I've been in this business for forty-two years! Forty-two years! I was sorting two-penny nails before your parents even said 'I do.' "

I edged along the perimeter of the store, scanning shelves for caulking guns and caulk. Nothing I spied as I peered up the dusty aisles inspired me with confidence that I would find anything I sought.

"I respect the experience you bring to the field—" This second voice sounded measurably calmer than the first, though easily as firm.

At the last aisle I resigned myself to the necessity of asking the hardware store owner for his assistance. It was impossible for the shop not to have a caulking gun. More than likely it was a behind-the-counter item. Still, I sensed this was not the best time to request help.

"*Respect?* You haven't shown me an ounce of respect since you and the rest of your *associates* first came in here, trying to snow me with stories of revitalization and renewal. Those were your words: *revitalization* and *renewal.* And look how far you *haven't* got since then."

Turning back the way I came, I tiptoed for the door.

"Mr. Edgers, a project of this scale takes careful organization and timing. I assure you we are going forward with construction as planned—"

"Oh, you assure me, do you? Funny, I don't seem to have any faith in your assurances anymore. I don't need promises, Himmel. I need you to place that order, or else."

"*Or else*, Mr. Edgers? That sounds almost like you're working your way to an ultimatum." The man's voice went all smooth and shrewd at the same time. A shiver worked its way up my spine in response.

There followed a quiet that was almost as unnerving as the shouting had been. I stopped and stood as still as

I could, unwilling to call attention to myself. I wanted to creep out quietly. But what with the bell and all, it was really too late for me to slip away unnoticed.

"And you. Whoever you are that's creeping around my store," Mr. Edgers called loudly, "I know you're here to back up your boss. You not man enough to show yourself?"

Was I not man enough? Lord, I hoped not. But I was woman enough to show myself even though I'd rather make a quick getaway. I had bigger things to fear than some guy in a hardware store—I hoped.

I moved into the aisle that gave me a clear view of the register at the back of the store, and the owner had a clear view of me. He had both palms flat on the battered wood counter before him, his wrinkled face drawn in a scowl. Some long-ingrained conditioning made me expect to see his expression shift into surprise when he saw I was a female. When his expression turned to one of distaste instead, I was the one surprised.

"What do you want?" he practically growled.

His unconcealed animosity rendered me speechless.

The man who stood facing him, the man I presumed to be Mr. Himmel, turned in my direction. He folded his arms across his chest, the soft fabric of his pale gray suit not making a sound, and tipped his head slightly as he regarded me with the bluest eyes I'd ever seen outside of a Tiffany stained glass window.

"Well?" Edgers snapped.

I flinched and took one cautious step forward. Great. A surpassingly handsome man stood at the end of the aisle, probably the guy who owned the Jaguar, and I was dressed for a day of errands and caulking the bathtub. Plus, you know, Little Orphan Annie. "I can come back," I said.

But Edgers's eyes narrowed. "Oh, hell. You're Georgia Kelly, aren't you? You're Pete's family."

I nodded, smiled a little. "Yeah, but that's okay, I can come back. I see you're busy." And there was a great big chain store just over an hour away. Suddenly, the long drive didn't seem like such an inconvenience.

"That's not the best idea you could have," Edgers snapped. "Didn't your granddad tell you anything? Didn't he tell you not to bother coming in here asking for my help?" He leaned closer over the counter, as though at any moment he might vault over it and make a mad grab for my throat.

I was in the twilight zone. And it was scary. Even Mr. Himmel looked all at once like he'd rather be elsewhere.

"I'm sorry," I said somewhat defensively. "He never mentioned any—"

"Now whose fault is that?"

"Whoa." I held up a hand. Mr. Himmel shifted his gaze to Edgers, lowered his brow in something that might have been thought. Or a migraine. "Enough already. I'm leaving. Happily."

I turned my back on the men and stomped toward the door. Of course, the stupid curls bouncing on my head probably took a measure of dignity out of my exit.

2

On the sidewalk I glared at the Jag. I thought about kicking the car. Probably the thing was alarmed. I shifted my focus to the tires. Tires weren't usually alarmed, were they? Seemed like I should have done something to show my displeasure at Himmel just standing there, watching Mr. Edgers spit vitriol at me, without so much as pretending he might step in and do something gentlemanly like defend my honor or my innocence or my right to unimpeded retail indulgence.

Jerks, the both of them.

I reined in my anger enough to retrieve the lamp from Aggie's Gifts and Antiques and stock up on fresh produce—and some ice cream—without lashing out at any of the *nice* people of Wenwood. Unfortunately, being alone in the car on the drive back to Grandy's allowed me to work up a good head of steam. By the time I pulled into the driveway and climbed out of the Jeep, I was seething.

Seriously, who talked like that to a customer? Who turned away potential business with insults? And what's more, who stood there and took that treatment and meekly ran away?

That last one would be me. And it was me I was most angry with. And disappointed. I was made of tougher stuff—or at least I had been. If this new mild me was an effect of having my life turned upside down, I was going to have some adjusting to do. Better yet, I was going to have to get over myself.

Grocery bag in hand, I slammed the back hatch on the Jeep. All things made of glass were best left untouched while rage was in the blood, so I left the damaged stained glass beauty for a calmer moment. Still, Grandy was at the threshold of the house, holding open the screen door and peering at me with concern.

"Go easy on the car, Georgia. It's only made of steel," he said. Grandy liked understatement. And sarcasm.

"Sorry, Grandy."

I slipped past him into the house, straight through the living room and on to the kitchen, where I had the presence of mind to rest the bag of produce on the worn Formica counter *gently*. I had deep-seated issues with bruised fruit.

"Want to tell me what happened?" Grandy leaned against the entryway to the kitchen, arms folded, one ankle crossed over the other. It was the pose of a younger man, not a man pushing eighty. But that's Grandy for you—always defying expectation and convention.

"You know your bathtub needs caulking," I said.

He nodded and hmm-ed as if he'd done career time as a therapist. "And what am I to infer from that? That you're angry with me?"

I wrenched open the door to the fridge and grabbed a pitcher of cold tea before meeting his eyes. "I was idiot enough to think you hadn't done it because you—" I didn't finish the thought, preferring instead to busy myself with pulling a cup from the age-stained maple cabinet and pouring the tea, buying time.

But Grandy unfolded his arms and stood straight. "Because you think I'm too old to maintain my own home?"

"Because your eyeglasses . . . because all the bending . . . all right, yes, because of your age." I closed my eyes for a second and let the guilt wash over me.

"You could have just said you thought I hadn't gotten around to it, you know," Grandy grumbled.

I didn't want to look at him. The idea of him being hurt because of something I said was bad enough. To have a visual to go along with it bordered on unbearable.

Still, I could hear the suspicion in his voice when he asked, "So you thought you would do it for me and not tell me? Say, on a night I'd be at the office?"

"Yes, okay? That's exactly what I thought." I didn't mention that I thought calling the movie theater "the office" was somewhat exaggerated. It was still work; he did own the place. And there was a room that functioned

17

as an office. Still . . . "So now that we've gotten that out of the way, how about you tell me why the cranky pants at the hardware store believes you should have warned me not to go in there?"

His expression blanked. "To the hardware store? Why shouldn't *you* go there?"

"You tell me." I took a breath, not wanting to sound argumentative. "I stopped in for a caulking gun."

"I have a caulking gun."

"Missing the point, Grandy. That guy took one look at me and knew exactly who I was and showed me the door." The anger bubbled up again. I grabbed a cantaloupe from the shopping bag, pulled a knife from the woodblock beneath the window slanting sunshine into the room. "Apparently Pete Keene's granddaughter is not welcome."

"He said that?"

"Not in those exact words, but the heartless intent was there."

Grandy remained quiet while I stabbed the cantaloupe and sliced open the sweet fruit. Tugging at a stubborn drawer with one hand and reaching for a paper towel with the other, I glanced his way.

If it were truly possible for a face to fill with storm clouds, Grandy's face would have shown a tornado forming. His lightly tanned, lightly wrinkled skin turned a blotchy red from his chin all the way up into his drastically receded hairline. He clenched his jaw to the point that his cheeks bulged, and I worried about the durability of his dentures. It was enough to snap me out of my own anger.

Abandoning the drawer, I wiped my hands on the paper towel and hurried over to him. "Don't worry about it, okay? Really, it's no big deal."

"Of course it's a big deal," he growled out. "Andrew Edgers has no right to talk to you or any of my family like that."

"Grandy, it's all right." I took hold of his elbow and squeezed gently, as though that action might loosen and expel the anger building in him. "I'm overreacting. It's . . . I haven't been sleeping well. It's so darn quiet here, who can sleep?" I joked. "It's fine."

"It's not fine," he grumbled. "You deserve to be treated with respect."

Oh, gosh. Where was Grandy when my engagement was falling apart? "I've had worse, believe me. I never should have said anything. Let it go, okay? I'm sorry I brought it up."

Though the tension relaxed out of the arm I held, his jaw remained tight. "Don't be sorry," he said. "You can tell me anything. I'm a tough old man. I didn't get to be this old by being weak."

That made me smile—a genuine, unforced smile. The idea of Grandy ever being weak was laughable. "All right. From now on you get all the humiliating, embarrassing details of my life, how's that?"

Shrewd brown eyes peered down at me, their color faded but no less arresting. "I don't want to hear about shoes or nail polish. I only want to hear the good stuff."

Turning back to the split cantaloupe awaiting me on the counter, I laughed, thinking Grandy was back to his calm, jovial self. Though a part of me was still curious about the issue between Grandy and Andrew Edgers, I figured if Grandy could let it go, so could I.

Yup. Sometimes I can be a complete fool.

The basement room in Grandy's house had once served as my grandmother's art studio. Being that the house was a split-level, the "basement" wasn't underground but at ground level. The two walls cornering into the yard had windows that caught the northern and eastern light. Grandma had kept her easel and paints against the wall shared with the garage. This allowed her to place her still life arrangements opposite, between the two full-size double-hung windows that filled the room with all-day sunshine.

It was there, in the corner between the windows, that I had dragged a battered old table and set upon it the mock-Tiffany lamp. Glass work benefited from every bit of available sunlight. I had spent the day before trimming back the vegetation outside the windows so that once again Grandma's corner delivered sunlight with rays to spare.

With a microfiber cloth, warm distilled water, and a little mild dish soap, I carefully wiped the dust and grime and—*ew!*—spiderwebs from the lamp. Each careful stroke of the cloth allowed a little more light to shine through, until the shade of the lamp was exposed as a tumult of blues and greens. Cornflower, azure, peri-winkle, and robin's egg mingled and tangled with moss, sage, emerald, and forest. The pattern was a classic Tiffany design, creating the illusion that the lamp shade itself had been formed by nature, dripping with leaves and blossoms, filled with beauty and life.

Of course, nature didn't have threads of lead separating leaf from petal. Even if it did, the lead wouldn't be dusty with oxidization. After tugging on one of the several pairs of disposable cotton gloves I kept in my work box, I broke into my trusty reserve of cotton swabs, and began the meticulous work of cleaning the dust from the lead.

Caught in the hypnotic effect of the work, I lost track of time. Only the setting of the sun and the loss of light clued me in to the late hour. Grandy had long since headed out to work; I vaguely remembered mumbling a good-bye when he called down the stairs. I still had full daylight then. He liked to get to the dine-in theater he owned a solid hour before the box office opened for the seven o'clock show. As much as he swore he trusted his management staff, several times a week he would review the establishment like a general inspecting his troops.

Since I was already on a roll, and Grandy was safely out of my hair, I made myself a quick dinner that didn't center on meat and potatoes, turned the radio up loud, and went to work cleaning the neglected portions of the house—the baseboards and ceilings, under the stove, behind the fridge . . . all the icky places.

Long past midnight I blindly threw all the rags and cleaning towels and clothes I'd been wearing into the washer but held off switching the machine on. I wanted to shower the grime off myself, scrub it out from underneath my fingernails, and otherwise wash away the day.

While the dirt and tension slid down the drain, I opened the door to the basement, where the wash waited, and made a critical error. I paused. I took a breath. And on the exhale I felt every muscle, every tendon go limp. I was tired and ready for bed and in no mood to trudge down the stairs. The washer held nothing I would need immediately. I decided the laundry could wait.

The next day followed the same path—stained glass work while the light was strong and housework while it wasn't. Grandy stayed well out of my way and left for the theater without a word. I kept going, not resting until the house was dust-free and every inch of wood polished to a gleam.

After two days of scrubbing, sleep claimed me quickly. Sometimes I thought I was catching up on the sleep I'd lost during years in a high-pressure job, juggling the books for Washington Heritage Financial, trying to keep a handle on the flow of billions of dollars. Sometimes I thought sleep was putting the final touches on the healing of my broken heart. Sometimes I was just tired.

But never had I woken up to a pounding on the door quite like the pounding that woke me in midmorning. Panic gripped my gut. Something was wrong. What could be wrong? Grandy. Something had happened to Grandy.

I flew out of bed and down the stairs, heedless of the faded T-shirt and gym shorts I wore in lieu of pajamas. Worse, heedless of the state my hair might be in after falling asleep with it wet. This was perhaps something I should have heeded. When I ripped open the door, the first thing I noticed was the look of utter horror on the face of the man standing on the porch. The second was the shiny gold badge he held at eye level. The third, a uniformed officer standing at his side.

The twisting in my gut got a little tighter. "Yes?" was all I could manage.

The man with the badge shook his head slightly as though calling himself back to the moment. "We're looking for Peter James Keene. Is he here?"

My mouth went dry. The police were looking for Grandy? Specifically? No way that could indicate a social call. I nodded and stepped back, gesturing for the gentlemen to come inside. "He should be—"

"What the blazes is going on here?" Grandy's voice boomed from the stairway.

I looked over my shoulder then scampered out of the way. Grandy stomped down the stairs, turning for the front door while cinching the belt on his old-fashioned dressing gown and glaring at the policemen.

The one in the suit brandished his badge again. "Detective Nolan, Pace County PD. Are you Peter James Keene?" he asked.

Grandy reached the threshold and stood toe-to-toe with the detective, glaring down at him. "And if I am?"

"I need to ask you to come with us, Mr. Keene. I have some questions I'd like to ask you."

"So ask." He folded his arms, straightened his spine. Amazing. Eighty years old, in plaid pajamas and a dressing gown, wearing slippers straight out of the fifties and still he was a tower of intimidation. Even the uniformed officer shifted nervously.

Detective Nolan kept it together. I guessed the gray peppering his dark hair and the faint wrinkles at the corners of his eyes were testament to his years of experience. "I'm afraid you'll have to come along with us down to the precinct."

"What's wrong with here?" Grandy asked.

Sweat prickled my scalp. I finally broke my silence. "What's going on? Grandy, did something happen at the theater?"

"I'm afraid your . . ." Detective Nolan hesitated, looking between Grandy and me.

"Grandfather," I supplied.

Nolan nodded. ". . . needs to answer some questions for us. And it would be best if he came along willingly and quietly."

A whole new knot made its presence known in my belly. This was worse than bad, even though I didn't know what worse than bad was called. Terrible? Horrible? Disastrous?

One question squeaked out. "Grandy?"

He looked to me, his expression softening as his posture relaxed. "I'm sure it's nothing, Georgia. Just some sort of, er, formality."

"Formality for what? What's going on?" I tried to move closer to Grandy, but Detective Nolan reached out a hand to stop me. "Hey."

Grandy turned to me with a slight smile. "It's all right, Georgia." He meant to reassure me, but the unease was clear in the pucker of his forehead, in the narrowing of his eyes. That only intensified my worry. "Why don't you give us a few minutes' head start and then follow? I'm sure we won't be long and I'll need you to drive me home."

This was even weirder than the police presence. "Are you actually going to leave the house in your dressing gown?"

Grandy turned his gaze to the detective, a question in the lift of his brow.

Nolan shook his head. "You're dressed enough."

"In that case, Georgia, when you come, bring me a shirt and trousers, will you?" He turned to the door, and the uniformed officer preceded him onto the porch, but glanced back over his shoulder. "And some shoes?"

Arms wrapped around my body, hugging myself, I nodded. All at once, reality was something I was observing, not participating in. My mind couldn't grasp any scenario in which Grandy would be taken in for questioning. What could he have done wrong? Mixed whiskey with his prune juice?

I stirred myself enough to cross to the open door. Outside, Detective Nolan shut himself inside a deep blue sedan while the uniformed officer assisted Grandy into the back of a squad car. Grandy didn't look my way, instead looking straight ahead with a calm sort of dignity.

Not until both cars had pulled away did I close the door and get it into gear. I didn't want Grandy sitting in the police station any longer than necessary.

I raced around the house, dressing, gathering clothes and shoes for Grandy, and shoving them into one of my trusty reusable shopping bags. With no time to do anything elaborate, I scraped my wild curls back into a soft ponytail. Flip-flops, purse, and keys to the Jeep and I was out of the house.

Crossing to the car, I spied the little cluster of gawkers across the street. Of course. Nothing brings neighbors together like a little police action.

"Everything okay?" one of the ladies called. "Pete all right?"

"Fine," I shouted back. "Thanks for asking." And I ducked into the car before any further questions could be lobbed in my direction.

I shoved the key in the ignition and wasted no time backing out of the driveway and racing down the street, away from curious neighbors.

Of course, once I reached the end of the street, I realized I had no idea where the police station was located. Yeah, I'd call that a flaw in the plan.

After putting some distance between me and Grandy's street, I steered the Jeep to the curb and threw it into park. With the engine's motor still running, and the dappled sunshine of a spreading maple tree shading me from the morning sun, I grabbed my smartphone out of my purse and did a map search for Wenwood Police Department.

The search returned no results. Drat. The jurisdiction must fall to the county. I closed my eyes and tried to recall the details of the uniform the officer wore to the house. My memory showed me a field of deep blue, a shield and name tag over the left breast. But it was the points of his collar I was interested in. I could visualize a precinct number there. The more I tried to focus, the more I worried my memory was painting in details from the city police uniform with which I had become so familiar.

Double drat.

I eased back onto the road and pointed the Jeep in the direction of the village. Someone there would be able to tell me where the station was, if I didn't get struck by luck and pass it along the way.

Less than fifteen minutes had passed before the Jeep bumped along the old cobbled road bisecting the village. I rolled slowly along, reading shop signs in search of one wherein I thought someone would be able to help. When I spied the bakery, I knew I'd found a solution. What I needed to find was a parking spot. What I found instead were two more police squad cars and a yellow caution-tape barrier preventing anyone from entering the hardware store.

That knot once again took hold of my stomach. I flipped a U-turn and parked the Jeep on the opposite side of the street. Grabbing my purse, I hurried to the sidewalk in front of the hardware store and peered through the plate glass display window. All the lights were on, but I could see nothing beyond the rows of shelves I had wandered through two days before.

Determined to get some info while at the same time afraid of what I might learn, I headed up the street a little. Ahead, in front of Village Grocery, a cluster of senior citizens stood as if in conference. It reminded me of the scene across the street from Grandy's house. Sweat prickled my scalp, from nerves or the heat or both, and I quick-timed it to Aggie's Gifts and Antiques and burst through the door.

"Carrie?" I called over the jingling of the bell. "Hello? Are you here?"

Impatient, I circled the perimeter of the store, passing by jewelry armoires, quilt racks, an old vanity table to where the register sat midway along the western wall. Back to me, she was climbing down from a step stool, feather duster in her hand, when I found her.

"Carrie," I said again.

Her eyes found me and opened wide. "Oh my gosh! Georgia, is it true? It's not true, is it? It just can't be."

"I—uh—is what true? No, wait." I squinched my eyes shut for a moment, as if that action alone could pause the conversation. "What happened at the hardware store?" I asked then opened my eyes.

Carrie's eyes remained wide, and were now accompanied by a slack jaw. "It's Andy Edgers," she said. "Bill Harper found him yesterday morning, dead in the back room with . . . with . . ." She swallowed hard, and I imagined she had a knot in her throat as big as the one in my stomach. "With his . . . head . . . bashed in. Murdered."

The knot burst open into a rush of queasiness. "Oh, my gosh," I murmured. "Murdered? Holy cow."

Okay, death did not stop the guy from being a jerk. Happily, I didn't think for a minute the guy had it coming. He was mean. He deserved to have his house TPed or maybe as far as having his car egged. But murdered . . . wow. Still . . . "He must have really pissed someone off," I murmured.

"Georgia." Carrie stepped close, took loose hold of my elbow.

As her worried gaze met mine, the pieces fell into place. "No," I said. Carrie asked if it was true. Andy Edgers dead. Grandy taken to the police station for questioning. "No, that can't be."

"Pete was in the shop the night before last. They're saying they had a big fight."

"Who are *they*?"

Carrie shrugged a little uneasily, took a tiny step back. "You know, people."

"People like who?"

Her smile was a little wobbly. "It's really not my place."

I shook my head to clear away the unimportant thoughts. I was chasing after the wrong fact. Who was spreading rumors wasn't the issue. "It doesn't matter. Gran—Pete didn't do anything."

"I didn't think so." She let out a breath as though she'd been holding it. "And, I mean, you would know, right? You're staying with him and all."

"But okay, listen. The police . . ." Oh, mercy. I certainly didn't want to announce Grandy had been picked up by The Detective and The Sidekick, but I needed to know which precinct house to go to. And if the town was talking, I didn't want to add any grist to the gossip mill by asking anyone else for information.

I began again. "You know that lamp you need restored? I'll do that job for free if you can give me some information and promise to keep a secret."

Carrie took another small step away from me and leaned back a little. She regarded me through half-closed eyes. "It isn't anything illegal, is it?"

"Oh, for heaven's sake, Carrie, of course not." I'd have stomped out right there but Carrie was the friendliest person I'd met. I needed to trust someone. Only time would tell if I'd made a good choice. If I hadn't . . . well, it couldn't get much worse, right? "I just need information and discretion. Deal?"

Again with the narrowed eyes. "I get to hear what you want before I agree."

Shrewd. "Fine," I said under a huff. "The police picked up Gra—Pete this morning and brought him to the station for questioning."

That made her eyes pop wide again. "No! So it *is* true."

"Just, don't tell anyone, okay? I need to go pick him up and I have no idea where to go. I don't know where he'll be. I don't know what precinct Wenwood is in." I stopped talking before the panic threatening within me escaped.

For longer than was comfortable for me, Carrie stood with eyes wide and her mouth slightly open. What seemed like forever later she shot into action, tossing the feather duster onto the checkout counter and racing to bolt the front door.

"I'll drive," she said, flipping the OPEN sign to CLOSED. "Come on. We'll go out the back."

"Wait. What?"

"Come on." She waved me along and bustled to the back of the shop.

Rushing to catch up, I called, "All I need is a precinct number, I swear. I can get directions off the map program on my phone."

In the back storeroom Carrie snatched a pair of sunglasses from a workbench and took her purse off a hook. "You need more than that. You're going to a police station. You don't want to do something like that alone. Forget the directions. You need a friend with you."

"I can't ask—"

"You didn't ask. I offered. Let's go." She pushed open the steel fire door and looked back at me. "Really, let's go."

Carrie was a virtual stranger. I mean, yeah, we'd gotten on okay when she showed me the lamp and all, but did I want to drive with her to the police station? Problem was, when she said I didn't want to go to the station alone? I was fine with the idea until she suggested it was unwise. After that, the anxiety in my bloodstream increased.

So I hurried out the door into the narrow strip of parking that ran behind the stores. Sunshine nearly blinded me, and I crossed the brief stretch of faded tarmac to stand beneath a tree overhanging the back fence. Comfortably in the shade, I waited while Carrie ducked back into the store—presumably to set an alarm—then popped back out to lock the series of deadbolts lining the door.

She locked, I waited, and something squeaked.

I glanced left and right, but aside from a few empty vehicles, we were alone in the lot.

"All set," Carrie said, turning away from the door.

She took three steps, I adjusted the purse on my shoulder, and something squeaked.

"Okay, hold it." I scanned the lot again, but saw nothing out of the expected.

"What is it?"

"Did you hear—" It came again, louder, longer. And a little twinge of alarm warned me I'd been looking in the wrong place.

I lowered to a crouch, and scanned the ground. Beside me, Carrie did the same. "What are we doing?" she asked. "Are we hiding?"

"We're looking." Duckwalking to the fence that divided the parking strip from the public park it bordered, I peered along the length of the fence where it met the ground. In the back of my mind I knew time was wasting. I needed to get to the police station to bring Grandy home. But if my instincts had been correct . . .

"What are we looking for?"

At last I spotted a beer carton, several cars away and tight up against the fence as though the box had been dropped over. And the box was moving.

I pushed to my feet. "Kitten, I think."

Carrie's face curled in disbelief. "Are you crazy? What would a kitten be doing back here?"

I didn't want to tell her I thought the kitten might be getting more than a little bit hungry, so I answered her with a shrug and headed along the fence in the direction of the beer carton.

"You must be imagining things. No one would abandon a kitten back here. Wenwood isn't that sort of town."

I paused to look over my shoulder at her. "You can have a murder but not a homeless feline?"

She huffed, waggled her fingers a bit. "Well . . ."

With a few more steps I was beside the box, peering inside. A teeny pair of blue eyes peered back at me, followed by that squeak I'd heard. Now the sound was clearly audible, and definitely the *mew* of a kitten.

What can I say? I melted. Grandfather in the clink, murder scene up the road, and I went all gooey over that teeny tiny *meeew*.

"Hey there," I said softly, "how did you get in that box?" I reached down and, one-handed, scooped up the kitten. A little ball of white fluff with a gray streak atop her head gazed up at me and mewed, and I tucked that fluff against my chest and I swear long-broken pieces of my heart began to mend.

"What are you doing? Don't pick it up. What if it's rabid?"

I turned the kitten's little face to her. "This is not the face of a rabid animal. This is the face of future world domination."

Carrie set a hand on her hip. "Unless it's a face that can give your grandfather an alibi, I suggest we get moving."

"Absolutely. There's just one thing I have to do first."

3

Not surprisingly, Carrie was opposed to standing
watch over the kitten while I ran down to Village
Grocery, but really we had little choice. I had no idea how
long it had taken for the little white puff with a tail to eat
the two tiny cans of food left in the box with it and I
couldn't let it dehydrate or starve now. As opposed as
Carrie was to watching the feline, she was more opposed
to buying supplies to keep it happy. Thus, Carrie waited,
I shopped.

Having no sound idea how much kittens eat, I grabbed
a few cans of moist food and a six-pack of bottled water.
With a packet of disposable plastic bowls, I hurried up to
the register and dropped the collection on the belt.

The cashier—a college-aged girl with yellow-blond
hair and black roots—reluctantly tore her gaze away from

the wide plate windows stretching across the front of the store. Her distracted gaze found mine. "Have you heard about Andy Edgers?" she asked.

I shoved the kitten food a little closer to her. Mention of Edgers renewed my urgency in getting to the police station and getting Grandy home. "I did hear, yes. Terrible," I muttered. "I don't need a bag for these."

She rang up the purchase in slow motion, pausing after each item to check the collection of townsfolk gathered in front of the store. "I hope no one takes over the hardware store," she said. "There should really be a music store here, you know? Classic vinyl and stuff. Wouldn't that be awesome?"

At a loss for words—seriously, poor Mr. Edgers hadn't been gone a day and already there were plans to take over his retail space?—I thrust some cash at the girl, shoved the cat food in my purse, and practically ran to the back exit.

I hurried Carrie into the car, and settled kitten and beer carton on the floorboards at my feet. The little miss (I checked) nibbled at the fresh can of food I had opened and placed inside the box, but it wasn't long before she was clambering out of her confines and into my lap. For a moment I worried she'd get in Carrie's way and we'd be put to the side of the road, but the kitten curled up happily in the crook of my arm and fell asleep shortly after we left the stretch of road Wenwood considered downtown.

"I can't believe you're planning on taking that thing

home," Carrie said on a resigned sigh. She'd already lost the battle about me bringing the kitten into the car.

"You don't like cats, I guess."

She slanted a glance at me. "I'm more of a dog person."

"But this is a kitten. Everyone loves kittens."

"Everyone except the person who threw it out like trash."

To her credit, she sounded angry. She might prefer a rottweiler, but there was a hint of stubborn animal lover about her that made me smile.

With the ball of fluff sleeping peacefully, I paid attention to the roads Carrie took on our way to the sixth precinct police station. The station could be reached by taking the interstate, Carrie informed me, but the road along the riverside was prettier and less prone to mysterious midday traffic snarls.

I felt the threat of guilt hovering over my shoulder—out of reach of contented kitten—as we cruised along the river road. The beauty of the area—pale summer sky stretched overhead, thick green leaves on the trees lining the road, the lush blue river rolling along speckled with small sailboats and large cabin cruisers—pushed the thought of Grandy in the police station into another realm. There along the road, a lazy summer day promised nothing but sunshine and good times.

We rounded a curve and a time-worn structure came into view. Wrapped by chain-link fencing with construction equipment huddling motionless inside the perimeter, a large wooden structure resembling an oversized barn sat partially demolished, its riverside wall open to the air. Bright, new wood virtually gleamed from the dark interior.

"What's going on over there?" I asked Carrie, tipping my head in the direction of the river.

A hint of sadness weighed down Carrie's response. "That's the old brickworks."

She didn't need to say more for me to understand her sadness. Once upon a time Wenwood was a thriving town. The Hudson River provided water, the riverbed below provided clay, and at the mill on the river's edge, brick after brick was molded, baked, and shipped across a young nation. Wenwood was a place for hardworking folk to build a good life.

The nation aged and the world expanded. Cheaper stone came in from Europe, and people started building with glass and aluminum, and brick making declined. Wenwood went from a bustling little village to a ghost of its former glory. And now it looked like even the old building was surrendering.

"What are they doing to it? Tearing it down?" I kept my voice soft, in the manner of someone speaking of a tragedy.

"To start with." Carrie shut her lips tight for a moment before continuing. "They're going to put a marina there, with a boatyard and a restaurant and everything. Figure it will attract some tourism to the area."

At a loss for words, I nodded. Tourism made sense. Wenwood was an old town, not without its charms, and the view along the river was certainly alluring. By the same token, you never knew what shape a town would take once it began relying on something like tourism for funds.

The kitten awoke and stretched and dug its claws into my forearm. I cursed soundly, and Carrie gave a triumphant sort of cackle and slowed for a left-hand turn. She guided the car away from the river, back inland. Seconds before I could ask how much farther, the police station came into view.

A boxy brick building, perhaps two stories, with windows at ground level indicating the presence of a basement, sat far back from the curb of an industrial-looking street. The front lawn featured a flagpole from which both the U.S. and the state flags flew, and a weathered bronze statue of a policeman stood watch over a half-grass, half-clover lawn.

Carrie steered the car into the lot running parallel to the station and pulled into a spot marked VISITOR, helpful since all the unmarked slots were taken by green and white squad cars. I swallowed against a rising sense of anxiety and climbed out of the car. My legs felt rubbery beneath me, not because we'd been sitting long or the heat of the day was getting to me, but because worry has a strange effect on musculature. I tucked the kitten back into her box and tucked the box under my arm.

"You're not bringing that thing into the station, are you?" Carrie stood at the back fender of the car. She dropped her keys into her purse and squinted at me like she could see the jelly my legs were made of.

"It's a kitten, not a nuclear device."

"Until it meets a K-9 unit."

"It'll be fine." I hitched my purse higher on my shoulder and marched toward the police station as proudly as I could manage while holding a somewhat fragrant carton emblazoned with a beer logo. Cheap beer at that.

The building that had appeared almost stately from the road looked a whole lot different close up. Weeds poked up below scraggly hedges, the sidewalk was cracked and uneven, and the brick building looked as if nothing more than a huff and a puff would blow the station house down.

"Is there some budget deficit in this county?" I asked, grimacing a little while gazing up at the building façade.

Carrie waved my question away. "Who can keep up with weeds this time of year? And after such a wet spring."

We shuffled up the steps—crumbled brick patched with mismatched mortar. "Not the weeds. The building. Why not replace the brick instead of filling it in with this ugly crap?" I toed a bit of concrete, and reached the top of the steps before realizing Carrie was no longer beside me.

She stood on the bottom step, her hand resting on the brick wall beside her as though it were resting over her heart. "These," she said fiercely, "are Wenwood bricks."

"Yeah, huh?"

She sighed. "Do you have any idea how old these bricks are?"

I peered at the brick dust collecting at the base of the wall. "Pretty old, I'm guessing."

"Georgia. These bricks are from the original Wenwood factory." Her tone was reverent, her eyes bright.

"Wenwood bricks have been used in historical buildings all along the East Coast, dating as far back as the early seventeen hundreds. They've housed presidents, for goodness' sake."

"Uh-huh." I nodded. "And right now they're housing my grandfather, so can we do the town pride parade later?"

Without waiting for her response, I tugged open the door to the station and stepped inside.

Moving from the bright morning outside to the dim station house interior required a moment's pause for my eyes to adjust. I shuffled forward enough for Carrie to enter behind me, but otherwise stood still and waited and blinked.

And yet, all the blinking and all the waiting had no effect. By the time I figured out the dim interior would be dim regardless of time of day or intensity of sunlight, Carrie was already across the pitted linoleum and rapping on the tall wooden desk at the far end of the narrow room. Paneling lined the walls, and here and there a community policy flyer was taped to the wall: Clean up after your dog, don't let trees interfere with power lines, possession of gunpowder is a prosecutable offense. Who knew?

The desk sergeant shuffled through a doorway behind the desk, in no particular hurry to assist. "Hey, Carrie," he said. "What brings you by today?"

"Steve, you guys have Pete Keene here?" she asked.

Sergeant Steve's lip curled suspiciously as he watched me approach. "Who's asking?"

"I am," Carrie and I both said at once.

"Pete's my grandfather." I stopped in front of the desk,

peered over the sergeant's shoulder to the doorway he'd come through. Racks with empty gun belts and radios ran from the ceiling to—presumably—the floor. "Detective Nolan came by the house this morning and brought him here for some questioning?" Before I'd finished speaking, the officer was nodding.

"Yeah, yeah, he's here. He's in the back."

I glanced to my left, where another doorway led to a hall that at some point in time—perhaps in an earlier century—had been painted a pale green. "Can I go back there?"

"Only if you're in handcuffs," he said.

"Oh. Well, we're here to drive him home," I said.

Sergeant Steve lowered his chin, looked at me from below his brows. "He's not available just yet." He narrowed his eyes. "Whatcha got in that box?"

"Nothing," Carrie said.

"Kitten," I said. Carrie shot me a quelling look and I shrugged. "What? Again, not a nuclear device."

Pointing a finger at the box, the desk sergeant said, "Open it up."

I can't be sure, but I think he was resting his hand on his gun. And I can't say as I blame him. I had just walked into a police station carrying a carton. All manner of objects could be concealed within its depths. But still, probably not . . . you know . . .

Using my body to brace the box against the counter, I lifted the loosely folded flaps and scooped out a wriggling puff of white fur. With no better option, I set the wee wonder on the top of the desk. The kitten blinked its wide blue eyes, sat, and let out a heartbreaking *meeew*.

Sergeant Steve made a noise typically reserved for women. It was something between an *oooh* and an *eeeh*, and I swear he melted where he stood. "Now that's the cutest little thing to come through those doors." His oversized man hand hovered above the kitten before he lowered a forefinger and stroked its head. "You just pick it up from a breeder or something?"

"Found it in a parking lot," I said.

The cop froze. All-business eyes looked down at me. "You found it?"

"In the parking lot," I repeated, somewhat less assured. "Will my grandfather be much longer?" I had a sinking feeling the kitten conversation wasn't going to end in my favor, and I really, truly wanted it to. Though new to the pet thing, I was on a crash course to understanding that there were few things in the world that couldn't be improved by the presence of an animal.

"What was it doing in a parking lot?"

"Hiding in a beer carton," Carrie murmured.

"Someone left this little guy in a box?" Outrage tinged Sergeant Steve's words. I wasn't sure if I was glimpsing Steve the cop or Steve the animal lover. Either way the thunder forming across his brow made me uneasy.

"Honestly, we don't know whether someone put the kitten in the box or the kitten got out of its house and found the box all on its own," I fibbed, hoping to defuse his impending wrath.

The officer pressed his lips into a tight line, making his cheeks bulge like a hamster storing seeds. He exhaled volubly through his nose, while somewhere off to my left a door creaked open. Subdued male chatter drifted in my direction. Neither of the voices had Grandy's natural growl.

"About my grandfather?" I prompted.

Sergeant Steve scooped up the kitten, gave it a rub between the ears, and handed it back to me. "He'll be at least another hour. At least." He nodded at the kitten. "Meantime you could get to work making signs, find out who that kitten belongs to."

My jaw dropped inelegantly. I was feeling very possessive toward the kitten, and pretty confident some hard-hearted human had discarded the little thing. But I was afraid if I admitted that last bit to the police, they'd make me leave it with them or, worse, bring it to a shelter, where it would be incarcerated with other homeless animals while it awaited trial—or whatever it is they have to wait for. And what if I didn't get custody?

"That's a great idea, Steve," Carrie said. She turned to me, eyes bright, smile wide. "We could make flyers, don't you think? And then the"—she waved at the creature—"*that* could be reunited with its rightful owner."

I squelched the urge to glare at her, focusing instead on setting the kitten back in its box. Since I had only one free hand, the flaps were presenting a problem.

"You," a male voice declared.

Keeping pressure on the carton with my hip, I turned to peer along the hallway to my left. Headed in my direction in the company of a uniformed officer was the blue-eyed guy from the hardware store.

He was stopped in the hallway—eyes narrowed, nostrils flaring, jaw muscles bulging—and he was pointing at me.

"Yeah, you," the blue-eyed man shouted, striding down the hallway.

In the movie of my life, this will be the moment where I look up and our eyes will meet while violins begin to play softly. His anger will fade away, replaced by a mischievous smile. "You," he'll repeat, "are the person I've been waiting for my whole life."

But this was reality. And in reality, his anger didn't fade as much as it intensified.

"You did this. Because of you, I've spent my whole morning in an interrogation room."

"What did I do?" I attempted to take a step backward, out of his direct line of fire. The motion disturbed the tension holding the box in place and the box crashed to the floor. An indignant *mrow* escaped from the box.

He closed the gap as I bent to retrieve the fallen carton. "You told the police I was in the hardware store the day Andy Edgers was killed. I don't know what you think you walked in on—"

"I never said anything to the police," I said. "Well, not about you anyway." My fingers caught the top of the carton. Rather than lifting cleanly, though, the carton tipped and I lost my grip. The box crashed back to the ground. A white ball of fluff streaked out and launched itself, claws extended, onto the gentleman's leg. "Oh, crap."

The man shouted a curse and jumped back. The kitten dug in and inched up.

"What did I tell you about bringing that thing in here?" Carrie asked. "Now look. It's attacking Tony."

I dived toward Tony, falling to my knees to better grab the kitten. My hands wrapped its little body in the split second before Tony's hands landed on mine. Together we prized the complaining cuteness off his knee while the uniformed officer looked on, hand over his mouth, shoulders shaking.

Clutching the kitten close to my heart, I stood. "Sorry about that."

Tony's eyes were wide, deep blue rimmed in bright white. His mouth opened but no words were forthcoming.

"Sorry," I whispered.

He blinked.

Carrie appeared beside me, holding the empty carton out to me, shaking it a bit. "Put it back."

"Someone threw it away," I said, quite forgetting Tony was mad at me even *before* the kitten attack.

The uniformed cop stepped forward. "Maybe best to put the cat back in the box for now, ma'am."

I did as I was told, but kept my gaze on Tony. I told myself this was because I needed to make him understand I hadn't been responsible for him being questioned. That was a much nobler reason than staring because he was irrationally easy on the eyes. "Really," I said. "It wasn't me."

He blinked again. "You're telling me you didn't drop a cat on me."

"Well, I didn't do that either. Not really."

"It was an accident," Carrie added.

A new voice broke into the fray. "Miss Kelly."

I had to lean left and peer around Tony's shoulder to see the source. Detective Nolan stood midway along the hallway, leaning half outside a door. "Me?" I asked for absolutely no logical reason.

The detective sighed. "Would you come with me, please?"

For the first time since Grandy left the house that morning, my muscles completely seized. Hands sweating, knees knocking, I froze.

"Miss Kelly?" Detective Nolan prompted. "Now, please. I need to ask you a few questions."

4

When I left the city and moved back to sleepy old Wenwood, I naturally had a lot of ideas how my days might go. Many of my visions involved sleeping late, creating stained glass masterpieces, even searching for my next job. None of my visions involved sitting in the police station with a boxed kitten under my chair, fighting to stay calm in the face of questioning.

It wasn't like I was in the middle of a *Law & Order* rerun—the station room lacked the noise and bustle of its television equivalent—yet nerves kept me from drawing a full breath and prevented me from holding my bouncing foot still. The detective whose desk I'd been deposited beside was the same detective who had driven off behind Grandy-in-a-squad-car earlier, though his suit jacket now hung from the back of his chair and his tie had gone askew.

"Where's my grandfather?" I peered around the small room, knowing I hadn't missed spotting him, but needing to double-check all the same. The walls were a vague blue, the desks consumed by stacks of paper and bulky computer monitors, and the only person other than the detective and me was a policewoman in shorts and a T-shirt apparently trying to bring some order to her desk.

"Mr. Keene didn't mention your visit to Edgers Hardware," the detective said.

"I don't see why he would. Where is he?"

Detective Nolan let out an annoyed little huff. "He's in an interview room. Having tea."

I bit the inside of my lip to keep from grinning. Grandy was more than a little particular about how to prepare his tea. If he had actually coerced the officers into bringing him a cup he was willing to drink, there was no need for me to worry about his well-being. Tough old guy. A bit of soft love warmed my heart and took away the chill of worry.

"Tell me about the hardware store."

"What about it?"

He glared at me from beneath lowered brows.

I shifted in my chair, wished I'd kept the kitten in my lap. "I don't mean to be difficult," I said. "I just need a more specific question. If you could."

Rubbing a hand across his forehead, eyes closed, he said, "Your visit to the hardware store. What happened?"

Still wasn't very specific. But maybe that's the way cops get the best information? Didn't seem right, being so vague and all, but what did I know? I was just a bean counter.

I took a breath. "I stopped into the hardware store to pick up a caulking gun and some caulk. The guy—the gentleman—who was just leaving, Himmel, was already in the store with Mr. Edgers."

"They were arguing?"

After a moment's thought I said, "Yes, I'd call it arguing."

"And they were arguing about . . ."

I shook my head, marking time while I worked to recall. "Some kind of order. I don't know what for. Mr. Edgers was . . ."

A new thought formed in my head.

"Mr. Edgers was?" he prompted.

Through my distraction, I replied, "He was disrespecting the other guy, you know, doing the whole 'I'm older and you should do what I say' thing." But my mind was chewing on one question. I wasn't the one who'd told the police Himmel had been arguing with Edgers. So who had? I had a sense Detective Nolan wouldn't tell me if I asked him. Not yet anyway. Maybe if he thought I was being extra helpful? "And something about revitalization and renewal. Or the other way around. It sounded like Mr. Edgers wasn't happy about it."

Detective Nolan scratched notes on the corner of an already crowded slip of paper. "Go on."

"Then Mr. Edgers said something about how Himmel had to place an order or else and Himmel said that sounded like an ultimatum."

Nolan's scratching paused. "And then?"

Anxiety morphed into residual anger. My toe stopped tapping and I crossed my arms over my chest, curled my hands into fists. "Then Mr. Edgers got a look at me and realized I was Pete Keene's granddaughter and—"

"How did he know that?"

I shrugged. "Small town? Big gossip? I'm pretty sure everyone knows that the newcomer with the crazy hair is Pete's granddaughter."

He looked for a moment like he wanted to protest, like he thought arguing the point would be the polite thing to do. In the end he let the protest slip away unspoken. He checked his hasty notes. "When the vict—that is, when Mr. Edgers realized who you were, did his demeanor change?"

That was a tough one. While I considered, I delayed my response long enough that Detective Nolan tossed me a more specific question. "Did he appear to regret that you heard the altercation?"

"Regret?" From beneath my chair, the kitten let out a pitiful meow, followed by the noise of claws on cardboard.

"Did he calm down? Did he look embarrassed?"

"No, he was just angry I was in his store." I bent to slide the box forward, tugging up a corner of the cardboard to peer inside.

"Why?"

"I don't know," I said. The stone of aggravation that had formed when Grandy refused to explain the feud between Edgers and him rattled through my gut. I reached blindly for the kitten, whether to soothe it or take comfort in its softness I couldn't say.

"Do you think it was because of anything you may have overheard?"

My seeking fingers found the surprisingly sharp claws of a kitten. "*Ow!*" I snatched my hand back, checked my finger for blood. "It was because I'm related to Pete."

"What makes you say that?"

I might have scowled, either at the detective, or at the point of pain on my fingertip. "That's what Mr..Edgers said. Not in so many words."

The detective's raised eyebrows were as good as a verbal prompt.

"I said I'd come back another time, and he told me that wouldn't be a good idea and my grandfather should have told me not to bother going to Edgers Hardware in the first place." The carton slid easily from below my chair, and I lifted it into my lap.

The raised eyebrows lowered, drew together over the bridge of Detective Nolan's nose. "But your grandfather didn't tell you that?"

Taking the kitten from the box, I shook my head. "When I asked him about it after, he told me it wasn't my business, that it was between him and Andy Edgers."

"You say *after*. After what?"

"After I got back from the store," I said.

"Can you tell me what time that was?"

I tried to snuggle the kitten against my shoulder, but it squirmed like a restless child. "I don't know. Twelve thirty? One?"

"Before he left for work then," the detective stated. He scribbled some more on his notepad, completely unconcerned by the presence of a quarter-grown cat in his squad room. "What time did he leave the house for work would you say?"

I shrugged. "I don't know. He left earlier than usual but I don't know exactly what time. I was . . ." I was in the basement, cleaning a stained glass lamp. I had no precise idea of when Grandy left for the dine-in theater.

It hit me then, the direction Detective Nolan's questioning had taken. We'd gone from focusing on the exchange between Himmel and Edgers, and slid right into what Grandy was doing in the hours before Edgers was found dead.

I'd gone to the police station to help Grandy. Instead, I'd done my fair share to destroy his alibi.

Back in Carrie's car, I leaned my elbow on the window frame and hid my face behind my hand. "I can't believe I did that," I said.

"I'm going to go out on a limb and suggest maybe—just maybe—the police have more experience getting information out of people than you have keeping secrets." She switched on the right blinker and turned the car into Willow Park Mall, another half-hour's drive beyond the Pace County PD. Detective Nolan, after he'd finished his "informal chat" with me, cautioned me he'd need another hour or more with Grandy. I'd tried to talk Carrie into taking me back to my car. There was no reason she should lose a day's business at the antiques shop to hang around a police station with me. I could only describe the look she gave me as a sarcastic glare. "You think there's a big demand for antiques on a Wednesday morning?" she'd asked.

We left the kitten under Sergeant Steve's dedicated attention and drove off to Willow Park, where a big chain pet store shared the exterior parking lot with the do-it-yourself home repair center.

As she cruised the parking lot for an ideal space, I continued to obsess. "I suppose having no experience being questioned by the police is a good thing. But I should have at least possessed enough presence of mind not to give them any more ammunition against Grandy."

Carrie snorted, an abbreviated sound somewhere between humor and disbelief. "The Pace County PD may look like teddy bears, but they do know what they're doing."

I peered at her from the corner of my eye. Detective Nolan had zero teddy bear qualities. As far as I knew. The wayward question of whether the good officer was covered in hair tumbled into my brain. I pushed it out with thoughts of Grandy sitting in a holding cell. That was enough to dispel all lesser horrors.

"Besides," Carrie went on, slowly guiding the car into a vacant spot, "I'm sure it's not as bad as you're making it sound."

My jaw fell. "I told Nolan about the fight I had with Andy Edgers. I told him how angry it made Grandy. Then I admitted to having no idea what time Grandy left the house." I choked back the next entry in my rant—that I had no idea what time it had been because I'd been entranced by a Tiffany-style lamp. Bad enough I felt the way I did about contributing to Grandy's status as a suspect, no need to invite Carrie into the guilt party.

"And you also told him you walked in on Andy arguing with Tony, right?"

"Tony?" I clambered out of the car, faced Carrie over the top of the sedan. "Oh, that's Himmel, right?"

She nodded briskly and started away from the car. "Anton Himmel." She reached over her shoulder, pointing her key fob at the sedan until its security system chirped in confident lockdown.

"All right but let's be clear on this. I only told Detective Nolan about that argument after they'd already questioned Himmel. I wasn't the one who brought it to their attention in the first place."

We paused outside the entrance to the pet supply store. "So then who did tell them?" Carrie asked. "Who told them to bring in Tony for questioning?"

I tilted my head, raised my brows. "That's what I'd like to know. Someone else who walked in on them maybe?"

But who else? The village of Wenwood wasn't exactly a high-traffic zone on a Monday morning. I'd only seen a few other people on the street. And even then, I had no idea who they were. Elderly man with alert antennae eyebrows. Teen girl already bored by summer. Two middle-aged mom types hooting over some outrageous joke. I remembered the sense I got from these people, not what they looked like. Even at that, I didn't think any of them the type to phone in tips to the police.

We wandered down the main aisle of the pet store, searching first left then right for signs of cat supplies. I pushed an empty cart, anticipating I was going to buy a lot of essentials. Carrie didn't share my enthusiasm.

"I wish I'd have noticed who was around that day," she said, following me down a likely-looking aisle.

"Nobody stopped into the store?" I asked.

Carrie treated me to another snort. "It's rare I get any business during the week. Thank God for Internet sales. They keep me in business."

I slowed beside a broad selection of hard plastic litter pans, hooded boxes, and something that looked like it required electric power. "Did you see anyone pass by, maybe on their way to the market?"

"You mean other than you?"

"Of course."

Carrie pulled an emery board from her purse and set about filing her nails while I fought to extract a pink pan from the stack of small-sized litter trays. As a red-haired girl, pink was a color I needed to be particularly careful with; I liked to incorporate it in other areas of my life, such as bath towels and . . . poop pans.

"Well. Tony passed by."

"Yeah, what about Tony? What's his deal? Where does he fit into the Wenwood landscape?"

"He kind of doesn't."

Completing the struggle, I threw the pan into the shopping cart and turned to consider the plethora of litter choices. "I don't understand. He was talking to Edgers like he knew him a long time."

"I wouldn't say a long time. Tony's in charge of the renovation on the old brickworks. You know, that building site we passed on the way up here?"

I made some sort of noise that indicated agreement.

"But that work's been going on since, I dunno, just before Christmas. They lost a lot of time what with the winter we had." Carrie shivered, apparently at the memory of a bad season. I remembered Grandy saying how happy he was he'd bought the Jeep when he did. His old sedan would never have been able to navigate the snowy roads. "I'd hoped they'd be further along by now. Town could sure use the business."

Considering all the choices in cat litter, I could just play eeny-meeny to choose one. Seemed to me my inability to make a decision centered more on trying to sort through what Carrie was telling me. "Explain to me how a marina will help business in the village." I hauled a plastic container of cat sand off a lower shelf and hefted it into my cart with a thud.

"The marina will be a destination. So the planners claim." She smirked to show her doubt. "It's meant to be a place for boaters to stretch their legs on dry land. Take in some sights, spend their money."

Wenwood had sights? Either I had been walking past them without realizing or I had been too familiar with the town to bother investigating. Though I had to admit, the stretch of land along the waterfront was probably breathtaking from the river. But at the moment, the village of Wenwood didn't appear to have much to offer to lure in visitors. Residents, sure. The necessary businesses were in place: grocery, bakery, luncheonette, pharmacy, and so forth. But a visitor to town wasn't likely to be drawn in by the Pour House bar or Danny's Taxes and Real Estate.

I rolled the cart forward and around the endcap, steering into the next aisle, where food, bowls, and toys lined the shelves. My mind worked hard to remember what little conversation I'd heard between Tony Himmel and Andy Edgers. The construction at the marina was at a standstill . . . What was holding it up? Did the *order* Edgers was waiting for impact work on the construction site?

Carrie ranged up beside me, slipping her emery board back into her bag and casually checking her watch in the process. Guilt washed over me. "I'm sorry," I said, grabbing the first set of little bowls I could reach even though they weren't pink. "I'm keeping you from the shop. Just some food and we'll be out of here."

I rolled the cart forward, yanked a small bag of crunchy kitten food from the shelf, and tossed it into the cart.

"I told you," she said, "people won't be banging down the door of the shop. They never do during weekdays."

Nodding in sympathy, I powered out of the aisle and turned for the registers at the front of the store. "But if there's no business during the week, why stay open? Why not take the days off, do something else?"

In a voice that sounded of surrender, she said, "Not a whole lot else to do."

"Come on. There's got to be something. Wenwood's quiet, but there's more to life than . . ." Than what? I'd spent most of my own time settling into Grandy's and sleeping like a drugged princess, sleeping away the weeks of stress and heartache I'd left behind. Surely there was more to life than that as well. Maybe I was looking for a clue.

"Business will pick up when the summer travel season starts. Families passing through on their way to Lake George. Everyone loves poking around an antiques shop. And then, Good Lord willing, once the marina opens, we can all get back in the black."

All? "What do you mean—" I began, but the upbeat tune on Carrie's cell phone cut short my question. She picked up the call while I guided the cart to the entrance of the checkout lane.

According to Carrie, it was Sergeant Steve on the phone telling us we could return to the station at any time. Grandy had finally lawyered up and was ready to go home.

The first words out of his mouth were, "Where are my clothes?"

While Sergeant Steve, Carrie, and Grandy's lawyer looked on, my memory flashed me an image of Grandy's khaki slacks and green button-down folded neatly on the front seat of his SUV, the SUV parked perhaps a tad haphazardly across the street from Aggie's Antiques.

"You forgot them, didn't you?" he grumbled.

I didn't realize it was possible to feel any guiltier. "Sorry, Grandy. Carrie gave me a ride up here and your clothes . . ."

"I've had a long day already, Georgia. And now you're

going to tell me the one thing I asked you to do was the one thing that escaped you?"

And even guiltier still. How low could I go?

"Don't worry about it, Mr. Keene," Carrie put in. "My car's right out front."

Despite Carrie's attempt at being helpful, Grandy turned his glower on me. He might have growled.

"Perhaps," his lawyer said, "we could exit out the back. Less uncomfortable for all concerned."

Grandy huffed and made the introductions. His lawyer, Drew Able, Esquire, took my hand in a firm but unremarkable grasp, his bland brown-eyed gaze sweeping me head to toe with no apparent conclusion drawn. I felt the same about him, in fact. Mid-forties, medium height, slim build, brown hair . . . his appearance gave me no insight into the type of man he might be.

"I suppose I have you to thank for making sure my grandfather isn't spending the night here?" I asked.

He flashed a surprisingly merry grin. "I think it's the officers who owe me the most thanks."

I glanced back to Grandy. He stood straight as a decorated soldier, clad in his blue thinning dressing gown, faded plaid pajamas, and Ozzie Nelson slippers. He held his chin high, his jaw clenched, his eyes piercing as he gazed into the cracked Sheetrock horizon of the waiting area. I couldn't keep back the smile or the sigh of relief. Nothing about spending the morning in a police station had impacted Grandy's pride. He was a tough old bear, even if he did have a bit of egg stuck to his lapel. Lawyer

Drew was no doubt correct—Grandy would have made the officers in the station house miserable if he'd had to spend the night.

"Well, let's get you home in a hurry and then you can give me a lecture on forgetting things, okay?" I suggested. Turning to Sergeant Steve, I motioned for him to hand me the box in which a kitten reportedly slept curled up on an old Pace County PD T-shirt.

"Just one thing." Waving a manila envelope, Detective Nolan strode into our midst, a pair of uniformed officers on his heels. "Search warrant. We'll be going along with you. I have a murder weapon to find."

5

We trailed in a convoy behind a Pace County PD squad car, like little sedan ducklings imprinting on a parent figure. Grandy rode with his lawyer, Detective Nolan took his own car, and I rode with Carrie back to her store, where I moved my pet shop haul and new fluffy kitten into Grandy's Jeep, thanked Carrie profusely, and hauled axle back to the house.

When I reached the house, I found Grandy and Drew reclining in Adirondack chairs on the front porch. Well, Drew reclined. Grandy managed to sit back in the chair and still look like he was prepared to attack. Steering the car into the driveway, I spied Detective Nolan overseeing his uniformed colleagues poking through the trash cans on the side of the house. Poor guys. There were sun-spoiled cantaloupe seeds in there.

I slid out of the Jeep with the beer carton in my arms. "What's going on?" I called.

Grandy stood from his chair. "I'm not in the habit of keeping spare house keys in my dressing gown."

He could have just said he was locked out. For the first time that day I got the uneasy sense perhaps Grandy wasn't taking things as calmly as he appeared. Yes, he could be formal, he could be proud, and he could be angry when crossed, but he wasn't the sort to be mean. He'd been short with me in the station. My own guilt had prevented me from seeing how out of character that was for him, how strange.

I crossed the lawn quickly, jogged up the few steps to the front door. Again bracing the box against one hip, I slid my key into the lock.

"Is that really beer in the box?" Drew Able asked.

Did I hear a hopeful note in his voice? Or was I imagining? Grinning, I pushed the door open. "Sorry, no beer."

"What is it?" Grandy asked as he shuffled to the door. He waved me in ahead of him, ever the gentleman.

"Small nuclear device." I set the box down on the worn, wingback chair to my left that demarcated the living room.

As the front door clicked shut, Grandy ranged up behind me. "What about my clothes?"

"In the car," I said. "Or upstairs in your room." White ball of fluff draped limp in my hand as I lifted its sleeping softness from the box.

"Georgia," Grandy growled.

Perhaps I should have given some thought to his

reaction to having an almost-cat in his house. But the kitten was a bright spot in what, at its core, had the potential to be a day from hell.

I lifted the kitten into Grandy's line of sight. A little *meew* of impending awareness broke free of the fluff.

"No." Grandy turned his back on the kitten and me and strode toward the staircase. "Tell Detective Nolan I'll be dressing," he said, reaching for the banister. A tremor shook his fingers in the split second before he closed his hand around the aged wood, a tremor that hadn't been present previously.

I tucked the kitten close and swallowed down the lump of uncertainty clogging my throat.

"Don't worry," Drew Able, Esquire, said. He slipped his hands in the pocket of his tan trousers, rocking back on his heels. "He's not himself right now. He'll be okay with the kitten. You'll see."

I sighed. It was kind of Drew to try and console me, but him explaining Grandy's behavior to me chafed a bit. Mumbling an excuse to Drew, I grabbed the PCPD T-shirt from the corner of the beer carton and carried it and the kitten into the bathroom. No way was the house ready for a kitten to run around unsupervised, so it needed to be safely confined somewhere—especially with the potential for police poking around.

I curled the shirt into an approximation of a bed in the corner where the wall met the bathtub. Lowering the kitten onto the coil of fabric, I admonished her to stay put, steeled my heart against her wide, innocent, please-love-me eyes, and ducked out of the bathroom.

With the door shut tight behind me, I returned to the living room just as Detective Nolan and his cohorts strode through the front door. Drew had taken a seat in a battered leather club chair that he'd turned to face the door. He stood as the detective approached, holding his hand out. "I'd like to see the warrant," he said.

Detective Nolan's brow crumpled and his lip curled in a disbelieving scowl, but he withdrew the warrant from the inside pocket of his suit jacket and passed it over to Drew.

"Aren't you hot in that jacket?" I asked.

The detective opened the left side of his jacket wide, revealing a shoulder holster and the gun snug inside.

"I can't ask any more questions or you'll shoot?" I guessed.

His scowl deepened. "Are you aware of the seriousness of this situation, Miss Kelly?"

Of course I was aware. Did he think I routinely watched my grandfather get accused of murder? Thing was, the whole situation, viewed from the comfort of the living room with its mixed generation furniture and worn-edged rug, reached a level beyond absurd. Given a few more moments, it would have started to feel like a waste of time.

But just out of sight of Detective Nolan, Drew Able, Esquire, moved his head a millimeter to the right, a millimeter to the left. That very slight motion warned me against straining the detective's patience.

I sucked in a loud breath. "Sorry. I can be inappropriate when I'm nervous."

I didn't know if that was the truth. My former fiancé

had accused me of being flippant when I needed to be serious, but after he revealed himself as one-sixteenth of the man I thought he was, everything he told me was cast in doubt. The me I understood myself to be when I was with him was a shadow now, and the person I truly was, yet to be discovered.

Drew refolded the warrant and passed it back to the detective. "Everything seems to be in order," he said. "You're searching for a murder weapon of unknown dimensions and bloodstained clothing."

The detective looked to me. "You have a utility space downstairs? Washer, dryer, tool bench, things of that nature?"

"Sure." One step was all it took for the memory of the washer full of my sweaty, grimy clothes to return to me. A twinge of embarrassment curled through my gut. I envisioned the thinner of the uniformed officers lifting the lid on the washer. The emanating fumes—somehow tinted green in my imagination—rise like coiled snakes to wrap around his head, the foul fragrance bringing him swiftly to his knees.

Heck. These were police officers. Surely they'd encountered worse aromas than that which might have been lurking in my laundry.

With a heavy sigh leaking out of my nostrils, I led the way down the half flight of steps, through the door to the garage. "Washer and dryer are that way." I pointed down the next half flight of stairs, tipped my head to indicate the work bench to my right. "Tools and whatnot are here."

Detective Nolan instructed the officers to split up—one

going downstairs, the other crossing to the workbench. Using the folded warrant as a pointer, he indicated the ground-floor art studio. "What's going on in here? Break something?"

I nearly smiled. "It came that way." The Tiffany-style lamp glinted atop its corner-set table, the missing section gapping like a broken heart. "The plan is to restore it, but I have to pull more of it apart before—"

"Detective." The skinny uniformed officer came to the foot of the stairs, looked up to meet his superior's gaze. "There's a bunch of clothes in the washer."

The embarrassment waiting in my gut spread from my belly, sent heat to my cheeks and flamed the back of my neck. "They're mine. From yesterday. I didn't turn the washer on yet."

Skinny officer shook his head. "Ma'am, these clothes are wet, possibly washed. Looks like a pair of boxer shorts sitting on top."

Okay, I didn't make it a habit to wash my prettier undergarments in the machine, even if it did have a cycle it pretended was gentle. But I would hardly describe my utilitarian cotton numbers as resembling boxer shorts. And I was sure I'd passed on starting the wash.

Feeling my forehead wrinkle as I fought for the memory, I hustled down the basement steps and double-timed it to the washer.

"Ma'am, please don't touch that," Skinny said.

I peered inside the old-school agitating cylinder machine.

"Ma'am." The officer was at my back, one hand hovering near my elbow as I took in the sight within the washer.

"I won't," I said on a breath. Just as he'd said, a pair of boxer shorts leered up from the depths of the washer. Woven among the tangle created by the spin cycle, my T-shirt twisted around Grandy's Dockers, my shorts peeked between the coiled sleeves of the blue and white shirt he'd worn the day before. His things must have been in the machine when I'd tossed my clothes in. I hadn't bothered to check.

Despite the presence of the officer, my promise not to touch anything, I reached forward, gripped the edge of the washer while I waited for the world to make sense. I hadn't started the washer, I was sure. Grandy's clothes weren't in there when I threw mine in with the cleaning rags, when I added the detergent. So he'd come home somewhere around 1 a.m. and started a load of wash?

"Anderson," Detective Nolan said. "Go out to the car and grab a couple of the large evidence bags, will ya?"

I turned, found Nolan lurking just over my shoulder, too far for me to have been aware he was standing there. "Evidence bags?"

Skinny Anderson strode across the room and bounced up the stairs.

"My laundry is evidence?"

Nolan grimaced. "A perpetrator commits murder, there's a good chance that perp got blood on his or her clothing."

I should have focused on that, on the belief neither I

nor Grandy were perpetrators of anything more than the occasional bad pun. But two thoughts fought for priority in my mind: uppermost, the question of what the laundry said about Grandy's guilt; second, and better to obsess over since it was a much less world-shattering issue, the knowledge that my lavender bra with the Pink Panther emblem would be seen by potentially half the population of the Pace County PD.

"You'll be able to know if there was blood even though the clothes have been washed?" I asked.

Nolan's smile was grim. "You'd be amazed how many times you can wash something and blood residue remains."

Well, that would be true if I weren't prone to cutting myself when getting careless with stained glass. I knew what it was to try and clean bloodstains from clothing. The fact that residue remained failed to amaze me.

The thump of footsteps overhead made the ceiling above us creak. Grandy was headed to the living room.

Without a word to Detective Nolan, I ducked out of the utility room and dashed up the steps. Grandy had gone through to the kitchen. He was rooting in the refrigerator, the cool air rolling through the heat of the room like a breeze off an iceberg.

"Georgia, where did you put the roast beef slices? You didn't throw them out, did you?"

"The police are searching the house and you want a sandwich?"

He glanced at me over his shoulder. "I'm hungry."

"Lunch can't wait?"

"I haven't even had breakfast," he said. "Let the police look. They're not going to find any of this evidence they're looking for. While they're searching for their unicorn, I may as well eat."

Drew Able, Esquire, ambled into the kitchen. He leaned his back against the edge of the corner sink and crossed his arms, as if this were his accustomed place, as if he were home.

"How can you be so calm?"

"Like I explained to your grandfather, he can't let any of this get in the way of his usual routine. It's best he go about his business as usual."

Grandy scowled at Drew. "Stop sounding like a therapist."

"Sorry, Pete. But I don't want you to forget how important it is for you to keep doing what you always do. Don't talk about the situation, but don't hide from it, either."

"I don't hide from things." Grandy swung shut the refrigerator door, a final burst of cold air pushing through the room. He smacked a jar of mayonnaise and a package of deli meat onto the counter. "I'm going to get myself a bite to eat and go to work."

"Work?" Jaw hanging open, I dropped into a kitchen chair. Though I heard every word Drew said about keeping things normal, I couldn't believe Grandy would have the desire to go to the dine-in, much less the energy.

For this outburst, Grandy turned his back on his lunch and leveled a disapproving gaze at me. "I have a business, Georgia, and a work ethic that I thought I'd managed to

71

instill in you. I'm not about to skip out on my staff because I've had an unexpected morning."

An unexpected morning? Being hauled into Pace County PD for questioning regarding a murder was unexpected?

"So I am going to the office tonight," he said, wrenching open the bread drawer, "and you are going to spend the evening finding a home for that feline you brought into my house without asking."

I gave him back the patented family scowl. "I don't think so," I said. "You're going to work, I'm going with you."

The Downtown Dine-In was not, in fact, located in downtown Wenwood. Instead, the restaurant/theater anchored one end of a strip mall forty-five minutes down the highway. An office supply store sat at the other end, with a string of predictable, if dull, stores in between—dry cleaners, foot doctor, insurance agency . . . the usual.

"I don't see why you insisted on accompanying me, Georgia." Grandy drove with his hands at ten and two, the radio tuned to the all-news station so he could be advised of a traffic jam before getting caught. Traffic reports aired every fifteen minutes. Between them, Grandy lowered the radio volume and turned his attention to me. "I'm not some weak old man who needs a nursemaid."

"I know you're not. I'm just worried about you."

"What's to worry about? So the police asked me a few questions. I answered them. End of story."

I wanted to remind him the police had custody of my

Pink Panther bra, but even I knew that wasn't the important element.

"But why did the police need to ask you questions? What happened between you and Andy Edgers?"

He took his eyes off the road long enough to shoot me a quelling glance. "I've already told you that's not your business."

"It wasn't my business yesterday," I said. "But don't you think today's a little different?"

"It's no different."

"Grandy, the man died. The police—"

"His death had nothing to do with me," he ground out.

My phone rang at that moment, saving either me or Grandy or both of us from the conversation. I dug the device out from the bottom corner of my purse it always seemed to gravitate to and checked the identity of the caller. Unknown. I considered ignoring the call, reluctant to get trapped into a sales pitch. But of the friends I'd left back in the city, a few kept their numbers private. I tapped the green button to accept the call.

The moment I heard the voice on the other end of the connection, I regretted the decision.

"Georgia, why haven't you returned any of my calls? Do you realize how late I've had to stay up just to be sure I'd get through to you?"

"Sorry, Mom." This was a habit. I'd long ago learned not to argue the question of responsibility. Far easier to assume the guilt for whatever her grievance was and apologize directly so the conversation could move along. "How's the trip going?"

"This is no simple trip, Georgia. This is my honeymoon. It's not as straightforward as a weekend getaway."

"Of course not. You've already been gone for a month. Where are you this week?"

Grandy harrumphed. "Your mother's calling from her wedding trip?"

"We're on the overnight train to Italy right now. Very romantic."

I wanted only to nod to Grandy. I ended up making a sour face. On the one hand, yes, Italy equaled romantic. On the other . . . "Mom, I'd really rather not think about you and Ben in any romantic setting." Eew.

"Oh, of course. I'm sorry dear. I forget how painful it must be for you not to have your own honeymoon to look forward to anymore." Her voice dripped with pity, and I cringed inwardly at her mistaken assumption over what troubled me. Up to that point I'd been mostly successful at burying the heartache that came with knowing my mother kept finding Prince Charmings and I succeeded only in finding the two-faced villain.

Mom always said that my dad—my real dad—had been the love of her life. After losing him, she figured the best she could hope for was someone who made her toes tingle. Too bad she never seemed to learn that eventually the tingle would dwindle. Four husbands since my dad passed away and still she kept hoping that first blush of love would last.

I may have envied her a little bit. Or a lot. But I'd never admit it.

"What can I do for you, Mom?"

"Not a word to her," Grandy put in, "about what's happening here."

I nodded again to show I'd heard him, even as Mom answered my question. "I just wanted to see how you were getting along in Wenwood. It can be a bit on the bland side after life in the city."

Outside my window, the highway bustled along. Cars roamed the parking lot of the big do-it-yourself home store and clustered around a chain restaurant known for steak and beer. And back in downtown Wenwood, the question of who killed Andy Edgers was likely hot on every tongue.

"It's . . . fine," I said. "I'm enjoying the quiet." This was true. The police station had a surprising hush that the city lacked.

Her sigh came across the phone in a tornado of static. "I wish you'd come to stay with Ben and I. You know the offer is still open."

Tough choice. Stick around Wenwood, where there was a killer on the loose, or meet my mother and her latest spouse in Italy. "Thanks, Mom, but I'm good here."

"If you say so."

"I say so."

"How is your grandfather?" she asked.

I slid my gaze in his direction. He kept a loose grip on the steering wheel, his eyes shifting smoothly from the road ahead to each of his mirrors, back to the road ahead. But despite his protests about how he wouldn't let the events of the morning slow him down, a vertical wrinkle bisected his brow, deep and stubborn and new. He didn't want me to mention anything to Mom, though. Maybe he was right. She could do nothing from Italy, and heaven knows I didn't want her and Ben descending on Grandy's house.

"He's fine," I said. My statement caught his attention and he glanced sternly at me, a reminder to tell her nothing. I scowled back. "He has a stash of devil dogs he thinks I don't know about. And a lifetime supply of butterscotch candies hidden inside the pressure cooker."

Grandy signaled for a turn and mumbled something about never letting me in his house again.

"See what you can do about that, Georgia. He needs to be careful with his sugar intake, not to mention his cholesterol."

"I know."

"I'm counting on you to look after him," she said.

Her words cut through me in a hot bolt of guilt. It was all I could do to assure her I'd keep an eye on him, without spilling the whole story of the Pace County PD. After that I rushed her off the phone. I shifted in my seat in an effort to look Grandy in the eye.

"We can't not tell her what's going on," I said.

"She doesn't need to know."

"She's your daughter. She worries about you."

"She's worried about me getting too fat for a coffin," he snapped.

"Grandy!"

He gripped the steering wheel tightly, leaned forward

in his seat. "There's no need to tell her about what happened this morning, that's all I'm saying."

"Why not? You didn't do anything. I don't see why the whole thing has to be a secret."

Guiding the car into the parking lot, dine-in dead ahead, Grandy said, "Let's make a bargain."

"A bargain?"

"You do your best to find the owner of that fleabag you brought home today. And if you can't find the owner, you can keep it, *provided* you say nothing to your mother."

There was a trick in there somewhere, I was certain. Keeping the kitten couldn't be as easy as keeping my mouth shut, could it? Okay, it could be, but it was wrong.

"Here's my counteroffer," I said. "I'll keep quiet, keep the kitten, but you have to tell Mom next time she calls."

He shook his head, slow and deliberate. "This is not a negotiation, Georgia."

"Of course it is." I waved my cell phone at him. "I can just hit *Dial last caller* and explain everything to your daughter right now. She'll be thrilled that I called her."

Huffing at me and not the effort of steering the Jeep, Grandy turned into a parking space behind the dine-in and switched off the engine. "You would so easily ruin your mother's honeymoon?"

It was on the tip of my tongue to suggest she'd have another honeymoon someday to make up for the one I ruined, but that was a pessimistic reflex. It would be nice if she had found her happily ever after, after all.

"Besides," Grandy said, "there's no sense bringing up the story until we know how it ends."

"What if we never know how it ends? What if Detective Nolan and his entourage never figure out who killed Andy Edgers?"

"Then your mother never has to know."

"I have a better idea," I said as I climbed out of the SUV. "Their trip is over in two and a half weeks. You can explain the whole thing when they come back from Europe, whether we know the perp's name or not. Deal?"

"Perp?"

"Deal?" I repeated.

Grandy let his chest puff out when he took a deep breath. "Deal." He took a step toward the back door of the dine-in but stopped and spun to face me. "But don't forget your end of this bargain. You have to find out who belongs to that cat."

6

Nearly twenty years ago, the Downtown Dine-In theater opened for business. A refurbished traditional movie house, in which the interior of the theater, the rows upon rows of seats, had been torn out, the dine-in's screening space now held rows of three-foot round tables, with swiveling club chairs tucked two by two at each table. Gray and burgundy dominated the theater interior, while the lobby featured a gray and navy patterned carpet and gray walls with burgundy accents painted like racing stripes erroneously applied to a stationary object.

Walking back into the dine-in sent me back to my childhood in a way walking into Grandy's house had failed to do. One sniff of the mix of faux-pine industrial cleanser and last night's French fry oil and I was sixteen years old again, wishing my grandfather ran the multiplex off the interstate so I could invite friends there—so I could *make* friends by inviting them to free movies—instead of the funky-fragranced single-screen dinosaur playing third-run movies and overcharging for chicken fingers. A lot of years separated me from the sixteen-year-old pariah I was, still the echo of my loneliness vibrated in my bones, bouncing off the high ceiling, circling the open space and reflecting from the blank screen. The emptiness sliced straight through me.

"Are you all right?" Grandy asked, doubling back to where I had stopped mid-lobby. His trim, salt and pepper brows pulled together; his frown announced his concern.

Hand over my heart, I managed a weak smile. "It takes me back, being here."

Unaware of the thoughts rolling through my head, not sensing the restimulation of heartache from sixteen-year-old me to six-month-ago me, Grandy grinned. He gazed around the lobby, pride squaring his shoulders, joy lightening his eyes. "Gets inside of you, doesn't it?"

"You could say that."

He continued scanning the space, a smile lifting the corners of his lips. "I thought when the brickworks finally closed, that would be the end of me. This place kept me going."

Following his gaze, I tried to see what he saw, tried to spy the salvation in the dark cloud gray of the walls. Seeing as how it was Grandy who was keeping *me* going, I wanted to understand what kept him getting out of bed every morning. That comprehension eluded me.

A metallic crash sounded from behind the closed doors of the kitchen. As I turned toward the noise, I caught the shift in Grandy's gaze, from pride to aggravation, with a surprising dip of sadness in between.

I trailed behind Grandy across the lobby and through two sets of swinging doors set a sufficient distance apart to prevent the light from the kitchen from encroaching too much into the theater during showtime. Behind the second set of doors, a cluster of white-clad cooks stood over an impressive spill of baking sheets, arguing with one another and threatening to report the shortest among them to Mr. Keene.

Grandy's voice boomed out in response, "Whatever it is you want to tell me, you'd better do it fast."

Two of the three cooks jumped, turning to face Grandy with worry widening their eyes and softening their jaws. The third huffed loudly, the edges of his mustache ruffling. He shook his head, smoothed his short beard, and turned away. "Would anybody care to explain what happened?" Grandy asked.

The shortest one spoke up. "Just a little accident, boss. We'll get it cleaned up."

"How many times have we talked about the need to be careful in the kitchen?" Grandy asked.

I wished I had the means to close my ears, wished I hadn't followed him into the kitchen. Witnessing the cooks receive a dressing-down wasn't on the top of my must-do list. The best I could do was look away, back slowly out the door. In keeping my gaze averted from the two cooks trying to explain themselves to Grandy, it was the third cook whose face I spotted—his jaw clenched, mouth pinched, nostrils flared. I reached the doors before I could judge whether his anger centered on Grandy or the two cooks. Wimp that I am, I escaped before things got worse, retreating to the lobby, continuing on to Grandy's office—luckily, unlocked.

A dusty stack of papers sat atop the computer keyboard, testament to Grandy's distrust of computers. He didn't avoid them as much as he ignored them. Tolerated more than accepted. Despite my and my mother's efforts over the years, he couldn't quite adapt. Now and again he would try—even going so far as updating the hardware—but I doubted he would ever embrace the technology.

With the papers cleared, I switched on the machine and waited for it to run through the boot-up. Though in reality only long minutes had passed, it seemed like hours before the computer displayed the factory-default desktop. Thus, it felt like days before I had a word processing program open and the draft of a flyer for the missing/found kitten to which I secretly hoped no one would respond.

I tilted my head and considered the text on the computer screen. Found: white kitten. Where: behind Aggie's Antiques. When: Wednesday morning.

Well, that wouldn't do. All it needed to read like a party invitation was an RSVP date.

I wiped out the *Where* and *When*, turned the *Found* into a title, and added a *Call* with my cell number. A quick clip art search allowed me to paste in a basic line drawing of a cat. Maybe an actual photograph of the kitten would have been more accurate. But she was a white kitten and

I was printing black and white notices to put up around town. She would be nothing more than a white blob center page. The line drawing would show more detail.

Shrinking the word processor window, I leaned back in the chair in Grandy's office and indulged in a stretch. The alluring aroma of burgers grilling and chicken frying snuck beneath the office door and wrapped around me like an embrace of temptation. To eat the food they were cooking up downstairs in the dine-in's kitchen would wreak havoc with my digestion, but mercy, it smelled divine.

Part of me wanted to be downstairs with Grandy, making sure none of the arriving patrons were looking sideways at him, or whispering about him. The bigger part of me knew he hadn't lived as long as he had without weathering some uncomfortable times, but feared he wouldn't want me to witness such treatment if it occurred.

Who was I kidding? I didn't want to witness anyone talking trash about Grandy. He was still bigger than life to me, invincible, infallible.

I wasn't ready yet to see him any other way.

Going to work with Grandy at night meant inadvertently adopting his waking time in the morning. Though my internal clock nudged me awake at its customary time of shortly past six, I successfully groaned, rolled over, and went back to sleep.

Somewhere past nine I found awareness again, when the formerly adorable ball of white fluff ceased being adorable by gnawing on my chin and digging her claws into my neck. And she had appeared so innocent while she slept.

Setting the kitten aside, I dragged myself out of bed and into the shower. Dressed and finally awake enough to function—I hoped—I made my way downstairs and to the kitchen. There was no sign of Grandy. I peered out the window; his Jeep sat undisturbed in the driveway.

In the process of making coffee, I urged my memory to cough up information from the night before. Had Grandy mentioned any plans? I didn't think so. I had spoken to him about borrowing his SUV, an idea he was fully in favor of since I needed the vehicle to drive up to the office store and pick up the flyers advertising a found kitten. If he had mentioned anything about meeting the boys in town for coffee or fishing or something equally rustic, I had clearly blanked it out.

With coffee prepared in a thermal travel mug and the address of the office supply store plugged into the GPS on my phone, I checked once more on the kitten and headed out to pick up the flyers.

While I followed the mechanical voice on my phone telling me when to turn and onto which street, my mind took up the unavoidable question of who might have told the police about Grandy's argument with Andy Edgers. I couldn't shake the idea that the answer to that question would help determine who had actually killed Edgers. Trouble was, I knew precious few people in town to begin with. Even if I had a name, how much good would it do me?

The GPS voice on the phone directed me to take a left and head north on Riverview. I recognized at once the picturesque road Carrie had driven on our way to the police station. The sun still glinted off the soft swells of the river that the road ran parallel to, though thick clouds were gathering in increasing numbers. Squinting at the sky, I tried to determine if there was rain on the way; driving someplace new was bad enough. Driving someplace new in the pouring rain was a whole other cause for stress.

I'd just about decided the clouds were of the nonthreatening variety when the old brickworks loomed into view. Hundreds of people had worked there at its peak, Grandy included, but the numbers steadily dwindled until the building was shuttered. Now a new business was moving in, one promising a renewed vigor for the towns along the river, Wenwood—the closest—chief among them. But again, the construction equipment within the fenced-in perimeter stood idle, and not a soul stirred. The only difference between the view I saw that day and the view the day before was that this time Anton Himmel's fancy car was parked beside a trailer inside the fence . . .

And the gates were open.

Even as I steered the Jeep through the open gates, the little voice in the back of my head declared me unreasonable and bordering on insane, while the little voice emanating from the GPS on my cell phone told me repeatedly to turn left. I ignored both and pulled the SUV parallel to the sports car, guilt and triumph warring within me at the sight of the clouds of dirt and dust the SUV kicked into the air around the Jaguar.

I shifted the vehicle into park and took hold of the ignition key. Doubt took hold of me. I was in the grips of a crazy idea, wondering what talking to Himmel would accomplish, wondering if I should back up the Jeep and return to the road.

I was reaching for the gear shift when Himmel stepped through the door of the trailer, eyes on me. Or eyes on the dust now settling over his Jag. Either way, he didn't look pleased.

Taking a breath for courage, I cut the ignition at last.

Feet clad in classic workman's boots, and knees stretching threadbare jeans, Himmel jogged down the few steps, came straight for the SUV, and pulled open my door before I'd even exhaled my courage.

"To what do I owe the pleasure?" he asked in a voice that indicated he was something other than pleased.

Shifting in my seat to face him, I said, "You know it wasn't me who told the police you were arguing with Andy Edgers, right? So why the animosity?"

"Why the visit?"

"Why the rushing out the door?"

"To keep you from getting out of the car."

"Then why did you open my door?"

Seeming as though the question caught him short, he straightened, but tipped his head slightly to the side. "Habit."

"You mean, as in opening a door for a lady kind of habit?" In my mind, the idea of Himmel as a gentleman contradicted the idea of Himmel as a jerk the way opposite poles of magnets repelled each other. Two such different ideas simply could not occupy the same space. "What brings you to my construction site, Miss Kelly?"

A zillion lame excuses occurred to me in one jumble. In the end, I went with the truth. "I was wondering if you would tell me why you were arguing with Andy the other day. What was that all about?"

He huffed and released the door. Turning away from the Jeep, he said, "I went all through this with the police."

Moving slowly, so as not to spook him, I lowered both feet to the ground and eased myself out of the SUV. "What did you tell them?"

He pushed a hand through his hair, and I mentally kicked myself for admiring the sureness of his motion, the way the blond strands brushed his collar, the definitive set of his jaw. "I explained to them about the project," he said.

I edged closer to him, conscious all the while of his potential to turn on me and order me off the property. And conscious, fleetingly, of the knowledge that the police had questioned Himmel in relation to Edgers's murder. Like Grandy, he was a person of interest. Unlike Grandy, I had no past experience with him to tell me whether he was innocent or guilty. "What about the project? What's that got to do with . . ."

He glanced over his shoulder at me. "This project." He waved an arm, the motion intended to encompass the construction site. "The rebuilt, revitalized waterfront."

"Umm . . ." To call the location *rebuilt* was some serious cart before the horse business. The grounds were crisscrossed with excavators and bulldozers, all idle, while gaps remained in the walls of the massive brickwork factory. Window frames lacked glass panes, and what was once the employee parking area was now a field of flowering weeds broken by patches of asphalt. In the deep recesses of my memory, snapshots from Grandma Keene's photo albums created my impression of the venerable brickworks where Grandy had spent his days. Neatly trimmed hedges had framed the main entrance, pallets of bricks peppered the side lot, waiting to be shipped out, and shiny cars filled the parking area. Now, only the shadow the building cast and the view of the river matched my recollections. Like Grandma Keene, the glory days of the brickworks had long ago been laid to rest.

"You have to picture it," Himmel said as he strode away from me, crossing the packed dirt expanse dividing the construction trailer from the water's edge. "We're starting with two small piers rather than long. That will give the impression right away of a well-trafficked location, and we can extend both piers or add more when the time comes."

Out on the water, rotting pilings jutted from the riverbed. I tried to picture piers stretching over the water where now there was only spoiled wood, tried to picture boats at dock—pleasure craft with families and fishermen. I had to admit it was a pleasing vision.

"The main building," he continued, shifting his stance to face the brickworks, "will have two floors, a marine shop below and restaurant above. We'll be cutting back the roofline to allow outdoor dining in milder weather."

"Which is boating weather anyway," I put in.

"Precisely." Himmel grinned. "Wenwood's location

makes it an ideal rest point for people spending the day sailing the Hudson. In good weather, you stop to enjoy a meal, maybe spend the weekend in Wenwood. In unexpected bad weather? Same thing."

"Sounds like you've got this all figured out," I said.

He nodded. "It's been a long time in planning." His gaze remained on the brickworks, as though he saw not what it was but what it would become. The spark in his eye and the eagerness in his stance nearly made me take a staggered step backward. Though his overall appearance was unchanged, the faraway look in his eye revealed another side of him—a side with plans and goals and dreams, a side that might even be considered admirable—a different sort of Anton Himmel than the scowling, angry man I'd met before.

But the equation wasn't adding up. "So if you've got everything worked out, why are you and I the only people here? Why is no one working?"

The contented, visionary expression vanished, replaced by the tight-lipped, narrow-eyed anger I'd first encountered. "Look around," he said. With a sweep of his arm, he encompassed the open, still area in which we stood. "What's missing here?"

I knew *workers* was the wrong answer, but I couldn't guess at the right one.

"You see any supplies here? You see pallets of lumber lined up and ready to go?"

"Umm, no?"

"Damn right *no*."

"But why not? Why is—"

"Tell me again why you're here," Himmel demanded.

"I . . . uh . . . was wondering why you were arguing with Andy Edgers the other day."

He raised his brows, inclined his head in a manner to suggest I already knew the answer.

The sun beat down on my head, raised prickles of sweat along the back of my neck while I worked to pull the pieces together. And then I had them. "Andy was supposed to supply the lumber."

"You're close."

Okay, so I *thought* I had them.

"Part of the agreement with the Town Council was that we would go through local channels in all possible instances. Mr. Edgers was supposed to process our supply orders for lumber, nails, asphalt, you name it."

"Is that typical?"

Himmel scowled—a response that required no words.

"So why aren't the supplies here?"

"There are some problems with the orders." He turned and walk back toward the Jeep.

Quick-timing to keep up with him, I asked, "Was that why you were arguing with Edgers? Did he know about the problems with the orders? Was it on his end or yours?"

He shoved one hand in his pocket and with the other opened the door to the Jeep. "If you'll excuse me, Miss Kelly, I need to get back to work."

Coming to a halt, I placed my hands on my hips. "Did he know about the problems, or what?"

"Miss Kelly . . ."

"Georgia."

"Georgia. I need to get back to ordering supplies from my own sources now so I can get this site working again. Thanks for stopping by."

He let go of the door to the SUV and hustled back to the trailer. I supposed *gentlemanly* only went so far when there were questions you didn't want to answer.

But why? Why would Edgers's familiarity with the problems surrounding the supply orders be enough for Himmel to send me on my way?

I climbed into the SUV, pulled the door shut, and started the engine. I didn't know how I would learn the answer to that question, but I was darn sure going to find a way.

Ⱥt the office supply store, I made fifty copies of my "Found: White Kitten" flyers and picked up a roll of tape. The problem, I realized as I set the flyers and tape in the car, was that a tiny voice in the back of my mind had already named the kitten Friday, because her soft cuddles soothed my tension the same way as a Friday afternoon of a stressful workweek. The possibility of returning her to someone who had either let her get loose or dropped her over a fence gnawed at my happiness . . . because having Grandy under suspicion of murder hadn't done enough damage.

Luckily, there was a glass shop in my future. Having that craft wonderland at the end of the road made the hour-plus drive along the interstate bearable. Either that or the miles of green foothills leading on to lush mountains soothed me in a way I hadn't anticipated. By the time I reached the shop, another half an hour east from the mountains and back toward the river, I felt as though I had truly escaped the troubles I'd left in Wenwood.

With the selection of pieces from the broken lamp wrapped in cloth and tucked in my ever-present reusable shopping bag, I rolled down the windows of Grandy's Jeep to keep the cab from becoming hell hot in the parking lot and headed for the store.

Colorful panels of stained glass art hung at intervals across the plate windows stretching the front of the shop. Images of waterfalls and waterfowl, fish and boats and lighthouses, decorated the panels, mixing the beauty of the glass craft with the flavor of the riverside town.

I pulled open the door, the electronic beep that alerted the shopkeep to my presence sounding harsh in my ears after the gentle tinkling of Wenwood's bells. I side-eyed the front window from inside the door, gratified to see tracks of the type used for sliding doors installed on the sills. Such a design made it possible to set one end of a piece of colored glass between the tracks, rest the opposite end against the window, and evaluate the glass based on the way the sun struck the colors.

"Afternoon," a woman called cheerfully.

Turning to the interior of the shop, I looked past the light table, past the cubby shelves of glass surrounding it, and found a reed-thin, dark-haired woman perched on a step stool. She held a clipboard in one hand, a pen in the other. Inventory, I guessed. I had interrupted her counting the shade forms stacked high on open-backed shelves.

"Hi there," I said. "I called about your selection of Kokomo?"

The woman nodded and pointed to the set of cubbies farthest to my right. "Over there," she said. "You need help, just let me know."

I nodded, turned away without answering. I was eager to get to the glass, to lose myself even further in the brilliance of the color, the white wisps pulled through to create soft swirls, the hint of opposite color blended in to make the hues bolder, brighter.

One by one I set samples from the broken lamp on the light table. The illumination from below revealed subtle shifts of color and patterns in the glass. It was this detail that I tried to find a replica for as I sifted through the sheets of glass filling the cubbies. I pulled shades of lavender, blends of white and periwinkle. Some sheets measured one foot square, others one foot by two feet. Sheets of three by three . . . well, those would be a last resort.

I lined the light table with smaller sheets, set the larger ones in the tracks on the windowsill at the front of the store. Once I had the blues, the greens, the whites, and the gold-threaded pinks and lavenders selected, I collected up my samples and carried the sheets to the checkout. The excitement of working with the glass I selected bubbled within me. With a plain lampshade form added to my haul, the shopkeep happily took my credit card, and I grinned past the specter of a dwindling bank account that came to hover over my shoulder and burst a couple of my bubbles.

Money concerns gnawed at the edge of my consciousness on the drive back to Wenwood. I was by no means in dire straits, and had sufficient funds to keep me a few more months if I was careful. But having been financially sound for so many years, the fear of losing that security had the power to get under my skin and ratchet up my anxiety.

I pushed it away as best I could, kept it in a dark corner of my mind while I unpacked the glass sheets in my work area at Grandy's house, the kitten looking on in wide-eyed fascination. But the echoing concern struck while I took the ride with Grandy to another night at the dine-in.

"What's got into you?" he asked. "You're not sulking about that cat again, are you?"

I'd left the flyers on the dining table, electing to delay their posting for one more day. "What have you got against Fri—the kitten? You never had a problem with pets before."

"I've gotten wiser in my old age."

"I would have thought this acquisition of wisdom would include the understanding that pets actually extend a person's life expectancy."

Steering the car into the parking lot, he said, "Georgia, having a cat under my feet would kill me."

"Grandy," I countered, "you're too tough to let one little cat get in your way."

He huffed. "Why did you have to bring home a cat? Can't you be like a normal person and bring home a stray dog?"

"I haven't come across one but I'll keep my eyes open. Fair enough?"

With the Jeep tucked into Grandy's usual parking space, he cut the engine and turned to me. "A deal's a deal, Georgia. If no one claims the little beast and your mother doesn't find out about my trip to the police station, you can keep it. Try and cheer up until we know for sure."

Sighing, I reached for the door handle. "It's not the kitten." I climbed from the SUV, reached back in to lift my laptop bag from the floor.

"What is it then? Have you gotten another message from that good for nothing you were engaged to?"

The thought of my former fiancé hit me like a fist to the gut. Any memory of him I kept locked securely in the farthest recess of my mind, undisturbed until someone else mentioned him to me, and then the lock sprang open and recollections—good and bad, joyful and painful—rushed out.

I leaned for a moment against the side of the Jeep, waiting for the surge of sorrow to pass.

"Georgia?" Grandy asked, a break in his voice. He took my elbow in his gentle yet sturdy grasp. "Something wrong? Are you all right?"

Forcing the memories back into the dark corners of my mind, I nodded, got my legs under me, and stood straight.

"I'm sorry, dear," he said, "I didn't mean to upset you." His face rumpled briefly in regret before he took a breath, schooled his expression, and looked to the sky. "He was a swine who didn't deserve you. Now let's go inside."

Silently I followed Grandy across the parking lot and waited while he unlocked one of the dine-in lobby doors. I clung tightly to my laptop bag, steeling myself against the residual tug of regret. I reminded myself I was through with the past, that it was time to look forward.

Accompanying Grandy into the lobby, I wandered ahead of him while he relocked the door—which inevitably included dropping the keys, cursing like I couldn't hear him, and starting over again.

Inside the burgundy and gray lobby, Grandy's head cook, Matthew, leaned against the darkened concession stand, back to me and white-knuckling a cell phone held against his ear. "Hey, I'm not happy about this . . . What am I supposed to do? The guy's . . . whaddaya call it . . . Teflon . . ." He lifted his head and sighed loudly. "Look, I don't know. You figure an old guy like that would spend less time working, not more. It's gonna take an act of Congress to get him to retire."

He glanced casually over his shoulder. On spotting me, he straightened, muttered, "I gotta go" into the phone, then turned toward me. "How did you get in?" he asked, eyes narrowed.

"Pete." I tipped my head toward the lobby, where the crash of keys hitting the marble floor and the following profanity repeated itself.

The cook swallowed, his prominent Adam's apple betraying his concern. He smoothed down the edges of his mustache, considering. "How long . . ."

Presuming he wanted to know how long I'd been witness to his conversation, I replied, "The whole time."

Of course I had only heard a snippet, and lying to him was unkind, but I didn't care for the way he spoke to Grandy. The wicked streak in me wanted to see the cook squirm.

"Have you just gotten here?" Grandy asked, striding into the lobby.

The cook slid his cell phone into the pocket of his chef's coat. "Just came out to take a peek at the weather."

"You have a door out the back of the kitchen, don't you?" Grandy asked. "Did you expect the front of the house to have different weather than the back of the house?"

With a shake of his head and a clenched jaw, Matthew turned his back on us and returned to the kitchen.

Okay, so maybe Grandy could get under a person's skin. Just because he was my granddad, that didn't make him a saint. But I was obligated to take his side, right?

"I don't think he likes you," I said once the passageway door to the kitchen swung closed.

"I don't like him much either," Grandy grumbled.

I stuck beside him until we reached his office then preceded him inside, switching on the overhead light and setting my laptop on his chair. The air in the space was close and warm, the air-conditioning having not yet dispelled the heat of the day. "If you don't like him, why is he still working for you?"

Grandy shrugged, pulled his chin to his chest. "He's my assistant manager's brother. I lose him, I lose the ability to take a night off. Plus, Matthew's a damn fine cook."

"This place serves burgers and chicken fingers. *I* could

prepare that." I dropped into the threadbare love seat opposite the desk. "And I wouldn't give you an attitude."

"Yes, you would." He moved my laptop bag to the floor and lowered himself into the desk chair.

"Yeah, I probably would. But I gotta tell you, Grandy, I'm starting to think I might be wrong about you. First I find out you and Andy Edgers have some old, nasty business between you, and now you and your head cook don't get along? How do you explain that?"

Keeping his back to me, he said, "How I run my business is not your business."

"Is that what you told the police?" I asked. "Did you tell them your relationship with Andy Edgers was none of their business?"

"Don't be ridiculous."

"So you'll tell perfect strangers what happened but not your own family?" I waited for a response from him. When only the faint squeak of his chair filled the silence, I went on. "Does my mother know?"

This brought an over-the-shoulder scowl. "Would you call to get the story from her if I said yes?"

I wouldn't and he knew it. He had me there. I needed to accept he wasn't going to share with me the Andy Edgers story. But one thing still bothered me—all right, more than one, but only one I could ask about. I kept quiet until Grandy seemed to settle into his nightly paperwork; the better to catch him off guard. "How did the police know you stopped at the hardware store?"

He stilled, let a full count of three pass between us before he answered. "It didn't come up."

"You didn't ask them?"

"I wasn't precisely in charge of the conversation."

I shifted forward in my seat, as though it would move me closer to an answer. "Well, why—"

"Georgia," he cut in loudly, "didn't you come here to accomplish something other than badgering me?"

Only a few simple words and suddenly I felt eight years old again and guilty of distracting Grandy from more important, adult things. I cleared the lump from my throat. "Yeah." I rose just enough to pull my laptop bag to the love seat. "I need to use your Wi-Fi here to look for a job."

He spun his chair so fast I feared he might complete a 360. "A job?"

"Sure." Tugging the laptop free of the bag, I slid back in my seat. "I'm supposed to be getting my life back on track. That means a job, a place to live . . . can't impose on you forever, can I?" I grinned to cover the anxiety gnawing at my confidence.

"No," Grandy said softly. "No, of course not." He spun the chair, putting his back to me again. "You've got your life ahead of you. Best get on with it."

After another disappointing night at the dine-in, with attendance far lower than a Bond film typically draws, the drive home was silent and despondent. Even my relief at having finally updated my résumé couldn't overcome the weight of the mood.

Call me a coward, but I woke up early the next morning and headed on foot into Wenwood village rather than risk the rumble of the Jeep luring Grandy from his slumber. The walk into the village was short enough to be pleasant but long enough to count as exercise.

I made my way along streets lined with oak and elm. Thick canopies kept the sun from my head. Below my feet, sidewalks lifted and dipped from the pressure of spreading tree roots. And the brick walks leading to gentle, old homes consisted invariably of worn, sun-faded brick stamped in the corner with a small WND. The history and legacy of Wenwood brickworks surrounded me, but its past way of life could no longer seep into my veins. I couldn't help wondering if the marina project would be enough to bring Wenwood back to a semblance of its former prosperity, and what would happen if it failed.

A single traffic light divided residential Wenwood from the little village of stores serving it. Adjusting the tote bag on my shoulder, I crossed against the light—there was no traffic to prevent this—and walked into town.

To my right stretched the windows of Village Grocery, the first stop on my path.

The entrance opened automatically at my approach, welcoming me to the bright lights and battered shopping carts of the market. Produce lay straight ahead, and for a moment I expected to find Bill there right where I'd left him days before. Of course, the only person in the produce aisle was a gray-haired woman surveying the cantaloupe.

I made the turn toward the checkout registers and stopped at the first lane. Again, the dyed blond cashier was on duty. "Hey," I said, pulling her attention away from the tabloid paper she was reading. "Is it okay if I put a flyer in your window?"

She lifted her head. "What kinda flyer?"

"I found a kitten out back." I tugged one of the revised flyers free of my tote bag and handed it over. Centered below the title "Found: White Kitten" I had relented, and instead of a piece of clip art, I'd used a picture of Friday, which owing to her extreme white fluffiness looked more like a photograph of a cotton ball with googly eyes.

The cashier took the flyer and studied the photocopied image. "What is that?" she asked.

"A kitten. See? Like it says?"

She adjusted her Village Grocery vest, straightening it so that her name tag became visible. Maura. Sort of an old-fashioned name for a girl whose appearance was so . . . progressive. "That's so sad that someone lost a kitten." She shook her head. "This town is getting crazy. First someone does in Mr. Edgers and now folks are los-ing pets? Crazy."

"Yeah, crazy. What about it? Can I put the flyer in the window?"

Maura glanced up, locked her gaze on mine. "If it was up to me, you could put up as many as you want. But you gotta ask the boss."

"Bill Harper?"

Nodding, she handed the flyer back to me. "He's in his office cursing at the books."

I thanked her and followed her pointed finger to the opposite side of the store, where wall paneling had been erected to block off the corner. A makeshift window cut into the paneling revealed Bill bent over a desk, pencil hanging from the corner of his mouth, fingers drumming against his chin.

I approached the office, forcing my feet to keep a steady pace instead of slowing. Last time I saw Mr. Harper, I hadn't made the best impression. Not that I would be heartsick if he told me I couldn't post my flyer in the street-facing windows, but I wasn't eager to have another negative encounter.

At the cutout window, I rapped my knuckles against the paneling below. As I should have expected, the wall shook. Something within the office clunked to the floor. And Mr. Harper jumped as if something had bitten his butt.

Hand over his heart, he glanced at the window, blew out a breath. "Georgia," he said. "What a surprise." With one hand he pushed the papers on his desk into a semblance of a stack and set a brick atop them. "What brings you by?"

"I . . . uh . . ." He was smiling at me. Like he was happy to see me.

"Mr. Harper," he offered, smile stuck in place.

"Right. Mr. Harper." Maybe he'd forgotten how annoyed he'd been with me? Or maybe he had some legitimate mental disorder that caused his moods to swing wildly from one day to the next? I couldn't guess at what had led to his change in the way he treated me, but I could certainly use it to my advantage. I held up a flyer. "Mind if I put this up in your window?" I threw in a big smile, in case his mood flipped the other way.

He stood and approached the cutout, leaning a bit so

he could see me through it. "Of course not, you go right ahead."

"Super, tha—"

"Say, how's Pete?"

"Fine."

"Good, good," he said. "I heard the police had him in custody, wondered how he was holding up."

Ah. Of course. The gossip grist for the rumor mill—goes in fact, comes out fiction. "He's fine," I repeated, more confidently this time. "He's not in custody, just had to answer some questions."

"Oh. Oh, I see." His brow creased as he adjusted to this information. "Well." He cleared his throat, loosening whatever words were caught there. "I'm glad to know that. Been thinking about him. Tough thing to have an old friendship that ended badly make a person look suspicious. Must be hard."

Nuts. On the odd times I'd retreat to this town with my mom as a kid, I thought folks were just being polite when they asked her about her plans. Now older, knowing the members of the town would all collect in one place to swap stories whether they had the facts or not, I felt my skin prickle. The sense that Bill Harper was looking for information, that he would pass it along at the first opportunity, gave me goose bumps.

I forced my mouth into a smile. "I'll let Pete know you were asking after him."

Mr. Harper grinned back. "You do that."

As I walked the length of the street-facing windows, the goose bumps got so bad it felt like a colony of ants were crawling across my skin. Stopping in front of a patch of window barren of oversized posters for special prices, I shuddered.

Maybe this was small town living. Maybe everyone got up in everyone else's business. And if they kept track of one another's lives out of kindness and concern, then that was the sort of thing from which the world could benefit. What worried me were the folk who kept tabs for less than friendly reasons. No, they weren't limited to small towns by any means. In big cities, though, those sorts of folk were easier to avoid. You could cut those folks out of your circle and still have friends to spare. Well, if you got custody of the friends in the breakup, that is.

I dropped my tote bag to the ground, fished around in its depths for the cellophane tape while my mind reviewed the friends I'd lost. All indications to the contrary, I didn't think my former fiancé had intentionally set about to separate me from my friends. He and they simply kept on with the life they were accustomed to living: dinners out, martinis at a downtown bar, brunches at the latest overpriced trendy spot. Out of work and money-conscious, I kept having to decline invitations. I couldn't really blame any of them for their failure to keep asking.

Of course, I could blame them for not being more sympathetic about my finances and not suggesting we meet at a place with a dollar menu. After all, I'm no saint.

I slapped the flyer against the window with somewhat more force than necessary and fixed it in place with enough tape to hold the paper immobile during a tornado. In the midst of my overachievement, my gaze fell on the bakery across the street. Fresh baked goods. Not over-priced and trendy. Just tasty. Probably fresh blueberries in the muffins.

Okay, so technically I was plotting to drown my friend-less sadness in warm, sweet carbs. I could have worse faults.

Flyer taped in place, I waved good-bye to Maura and went straight from the grocer's to the bakery across the street.

8

Grandy had brought me by the bakery on my first weekend after arriving in Wenwood. Or returning to Wenwood as the case may be. He introduced me to what felt like the entire population of the town, but the only name I remembered was Rozelle. Hey, if you're going to remember a name, remember the owner's.

The bell over the door that announced my arrival in the bakery sounded magical. Pretty much any tinkling sound would be mistaken for magic in the presence of decorated pastries, king-sized muffins, and the knee-buckling aroma of freshly baking bread. Saliva accumulated in the back of my mouth. I couldn't get my wallet out of my tote fast enough.

A "be right there" carried from the back of the bakery. I shouted an okay and rested my hands on the edge of a display case featuring shelf after shelf of cookies. Sprinkles, frosting, layers, and sweet centers, all in a heady range of colors, sizes, and shapes—how was I expected to resist?

"I'll just be another minute," the woman from the back called. "It's tricky timing. What is it you were interested in?"

I shuffled toward the back of the sales floor, closer to the door that led to the back rooms. "Some blueberry muffins?"

"Yup. I should still have those. Check by the front." Her words were followed instantly by the buzz of a timer and something that sounded suspiciously like "yippee."

Smiling, I wandered back toward the front, admiring the display of old-fashioned teacups and cake plates tucked into cubbies opposite the display cases. I had an absurd vision in my head of pouring cream into one of the pretty little saucers and presenting the treat to Friday. Not that cream was at all healthy for cats; it still made a cute picture in my imagination.

"Now, then, I should have some—"

I spun at the sound of the woman's voice. Sure enough, the owner, Rozelle, had appeared from the back room, her gray hair barely visible above the top of the tall pastry cases.

"Oh. Georgia," she said. "It's you." Her face went pale as flour, her eyes as wide as the saucers.

Panic threatened. What if she was having some sort of spell? Or a heart attack? Or a stroke? "Are you all right?"

"I'm . . . uh . . ." She rubbed her palms against her apron.

"Rozelle?"

"I'm all out of muffins," she blurted out, and bustled

to the pass-through at the front end of the display case. "You'll have to get them at another bakery."

"There is no other bakery." Was she confused, or was I?

"Well . . . I . . . Try the grocery." She took hold of my elbow and tugged me toward the door.

"Rozelle, what—"

"It's just across the way."

"But—"

"You won't have any problem finding it." She released me at the threshold, pushed the door open, and waved me through. "Have a nice day!" she said, a strained smile on her face.

Out on the sidewalk, I jumped clear of the path of a patron heading into the bakery before turning to gaze at the display window in confusion. All I wanted was a muffin. With blueberries. Why had Rozelle given me the bum's rush?

Wait. *The bum's rush?* Clearly I'd been spending too much time with Grandy.

Grandy.

I took one last look at the bakery window and shuffled away. Had Rozelle heard about Grandy's arrest? Could she possibly believe he was guilty? She couldn't. Could she?

Still craving a muffin, now caught in confusion, I picked up my pace and hurried away. I hadn't even had a chance to ask about putting a flyer in the window.

I crossed the access driveway that led to the parking behind the businesses on the north side of the road. The glorious scent of the bakery hung in the air around me.

My stomach gave a grumble of protest. Suddenly convinced I wouldn't have the strength to hang flyers without a dose of sustenance—and unwilling to buy supermarket muffins when my taste buds were primed for fresh made—I paused as long as it took to tape a flyer to the window of a vacant storefront, and eagerly passed through the door of the luncheonette.

Two steps in, the floor creaked, the same way it had done since I was a kid. The tiles beneath my feet were that same green linoleum with black and silver speckles, the stools at the counter the same avocado green. Wrapping my mind around the idea of those elements being the same for the past twenty-odd years took no small effort.

Of course, back when I was a kid, the six booths lining one side of the shop were always full; the small assortment of greeting cards and office supplies lining the other side of the shop were always crisp and white and free of dust. The shock of seeing the luncheonette through older eyes, without the veil of memory, without full tables and with a thin layer of dust, was enough to steal a breath.

"Sit anywhere you like."

I snapped my gaze to the left. A woman in a robin's egg blue waitress dress stood refilling a cup of coffee for an older gent at the counter and grinning at me. "I'll just . . ." I pointed to an empty stool, and she nodded.

Lowering my tote to the floor, I slid onto the stool with none of the effort I remembered from my youth.

"Coffee, hon?" she asked.

My memory, stimulated to peak efficiency by my surroundings, offered up her name. "Thanks, Grace."

She produced a white earthenware mug with the kind of efficiency that made me think she'd pulled it from her pocket. "Need to see a menu?" she asked.

"Any chance you have a blueberry muffin?"

Grace shook her head. "You're welcome to grab one at Rozelle's and eat it here. I won't mind."

"That"—did not sound particularly business savvy—"is very nice of you, but . . . a menu would be fine."

Evidently these were kept elsewhere. Bustling off to the opposite end of the counter, Grace hummed an unrecognizable tune.

Lifting the mug of coffee, I sent a breath across its hot surface and gazed out the window running behind the back counter. The steady, cooling stream of air I had going turned into a splutter. Straight across the way was the front entrance of Edgers Hardware.

The yellow sticker the police had used to seal the door appeared to be intact, though I'd need binoculars to be sure. The windows flanking the door provided a clear view of the shelves inside the store, despite the presence of a few sun-faded power tool boxes that once were probably an appealing display. From where I sat, the sign on the aisle endcap announcing a sale on liquid drain cleaner was easily visible.

I took a tentative sip of coffee, more for temperature than for taste. Neither registered. My mind was racing with the knowledge that my seat at the luncheon counter gave me an unimpeded view of the hardware store.

Grace returned, sliding a menu onto the counter in front of me. "Just give me a shout," she said.

She had turned away before I found my voice. "Grace, can I ask you something?"

The brow over her right eye lowered and gave a slight twitch. "You're not going to ask how many calories are in my tuna melt, are you?"

I didn't even want a tuna melt.

I smiled and set my cup down. "How late do you stay open?"

"Till six thirty Sunday through Thursday and eight thirty Friday and Saturday, just like it says on the door," she said.

Not that I could see the door from where I sat. "One more question?"

At that, both eyebrows lowered, but no twitch revealed itself. "It's not about calories, right?"

Again I smiled. "You know my granddad, Pete Keene?"

The gentleman at the other end of the counter perked up. "Everyone knows Pete," he offered.

"You know I do," Grace said.

Uh-oh. I riffled through the pages of my memory, but nothing sprang to mind. No recollections of Grace beyond the dim images of my youth, and not even a guess at who the guy was at the end of the counter.

One hand on her hip, Grace glared at me good-naturedly. "You don't remember, do you?"

I clutched the handle of my coffee cup. There was no good answer. I didn't want to own up to forgetting whatever it was she was thinking of. Even faking it . . . somehow I knew Grace would see right through my evasions and spot the truth.

In the end, I lowered my head in shame. "I'm sorry."

"You went to middle school with my niece, Diana. The two of you tried out for cheerleading at the start of the school year. Diana made the cheer squad and you got pep squad."

Of course it all came crashing back, every clap, every stomp, every split, every tear. Even Diana's face returned to my mind—her neat dark hair, big bright eyes, perfect elfin nose, gleaming white smile.

Okay, so maybe my imagination and fragile self-esteem exaggerated on the nose and teeth. Bottom line, I remembered Diana. I remembered her as the first girl who made me feel not good enough.

With age, I came to understand Diana hadn't intended for me to feel inferior. But the emotion of those days wasn't given to understanding.

I made myself smile. "Thanks so much for reminding me of my awkward and disappointing childhood."

The gentleman at the end of the counter barked out a laugh. Grace waved a dish towel at him. "You keep out of this, Tom. Eat your cookie."

"Don't listen to her, Tom," I said. "I may need an ally."

"Why do you think you need him for an ally?" Grace asked. "You forget who served you up a piece of apple pie with strawberry ice cream the day you heard the news? You sat right there with your Granddad Pete and he insisted you have whatever it was Diana was having to celebrate, because you were every bit as talented as she was."

As she spoke, the day came back to me in a rush: the late summer sunshine, the after-school crowd filling the luncheonette, and Grandy on the stool beside me, his hair only beginning to thin.

"Whose idea was apple pie and strawberry ice cream? Those are not two flavors that belong together."

She lifted a shoulder. "That was Diana's favorite."

My stomach rolled, either from the thought of the dessert or the memory of an event I'd happily repressed. "Grandy was always good to me," I conceded. "Speaking of, did you happen to see him going into the hardware store on Monday?"

Tom leaned left in my direction. "You mean the day ol' Andy was murdered," he shouted.

I froze. It felt somehow disrespectful to announce such a horrible thing using an outdoor voice. Seemed like the kind of thing that invited a bolt of retribution from heaven.

"That what you're asking?" Grace said.

"I'm just curious," I began. "Grandy—Pete—said he stopped by the store on his way to work."

"And you're doubting that?"

Esh. The guilt. The guilt. "I don't doubt it," I said as firmly as I could muster. Because I didn't doubt it. I knew he was there. It troubled me, though, to have the townsfolk think I doubted Grandy. "I just wondered what time."

I could ask Detective Nolan what time he had on his report. But the issue wasn't a matter of what time. The issue was a matter of who saw Grandy, of who told the police they had seen him there.

Gripping tightly to the coffee, I lifted the mug to my lips. I didn't doubt Grandy. I didn't. Not for a second did I even suspect he was guilty of what the police thought he was, of murdering Andy Edgers. None of my beliefs, however, changed the fact that someone had killed the man. I didn't think it was too far-fetched to suspect the guilty party of trying to make Grandy out to be the perpetrator.

But Grace shook her head. "I don't much remember. Sorry, Georgia." She pulled a dish towel from where its corner was tucked into her apron and set to wiping down the counter. "We can get quite the rush here toward the end of the day."

"Gets crowded," Tom affirmed, again with the outdoor voice. "Diana helps."

One eye on Tom, Grace nodded. "Diana helps out if she stops here for dinner, mostly handles the tables."

I glanced behind me at the six vacant tables, tried to wrap my mind around their capacity being considered a rush. I figured in time I would get there. In time I would adjust to the small-scale, slow pace of Wenwood. Portions of my mind—like my imagination, for instance—were still stuck on city settings. All I needed was some time to grow accustomed to the pace of my surroundings. Problem was, sticking around long enough for that to happen was not part of my plan.

"Terry's here," Tom announced. He patted the empty stool beside him. "And Dave stops for coffee. Andy won't come anymore."

Tom's gaze rested on the window, but I doubted he saw the same scene I did. I glanced at Grace and she gave the slightest shake of her head. "Terry's gone almost a year now, Tom, remember?" she asked.

Tom shifted his attention to Grace and the present. "Gone?"

"Gone down to North Carolina with his daughter, remember?"

For a moment the only sound in the luncheonette was the clang of pots and shush of water from the kitchen.

"Oh, sure," Tom said. "Sure." He lowered his head, focused on the half cookie in front of him. So complete was the motion that it felt almost as though a light had gone off, or a door closed. Tom had somehow left, even though he stayed in place.

"You may want to ask Diana when she comes in later," Grace said. "She might have noticed Pete stopping at the hardware." She brightened. "Plus it would be nice for you two to catch up."

Nice for who? I suppressed a shudder. Catching up implied sharing with another human being—for all intents and purposes a stranger—the downward spiral my life had been on for the past half a year. I didn't like to think about it on my own, much less share it with someone. "I might do that," I told Grace.

She gave a firm nod, as though the matter was settled. "You let me know when you're ready to order."

She retreated to the far end of the counter—which wasn't very far, comparatively—and shimmied up onto a stool. Lifting a newspaper from the counter and withdrawing a pencil from behind her ear, she bent her head over the paper and moved her lips as she read. My money was on the crossword puzzle.

I gave the menu a cursory glance; none of the options

jumped out and made my stomach growl. I still wanted that blueberry muffin. And still wondered why Rozelle had all but thrown me out of her store. I gave a split-second's consideration to asking Grace what would make Rozelle toss a customer out on her ass. Fortunately for all parties, the chime of my cell phone put an end to that idea.

The response to my inquiring "Hello?" was Carrie's barely restrained laughter. "You would rather sit around the luncheonette while Tom Harris comes in and out of coherence than come share a cup of coffee with me?"

I recalled the coffeemaker stashed in the back room of Aggie's Antiques. "That coffeemaker actually works?"

Her laughter escaped. "Unfortunately, no. Bring me a cup."

"And I would do this because . . ."

"Because I'm rescuing you, you just don't realize it yet."

"I don't—"

"Five-letter word for gravy," Grace said.

"Heinz," Tom shouted.

"Heinz isn't gravy."

"They don't make Heinz anymore?"

"They make Heinz," Grace snapped. "But not gravy."

I clutched the phone a little tighter. "How do you take your coffee?"

9

"Are you sure you didn't hear anything the night Andy Edgers was killed?" Sitting behind the cash wrap counter at Aggie's, I stared at the wall the antiques shop shared with the hardware store.

"For the thousandth time, no."

"Are you sure?"

Carrie glared at me from beneath lowered brows. "The wall you're leaning against? I share it with the pharmacy, and they're open right now. Can you hear anything?"

I gave the old *listening harder* a shot—stilled my breathing, turned my head, leaned closer to the wall.

Nothing.

"That's just crazy," I grumbled.

"That's brick," Carrie said.

"Wenwood brick?"

I'm pretty sure her nostrils flared. "Of course *Wenwood* brick. What kind of question is that?"

I shook my head. "I don't quite understand the boundless devotion to Wenwood brick. Like, take the police station. Their steps are in serious need of repair, serious need. But—"

"But they won't mix Wenwood brick with imported brick." Carrie nodded. "They'll stick with those steps until they have no choice and then they'll put in a concrete walk." Her shoulders sagged as the breath went out of her.

"I just don't see . . ."

She gave me a sad little smile. "You haven't lived here your whole life. It won't make sense to you."

"I've lived here enough."

"But on and off, right? At least, that's what Pete said."

"I suppose I would feel differently if I were truly a resident."

Carrie froze. "What do you mean *if*? You're a resident. Pete said . . ."

"Pete said what? That I was here to stay?"

While Carrie nodded, I struggled to determine what to do with that concept. Grandy knew I wasn't staying permanently. He knew I planned to stick around Wenwood only as long as it took for me to get my life back on track. We'd talked about just that plan.

Well, I talked. Grandy listened. Agreed. Said all the supportive words.

But did he believe it?

Moreover, did I?

I shook the wayward thoughts from my mind. "However it turns out," I said, "I didn't grow up in Wenwood. A few months out of a few school years clearly weren't enough to bind me heart and soul to Wenwood brick. It's going to be harder for me to understand."

Carrie busied herself straightening pens in a cup beside the register, tidying the little display of business cards for customers to take. "I suppose I could understand that."

"Thanks." I swirled the last dregs of coffee in the bottom of my cup. Hometown pride. That was something I lacked. As a kid I'd moved so much with my mother, passed from stepfather to stepfather, town to town, that I didn't really feel tied enough to one place to fight for the preservation of its legacy.

"By the way," Carrie said, casual as you please. "What do you have planned for tonight? Anything?"

Aside from trailing along to the dine-in if Grandy went, checking the Internet for leads on a job, and perhaps cleaning out the garage in search of a caulking gun, I was without appealing plans. "Not a thing," I said on a sigh. "My Friday nights aren't exactly action-packed these days."

Carrie smiled, the corners of her mouth lifting to highlight the hopeful glint in her eye. "Come with me to the wake?"

"I'm sor—the what?"

"The wake. For Andy. It's tonight and I seriously don't want to have to walk in there by myself."

Okay, this was getting a little weird. Did this woman

not have any friends? Surely there was someone else in her life more suitable for keeping her company at a wake.

"Look," she said, sinking her weight against the counter, "here's the thing. I got divorced. Almost five months ago."

"And your ex is going to be there?"

Her eyes slipped closed as she nodded. "And basically when we divided things in the settlement, I got the house and he got the friends. I have to go to this wake. I mean . . ." She gestured to the wall her store shared with Andy Edgers's. "I just really don't want to go alone."

Had she needed to come up with a sob story to get me to agree, she couldn't have come up with anything more likely to make me cave. That she explained her situation with the same shame-and-guilt-tinged tone I heard in my own speech all too often guaranteed my agreement.

I had no particular hesitation about attending the wake. Andy Edgers maybe hadn't been too fond of me, seeing as I was a member of the Keene family and all, but no one would fault me for turning up to pay my respects.

The biggest impediment was, of course, Grandy, and the booming displeasure he let loose when I made the mistake of telling him why I wasn't going with him to the dine-in.

I started by trying to simply dodge the question. "Just *out*," I said. "Nowhere special."

"If you're not going anywhere special," Grandy said, leaning against the jamb of the open bathroom door, "why are you using that thing to squeeze every curl out of your hair?"

"It's called a flatiron." And an expensive one, too. For

what it had cost, the iron should have straightened my hair with less effort than I needed to apply polish to my nails.

Grandy narrowed his eyes. "Have you got a date?"

"Hanging out with Carrie is not a date, I promise." I relaxed my grip on the flatiron, releasing a hank of hair that should have been pin straight and glossy. It was squiggly, with a dull sheen.

"Has that horse's ass you blessedly didn't marry finally turned up to apologize? You're not planning to see him, are you?"

I lifted a lock of hair away from my head and clamped it between the plates of the hot iron. "I'm not seeing him. Where do you get these ideas?"

"Then where are you going? There's no need to get all fancied up just for a couple of beers at the Pour House."

"Geez, Grandy, I'm going to Andy Edgers's wake, okay?"

The breath he sucked in through his teeth helped him to stand taller, broader, scarier. "Andy Edgers's wake?"

"See? This is why I didn't want to tell you."

"Why in heaven's name would you do such a thing?"

"I should have closed the door," I muttered.

"You know I didn't get on with Andy."

"Yeah, I do know that, but I don't know *why*."

"And the police have questioned me about his murder."

"Yeah, I remember."

"I bet half the town thinks I did it."

"Don't be ridiculous, Grandy." I selected a new lock of hair to squeeze the life out of. "No one thinks you killed Andy."

"Then why . . ."

He said no more, letting the silence grow until I turned to him. "Why what?" I asked.

He cleared his throat, shuffled his feet. "I could really use your help at the theater," he said. "I've got to get the payroll done and my head's not in it. Thought you might lend a hand."

I took a breath. Setting the flatiron down on the edge of the sink, I turned my full attention to Grandy. "I'll go tomorrow in the morning to do your payroll, okay?"

"That's not all—"

"I know." I reached and wrapped my hand around his forearm. "I know you'd rather I don't go tonight, but I promised Carrie. She helped me out. I need to return the favor. Besides, paying my respects is the right thing to do. Isn't that how these small towns work?"

He grumbled a bit but rested his hand atop mine. "Fine. Go this evening. Just remember, there's two sides to every story."

"What's that supposed to mean?"

He merely tapped a finger against the side of his nose and strode away down the hall.

Possessed of a college education and the common sense God gave to all beings not composed of Styrofoam, I understood the meaning behind the phrase *two sides to every story*. What puzzled me was why Grandy had felt the need to share that wisdom with me—and what he was hiding that had prompted his reminder.

His words settled in the back of my mind. There the puzzle stayed, beyond Carrie's picking me up, beyond the drive out of the neighborhood and out to the highway. We'd taken the turn south and zoomed up to highway speed by the time the curiosity morphed into the conviction that attending the wake was a less-than-brilliant plan. If I'd been driving, I could have hit the brakes and reversed direction and decision and gone home. Of course, Carrie was driving.

"Thank you so, so, so much for coming with me," she said for the bazillionth time.

I was running out of responses. *No problem* was sounding flippant, and *my pleasure* was downright untrue. I settled for, "It's the least I can do."

She nodded, more, I supposed, as a means of creating a suitable break in the conversation than as a sign of agreement. "Any news from the police?"

"Not that I know of. Why would they . . ."

"Oh, I don't know, just thought maybe . . ."

"They haven't stopped by to arrest Grandy if that's what you're wondering." I flipped down the visor and peeked at my reflection in the mirror. What was that crease running down the center of my forehead?

She shot a glance my way. "That's not what I meant at all. I was hoping maybe they had called to say they were no longer considering Pete a suspect."

"I'm sorry." Folding the visor up, I put my fingertips to my forehead and rubbed at the tension gathering there. "I'm a little preoccupied."

I kept my thoughts to myself as we were passed on the highway by a tractor trailer, a minivan, and a Japanese-made compact car that rolled out of the last century.

Maybe it was the last one, the reminder of things from another time that pushed the thoughts free.

"I'm just trying to figure out something Grandy said to me." I turned toward her; she kept her gaze focused on the road. "He said there's two sides to every story, and I should keep that in mind. I can't figure out what he meant."

"I think it's pretty self-explanatory. It's just good advice, isn't it? One of those pieces of life wisdom the older generations get such a thrill out of sharing?"

"Maybe," I said, "but I think that's the less likely explanation."

Steering the car smoothly onto the ramp to the access road, Carrie asked, "You think he was talking about something specific?"

"I do." I opened my mouth to elaborate, to explain my concern that Grandy's comment related to the mysterious something dividing him and Andy Edgers, but thought better of it. If Grandy didn't want to talk to me about whatever had transpired between him and Andy, it certainly wasn't something he'd welcome me discussing with Carrie.

"Or maybe I don't." I shook my head, forced a dry laugh. "I don't know what to think anymore." I gazed out the window at the passing neighborhood—houses larger than those in Wenwood, lawns manicured to magazine-spread standards, no car older than two years occupying flagstone driveways.

In an earlier time, a little blue house at the corner of the main road served as Wenwood's funeral parlor. Now the space was home to the Pour House, and Wenwood's dearly departed were laid out at an elegant, sprawling homage to Margaret Mitchell's iconic creation, Twelve Oaks. Only this one was the Palmer Funeral Home.

"Now remember," Carrie said as we circled to the back of the estate to find a vacant parking spot, "when you see Russ, pretend we don't see him."

"You know that sounds illogical, right?"

"Just give him the cold shoulder treatment," she continued.

With the car parked and the engine switched off, Carrie crawled out of the car with the speed of someone who had been superglued to their seat. "Let's get this over with."

"I don't know what you're worried about." I tugged my skirt away from where it had adhered to the backs of my legs on the car ride over. "You probably won't even see Russ."

Carrie shot me an incredulous look.

"What?" I asked. Would she be unable to resist looking for him? Did she expect him to seek her out? Why the disbelief?

But she only shook her head as we drew level with a family of mourners, none of whom looked familiar. As a group we entered the funeral parlor, silent aside from the occasional hiss of a whisper.

The last wake I had attended was for a coworker, a well-liked administrative assistant who had suffered an aneurism on a train platform—the sort of freak tragedy that made everyone realize how tenuous life truly is. Her viewing was standing room only. When my grandmother had passed, she'd been laid out at the tiny old Wenwood parlor, and the mourners had spilled onto the street. With these sorts of indelible memories, I supposed it was only natural that once inside the Palmer, I migrated toward the most crowded room and joined the end of the line of waiting mourners.

Carrie set a gentle hand on my elbow. "I think Andy's in the next one."

Of course she was right. The person whose line I was waiting on turned out to be someone whose name featured a lot of *M*'s and *W*'s and was most likely female. Andy's parlor was at the end of the hallway running the length of the mansion. The farther along the hallway we walked, the quieter the space became until I could have sworn I heard the crunch of the foot pad in my shoe.

"Ten minutes," Carrie whispered. "We're in and we're out."

I gave her a thumbs-up and followed her into the room.

The absence of a crowd gave me a new understanding of Carrie's concern over seeing Russ, and gave me new regret over Andy Edgers's passing. There seemed so few to remember him.

We were half an hour into viewing hours already and still several rows of seats remained empty. The few occupied chairs were taken by folks whose faces I'd begun to recognize as Wenwood locals. Grace from the luncheonette sat chatting quietly with Rozelle, her hand on Rozelle's shoulder as though comforting her. One of the clerks from the pharmacy kept her head bent over her rosary. And at the far side of the room, hands in pockets as he studied one of the bereavement bouquets, stood Tony Himmel.

"Thank God." Carrie seemed to shrink six inches all around as the tension left her. "I don't see Russ."

It was my turn to speak, but my gaze and my thoughts were focused on Himmel. I should have been wondering why he was present. Instead I wondered where he got his suits. Were they store-bought and well-tailored? Or custom-made? What kind of fabric was it that hung so well?

A motion to my left brought me back from my study of Himmel's silhouette. A gentleman approaching, balding head lowered, hand extended. "Thank you for coming," he said.

I did my best to elbow Carrie forward without being too obvious. She reached to take the man's hand. "Carrie Stanford," she said. "I have the store next to Andy's."

"My dad's spoken of you." The gentleman turned to me, again with his hand out.

"Georgia. Kelly," I added. I watched his eyes for a reaction, some narrowing or widening that might indicate he knew Grandy, or had knowledge of whatever had transpired between our ancestors.

But my name clearly sparked no interest in him. He turned back to Carrie with attention brightening his eyes. "You're next door to the hardware store?"

"Aggie's Antiques," Carrie said.

With that information, poor Carrie was stuck answering again all the questions I'd asked her about whether or not she'd heard anything the night Andy was killed.

Rather than standing beside them like a silent

interloper, I slipped away and walked sedately to the closed casket at the front of the room.

Calling on dim memories of childhood, I made the sign of the cross and knelt on the prayer stool. Religion—much to Grandy's frustration—had been a haphazard affair, and the prayers I may once have known were no longer in my memory. In my mind I put together a makeshift prayer— an entreaty to God to keep Andy close in heaven, and to bless with peace those he left behind.

I was struggling for some sort of closing when first the scent of woodsy, spicy cologne broke through the fragrant haze of lily and the prayer kneeler canted to the right.

Having made the trip to the funeral parlor with Carrie, I stood no chance of mistaking her flowery perfume for the scent occupying the air beside me. Eyes wide, I gaped at the man sharing the kneeler with me.

Tony Himmel held my gaze for as long as it took to bless himself then turned to the casket as his eyes closed.

What in heaven . . . Who does that?

Regaining my feet, I smoothed my skirt as though that surface motion would sooth the jangle of my nerves.

At that last wake, my former fiancé had accompanied me to the viewing. He'd held my hand while we walked in, kept his fingers at the small of my back while I offered condolences. He'd knelt beside me as I fumbled through prayers at the casket. That's what the people who love and care for you do. Sharing a prayer stool with someone you just met and tended to argue with was *not* the behavior of a casual acquaintance.

Of course, the front of a viewing room was not the

place to take Himmel to task for his personal-boundary-breaking behavior. I was limited to shooting daggers at him before turning fully and seeking a seat.

It was then, as I turned, that I spotted Detective Nolan meandering through the door. Perhaps it was my frozen-in-shock response that cued the other attendees to something unusual happening. I was, after all, standing at the front of the room. Or perhaps it was an instinct for drama. In either case, the few gathered in the room shifted in their seats and watched the detective stroll to the chairs lining the back wall. With an audible sigh, Nolan lowered himself into a chair, his gaze on nothing in particular.

Behind me, the prayer stool creaked as Tony stood. I shifted my weight. No one spoke a word. No one made eye contact. I'm fairly certain everyone held their breath.

Did they all know who Detective Nolan was? Or did his status as a nonresident of Wenwood brand him as suspicious?

Twinges of nerves I'd tried to smooth down flared to life. Detective Nolan's presence was one more chance for me to say something stupid that might implicate Grandy further. Super. Problematic detective ahead of me, personal-space-invading contractor behind me. And for crying out loud, where had Carrie gotten off to? She'd said ten minutes tops, but I doubted she had left me behind in her eagerness to keep our time short.

That moment's hesitation gave Tony all the time he needed. His hand slid around the curve of my shoulder. His voice, little more than a whisper of wind in my ear. "If I could speak with you . . ."

I should have flinched away from him. Instead I scolded myself for feeling the urge to melt into his touch. Stepping out of his reach helped. Storming away from him was also good. Not until I arrived at the love seat in an adjacent alcove did I risk facing him again.

Sitting was out of the question. Sitting invited the sort of cozy companionship we'd shared at the casket. Instead I stood and folded my arms so my forearms covered my belly. I held a breath, waiting for Tony to speak.

He took a look at the way I was standing, eyes sweeping from my patiently straightened hair to my pump-pinched toes, and puffed out a sigh. "Relax, please. I want to apologize, not upset you."

Damn. I lowered my hands to my sides while silently berating myself for letting my emotion show in my posture. When had I lost the ability to stand impassively through any situation, never giving anything away? Had I lost that skill with my job? Or had it fallen victim to a failed engagement and the loss of my old life? Behind my back, my hands came together, fingers twining.

"I shouldn't have been so harsh with you yesterday. My troubles with Andy . . ." He paused, tipped his head slightly in the direction of the casket. When his gaze came back to mine, the earnestness held me immobile. "They were nothing you caused, nothing I should have treated you badly over."

I caught the inside of my lip between my teeth. Should I accept his apology? He hadn't actually said he was sorry. My fingers untwined and my arms slid to my sides. "And the police station? You weren't exactly kind and gentle-manly there either."

His smile stretched tightly across his face, an expres-sion of chagrin more than joy. "That was . . . It hasn't been an easy week, Miss Kelly."

"Georgia," I said automatically.

He nodded. "Tony."

I took the hand he offered. A strong grip and calloused palms gave me the impression he didn't spend all his time sitting in an office wearing expensive suits. Before my imagination explored the potential behind those strong hands, I asked, "If Andy created such a problem for you on your construction site, why are you here?" And what was it Hollywood would have us believe? That the mur-derer always attended the services? Was that what had brought Detective Nolan to the Palmer?

Tony pulled in a deep breath and folded his arms across his chest. "I wanted to pay my respects. He may not have been the best businessman, but he had his share of good qualities."

"I'm kind of thinking that people with an abundance of good qualities don't get murdered."

"Good people get murdered all the time," he said. "If bad guys were the only ones who died, the world would make sense. And wouldn't that confuse us all?"

My search for an appropriate response led me not to a logical comment, but to a question that had been gnawing quietly at the back of my mind. "Speaking of confusing, there's something I don't understand. If construction on the marina was held up because you didn't have the supplies, why not push the orders through, either through Edgers or somewhere else?"

Tony's eyes flared wide and his lips pressed tight, as though I dared speak ill of the dead at the worst moment in the most inappropriate location possible.

"That day at the store. Andy said he needed you to place an order. Why didn't you? Why let—"

"There you are." Carrie arrived in the alcove, anxiety filling the air around her. "We have to go. Oh, hi, Tony. You ready, Georgia?"

"Yes," I said, "I just—"

"Price," Tony said. "Hello, Carrie."

"What? Price?" I repeated.

He unfolded his arms, stuffed his hands in his pockets. "It may be impolite to speak ill of the dead, but I wasn't getting a fair price from Andy's supplier. It's one thing to pay a little extra to keep a small business going or keep the money in a community. But there's extra, and there's unfair. A project the size of the marina, overpriced anything can blow your budget to pieces."

Carrie's eyes widened. "You're not suggesting Andy cheated you?"

"Not suggesting anything." Tony's cheeks flushed an angry red. "I'm saying I wanted a fair price. If I couldn't get a fair-price quote from Andy, my project would go so far over budget the marina would be at risk. This town needs the marina, Carrie, you know that. And Andy Edgers needed the business as much as I need the supplies. We should have been able to negotiate."

"But you made a *deal* with the town," Carrie said. "You agreed to—"

Bill Harper popped his head around the corner. "Hiya, kids. Getting a little loud in here." He bounced his eyebrows as if to lessen the sting of his reprimand. Not that it helped. I hadn't even been the one arguing and still my shame took me back to my childhood. Blast this town.

"Mr. Harper," Carrie began, waving him in, "the Town Council's agreement with Stone Mountain Construction requires the marina materials be sourced from Wenwood, right?"

Straightening his spine as he joined our little group, Mr. Harper cast his gaze momentarily to the ceiling, seeking his memory there. "Ahh-uh, yes, I believe it does."

"See?" Carrie arched her brows, glaring triumphantly at Tony.

"I'm aware of the agreement." Amazing how clearly he spoke despite the clenched jaw. "But it also allows me to seek supplies throughout Pace County if Wenwood is unable to accommodate our requirements. And forgive me for saying this, but with no one running the hardware supply now, we're free to source our materials elsewhere. I may be a lot of things, folks." He glared at each of us in turn. "But the one thing I'm not is a dishonest businessman. Now if you'll excuse me."

He ducked out of the alcove, leaving us silent in his wake.

"It appears you struck a nerve there, Carrie," Mr. Harper said.

She shook her head, lowered her gaze to the floor. "He

agreed to the terms, Bill. He has no right to be looking for other suppliers."

"Is this a legal agreement? Is it on file somewhere?" I asked. The issue aroused my curiosity. What exactly were the terms of the agreement? What were the contingency provisions? How much was at stake? If Andy Edgers couldn't fill the orders for Stone Mountain, they were free to find another supplier. Was supplying material to the marina project enough to kill for? Was there another small town hardware store out there for whom the commission on the supply order would make or break the bottom line?

"Certainly," Bill said. "Wenwood may not be the big city you're accustomed to, Georgia, but we're not a back creek town either. The papers are on file at Town Hall."

I looked to Carrie, who nodded. "I'll give you the address."

"Thanks." I turned back to Bill. "And they're available there for anyone to review?"

Mr. Harper tipped his head like a puzzled bulldog. "Whatever would you want to be looking at those for? I'm sure they make for very dry reading. Nothing to concern yourself with."

At least he didn't tell me not to worry my pretty little head. "I'd like to see them. I'd like to understand more about Wenwood."

"You can't understand Wenwood by reading its building codes," he said.

"No, but how the town does its business isn't a bad start." I kept my voice as light as possible, but Bill Harper's eyes narrowed and his jaw tensed.

"To understand Wenwood, you have to live here," he ground out. "You have to be a part of it. You have to love it. Someone whose heart isn't in this town can never understand."

My heart wasn't in Wenwood. I hadn't realized that showed. Bill Harper saw it, though. And he scowled and shook his head as he left Carrie and me in the alcove.

"We're getting under everyone's skin here, huh?" Carrie joked, but she twined a curl of hair around her finger, an action I was beginning to suspect indicated a momentary lack of confidence.

I sighed. "It's a gift." Wrapping my fingers around my elbows, I asked, "What do you know about the agreement between Tony's company and Wenwood?"

She frowned. "Not enough."

If I wanted to understand the agreement, I would have to go to Town Hall. But I was afraid the agreement was only half the puzzle. What I needed to see were Andy Edgers's sales records. If his lumber prices were above fair market, how much would ordering supplies through Edgers cost Tony Himmel in overages? And what lengths would Himmel go to in order to see his project completed on time and on budget?

I peeked past the corner of the alcove to where Andy Edgers's closed casket was flanked by funereal flowers. I reminded myself I didn't doubt Grandy's innocence in the matter of Andy's murder. Still, I'd feel better if I knew who *did* kill Andy. And, I figured, the first step to figuring out who was figuring out why.

10

With clear morning sunshine slanting through the windows, I slid the sheet of opalescent glass free of its protective newspaper wrapping and held it up to the light. Lavenders and blues, pinks and purples flared across the textured plane. I carefully tipped the sheet of glass against the window, studying it, looking for the bright spots and soft spots, the direction of any visible wisp lines. It was one of my favorite parts of the process. Those were the moments that allowed me to put aside the worries of the day and focus on the craft at my fingers. Those were the moments when all else disappeared for me, and all I knew was the pattern of the glass and where its truest colors lay.

But as I placed the glass on the worktable and began taping down the pattern pieces I'd copied from the intact side of the lampshade, the usual sense of peace and focus eluded me. Reaching for my marker, I tried to turn away the thoughts campaigning to be admitted to my consciousness. With each pattern line I traced on the glass, I tried to push aside the questions troubling me: How did one go about discovering the fair price of lumber? And why would Andy Edgers charge above it?

With the pattern drawn on the glass and the pieces removed, I lifted my glass cutter from the old olive jar it rested in, a pool of kerosene lining the bottom. Deliberately, I ran the cutter in a straight line, scoring the glass from one side of the sheet to the other, dividing the sheet to make it easier to cut the pattern pieces.

And still the question of whether Tony Himmel wanted his marina built so badly he would . . .

I set down the cutter and lifted the sheet. The next step required breaking the glass along the score, using even pressure on both sides of the score. Thumbs on either side of the score, I applied the required pressure and snapped the glass.

The glass broke clean along the score line—for a while—then veered off at a thirty-degree angle, breaking through one of the marked pattern pieces.

I cursed quietly. I'd blown the score, had failed to apply even pressure. Damn. So many thoughts swirling through my head . . . My mind just wasn't in it. The ride to the glass shop was too long to have to repeat because I had wasted glass trying to break it when I had no business doing so.

I stared at the split sheet on the table, at the glancing

sunlight on its gentle peaks, the subtle shadows in its textured valleys. I took a deep breath in, held it, and released it slow and even. My gaze never wavered from the glass, but my thoughts continued to stray. Thoughts of Andy Edgers's receipts, his order book. If I wanted answers, if I wanted a way to prove Grandy had nothing to do with Edgers's death, I needed to see those books.

Friday came bouncing down the stairs, pausing on each step before continuing to the next. Big blue eyes in a fluffy white face, she looked at me as though trying to implant a telepathic thought in my mind. Really, though, what sort of thoughts would a kitten have? Food, water, play about summed up her repertoire to date.

In surrender to a wandering mind, I decided to pack it in for the day. I closed the cover on the kerosene jar and stored it under the table, then lay a bedsheet over the top of my worktable, folded so no tempting linen edges were exposed from a kitten's eye view.

On my way up the stairs, I scooped her up and tucked her against my chest. Thus far the flyers I'd hung had yielded no result. As Friday snuggled under my chin, I felt a little thrill at the prospect of learning just how far I'd have to drive to get her to a vet. I almost regretted putting my real phone number on the flyers. But if she was truly someone else's lost kitten, I was sure that person was heartbroken.

In the kitchen I set Friday down and scribbled a quick note to Grandy assuring him I would be back in time to help him out with payroll. I grabbed the keys and headed out, wondering if the combination of curiosity, doubt, and anxiety I felt was the same emotional mix investigative reporters felt. Of course, they probably didn't go hunting down information wearing walking shorts and flip-flops.

With the radio retuned to a station that played more than the headline news Grandy favored, I followed the roads Carrie had driven days earlier, out of Wenwood and north along the river road, past Himmel's idle construction site then inland again to the Pace County Police Department.

The butterflies in my belly went into a frenzy as I parked the car and made my way to the front door. I tried to assure myself the worst that could happen was that Detective Nolan would deny my request, but my self wasn't listening and apparently butterflies are not conversant in English.

Three quick—thus nowhere near deep and soothing—breaths and I was inside the station house. And Sergeant Steve, my cat-loving ally, was nowhere to be seen. In his place . . .

"Diana?" I squeaked.

Her dark eyes met mine, and as I closed the gap between door and desk, I understood what had surprised me so—apart from the police uniform, that is.

Her sleek hair was pulled back in a low, almost schoolmarmish bun, and her face appeared entirely devoid of makeup. Years in the sun had not been kind. But among the wrinkles were an encouraging abundance of laugh lines. Or was it all those cheerleading smiles and not true happiness that had carved them?

"Georgia Kelly," she responded, straightening. The movement of her arm indicated she was reaching for her gun. I froze, butterflies suddenly smug, having known all along this was a bad idea.

But Diana's gun never appeared. She kept her hand braced against the grip of the gun, the most intimidating hand-on-hip pose known to man.

"Um." That was all I could manage.

"Go ahead, say it."

"Say what?"

She tipped her head and popped her eyes wide. In a mocking voice she said, "Oh, my gosh, Diana Davis. You're a cop? What went wrong?" She resumed her natural pose and glared at me, waiting.

"Okay, I'm surprised to see you as a police officer, so you're right on that. But the other part I don't know what you're talking about."

Her brows rose, disbelief writ in evenly plucked arches.

"And I was just at the luncheonette yesterday. Your Aunt Grace never mentioned—"

"Give it up, Georgia. What do you need?"

I needed a favor. I didn't think she was disposed to assisting me, though. Time to invent a Plan B.

Leaning my forearm on the desk, I said, "Honestly, Diana, I don't know about anything *going wrong*. I think it's great you're a police officer, really. I mean, it's not like you could be a cheerleader for the rest of your life, right? Not much chance for a career there, hey?"

Her eyes darkened, lips pinched, nostrils flared.

"Oh, crap." I hung my head. "This really could not have gone any worse." And she still had a hand on her gun. Terrific. "I'm sorry for everything, okay? The cop thing, the cheerleader thing, global warming, root rot, everything. Just . . . is Detective Nolan here?"

"No."

"Any chance you can tell him I stopped by?"

Against all odds, her eyes narrowed further. "Of course. I don't let personal feelings get in the way of doing my job."

I nodded and stood back. "Thanks." The butterflies were eager to get me the heck out of Dodge, but I couldn't go without one last attempt. "For what it's worth, I really don't know anything about your life after, like, sophomore year in high school. And even then I was only here a few months. My grandfather's not much for town gossip, and your aunt didn't breathe a word. Next time we meet up, maybe you'll give me the benefit of the doubt, huh?"

I rushed from the station, down the patched steps, across the pitted parking lot. No doubt I should have asked Carrie if she knew what days Sergeant Steve was on the desk. I needed an ally in the station, not a grade-school rival.

Inside the SUV, windows rolled down, my mind scrambled for the next step, the Plan B. Even if Detective Nolan called to see why I'd stopped by, there was no guarantee he'd give me the information I wanted.

Gripping the steering wheel, I waited for my nerves to calm before starting the engine. Judging by the clock on the dash, I had more than enough time to make an unscheduled stop. With luck, I could do a little digging before heading home to get Grandy to work.

In the span of twelve miles, the GPS and *Find It* functions on my smartphone became my favorite things. After the simple step of switching on the locator then typing "hardware store" in the *Find It* search bar, I followed the instructions of the soothing phone voice to the one privately owned store between the police station and downtown Wenwood. Two more shops were situated in northern Pace County, and one off to the west, but I could only do so much in one morning.

Unlike the village of Wenwood, which despite being peppered with empty storefronts could still be described as picturesque, the stretch of stores that soothing phone voice led me to was a characterless strip mall. Dry cleaner, pharmacy, packing store . . . each shop stretched the same width, each had an entrance door set to the right, each had the same aluminum-trimmed windows—except the shop I was there to see. Prince Hardware occupied a space twice the width of the other stores and the double-door entrance sat smack in the center.

Parking in the little lot facing the strip mall was limited, and I was forced to circle the lot twice before a gentleman carrying his dry cleaning vacated his spot. Even as I zipped into the spot, my stomach began to hollow with doubt. A packed parking lot, a double-wide lot, and clutter-free windows gave me the impression that Prince Hardware wasn't suffering. Still, impressions could be misleading.

Purse over my shoulder, I climbed out of the SUV, tugged the legs of my shorts back to a decent length, and headed for the hardware store.

As I drew closer, the colorful spots in their window resolved themselves as packets of flower and vegetable seeds. Garden tools with bright green grips and bags of fertilizer filled out the display. I paused at the edge of the sidewalk, wondering if it was too late to plant vegetables out back of Grandy's house, or if the seeds would have to have been planted before the end of May.

I was lost in indecision as the door to Prince Hardware swung outward and Detective Nolan stepped into the sunshine.

"Well." He half smiled. "Miss Kelly."

I rolled my eyes. "Just Georgia."

Smile fading, he asked, "Should I ask what brings you here?"

Probably it wasn't a good idea to tell the police you were in the midst of doing your own investigating. "I need a caulking gun," I blurted out. I nodded at the Prince Hardware sign. "This place was on my way."

"A caulking gun. Still." He nodded slowly, almost sagely, lips pursed, sunshine silvering the gray in his hair. "No chance you were planning to nose around Andy Edgers's competition for supplying materials to the marina project?"

I adjusted the purse strap across my shoulder and tried to make my face look innocent, which felt a lot like smiling foolishly. "Why would I do that?"

"If I had to guess, I'd say because you think someone

other than your grandfather belongs in jail. And wouldn't it be convenient if some other hardware store owner had a motive for killing ol' Andy."

"My grandfather doesn't belong in jail," I said.

He folded his arms, looking me over head to toe. "Where is it you said you were going before you stopped here?"

"Did I say? I don't think so," I said, also folding my arms and trying to give him the same once-over he had given me. "I was at the police station, in fact, looking for you."

"Is that so?" One step backward and he took hold of the door. "And now you've found me, the least I can do is help you find a caulking gun." Pulling the door open, he swept his free arm toward the entrance in invitation.

I tried to dismiss the fleeting feeling that this was some sort of trap. I'd done nothing wrong. Even my plan to poke around the store, just as Detective Nolan suggested, was more curious than illegal. Still, a corner of my belly curdled with unease as I ducked into the store.

The cool air inside instantly chilled me. Little beads of sweat I didn't realize had gathered while I was speaking to the detective seemed to freeze against my skin. When he set his hand against my shoulder to guide me, I shivered, though I was not entirely sure why.

"This way." He slipped past me, moving quickly into the center aisle that divided the store. Shelving ran east to west on either side, each aisle clearly marked, with well-stocked endcaps and signs for special deals on things like garden hoses and citronella candles.

Detective Nolan ducked into an aisle to our left and

slowed. An impatient glance over his shoulder made me rush to catch up to him. Checking the floor for chip marks (none) and the endcap products for dust (also none) had clearly slowed me down.

"Sorry," I muttered, coming to a stop beside him.

With a wave of his hand, he indicated the lowest shelf, where metal bins displayed a variety of caulking guns. "There you go," he said. "You even have your choice of color."

"Green or darker green." I squatted in front of the bins, examined the guns for some difference other than price, and tried to find the best way to start the conversation I wanted to have.

Before I could, Detective Nolan shifted to his left, making it easier for me to reach the devices at his feet, and said, "You should go ahead and buy one of those. You won't find anything different at Miller's Hardware."

I held a caulking gun in each hand, feeling the difference in grip, the difference in weight, pretending I cared deeply. "I might," I said.

"Trust me. I went by earlier and there's nothing different between there and here." I tossed the guns back in their bins and stood. "How do you know? Were you looking for caulking supplies?"

He shook his head, eyeing me as though I'd disappointed him somehow. "Look, Miss Kelly—"

"Georgia."

"Miss Kelly. You and I both know you're here to check out the potential heirs to the marina supply contract. So let me put your mind at ease. The department has already spoken with the owners at Miller's and here at Prince and we don't consider them as suspects."

Though I really did need to get that bathtub caulked, I let go of the pretense of why I was there. "How does that put my mind at ease?"

Lips pressed tight, he tipped his head side to side, considering. "Okay, so it puts my mind at ease. I don't need a civilian poking her nose in police business."

"So I'm just supposed to sit back while you continue to wrongly keep my grandfather's name in the suspect column?"

"Georgia," he said on a sigh.

"Now it's Georgia? This is my grandfather. He might hurt his share of flies and do serious damage to a box of cupcakes, but he's more the type to shout and glower than pummel and bludgeon."

Too late I realized someone had come up behind me. Detective Nolan gave a young mother, baby in her arms, a tight smile and a nod. She scurried back the way she'd come, leaving us alone again surrounded by plumbing supplies.

"Is this why you were at the station looking for me? To tell me about Pete Keene's . . . cupcake habit?"

The slightest hint of a smile twitching at the corner of his mouth did little to slow me. "I wanted to know who it was that told you they'd seen him leave the hardware store that afternoon."

"Is that all?" His eyebrows rose. "Now why would I tell you that?"

I couldn't even claim he should tell me because I asked

nicely. I ducked, grabbed a caulking gun from the bin, and pointed it at the detective.

His eyebrows rose higher. Gaze on the caulking gun, he had no need for words.

I lowered my arm, letting the device fall to my side. "Please. Will you tell me who said they saw Grandy?"

"I'm sorry, Georgia. I can't." He paused while a voice on the overhead speaker requested someone go to custom paint. "That's confidential information. Part of the investigation."

I breathed out a mild curse.

"Sorry you made the trip for nothing."

"Yeah," I conceded, lowering my head. Someone had told the police they'd seen Grandy leave, had told them they saw Tony Himmel. Who would see? Or was the person who claimed to see really the person who killed Andy Edgers, giving the police false suspects to divert attention from himself?

Detective Nolan ran his hand around the back of his neck. "If there's anything else I can help you with . . ."

I nodded slowly, resigning myself to the fact that I would have to learn another way who gave the police Grandy's name. I wasn't sure how. I had to figure out a way. In the meantime, I met the detective's surprisingly friendly gaze. "As a matter of fact," I said, "what do you know about caulking bathtubs?"

Wenwood Town Hall occupied a slight rise several blocks south of the town center. Like so many of the structures in town, it had been built of homegrown

Wenwood brick over a century earlier. Unlike other historic buildings in town, though, there were no gaps or concrete patches, no sign of crumbling brick or pockmarked mortar.

Walking from the parking lot at the back around to the front of the building, I tried to see the façade the way a native of Wenwood might. But I hadn't lived my life surrounded by Wenwood brick, hadn't gazed on it or walked on it every waking day. If I had, would I look on this building with pride? With a sense of tradition and maybe a feeling of home?

I stopped and stared. With the sun warming my shoulders, I focused my gaze on brick after brick, waiting for some sense of connection to the town to bloom within me. Instead, all I felt was hot, and all I really saw was new brick and mortar within its time- and weather-worn surroundings.

Neatly trimmed hedges appeared to wrap the building, but appearances can mislead. An almost two-foot gap separated the hedges from the wall, easily wide enough for one curious redhead to squeeze in between.

I backtracked to the back corner of the building, where some variety of machinery—likely an air-conditioning unit—prevented any plantings. From there it was a simple matter to sidestep the length of the wall with the bushes to my back. My exposed legs took no small amount of abuse from prickly branches, and each step I took included hisses, ouches, and a selection of muttered curses.

Before long I reached a patched section of wall, the brick below a window that perhaps had been itself replaced. I ran my hand across both old and new brick, seeking some difference in their texture. But fingertips accustomed to the smooth shift of surfaces in glass proved incapable of sensing a difference in brick. Or maybe all brick always felt the same? I didn't know enough. Grandy would know, but the information wouldn't help after I left my spot outside Town Hall.

What I did know was the richer, darker color of the brick meant they were recently placed. But why would Town Hall use non-Wenwood brick when even the Pace County Police Station refused?

As I shifted to return to the back of the building and escape the shrubbery prison, from the corner of my eye I caught sight of one of the bricks at the lowest line of repair. In its corner, the distinct WND stamp. A Wenwood brick. An old brick newly reset?

Bending to bring my line of sight even with the brick, I used both my eyes and my fingertips to explore the edges of the brick. If someone had simply relaid an old brick, would its edges be smooth and sharp? Or rough and crumbly?

Yet the brick must have been reused. There were no more new bricks.

Running a hand around the back of my neck, clearing away the perspiration gathered there, I shook my head. Too long in the sun could inspire freckling in people like me.

I extracted myself from the shrubbery and returned to the pathway leading to the front of Town Hall. Head down to keep myself from getting distracted, I marched up the few marble steps and through the mullion-windowed doors.

For a moment I remained still, letting the air-conditioning cool my skin. A quick review of my arms and legs showed an assortment of crisscrossed scratches, but thankfully no blood. Given the damage Friday had already done to my legs, a few more scratches would complete the look.

A set of double doors was ahead, with a plaque beside them that read COURTROOM. On the opposite side, a pegboard directory listed various offices and their locations. For such a small town, there were an impressive number of entries on the list. I moved closer to locate the number for my destination. No matter how many times I read through the list, no "Department of Gentlemanly Agreements" turned up.

Settling for the Department of Community Services as a good enough place to start, I followed the appropriate arrows to the staircase and down the hall to Room 203. As I pushed through the door, the big-haired brunette behind a utilitarian steel desk stood and settled her purse on her shoulder. She looked up at my entrance, jaw slackening enough to display her disbelief at her own bad luck.

"Sorry," I said. "Were you going to lunch?"

"Twelve to one, every day."

I'd left Grandy's Jeep in the lot at eleven twenty. Even with the brick-studying delay, no way had it taken me forty minutes to reach this woman's desk. I tugged my cross-body bag around to my front from where it had migrated to my back and unzipped it with the intent of pulling out my cell phone and checking the time. "I really just have a quest—"

The brunette huffed and dropped her purse on the desk. "Fine," she said. "You have fifteen minutes."

"I don't even know if I'm in the right place," I said, cell phone in hand. "And you're all leaving in fifteen minutes? Everyone takes the same lunch?"

"What can I help you with?"

"I was wondering if I could look at an . . . an agreement or contract or . . ."

She sighed and sat, as though my request was already exhausting her.

I began again, explaining in as many words as I could muster that I wanted to see the agreement between the Wenwood Town Council and the new construction at the old brickworks.

"The marina project?" she asked, rising.

"Umm, yeah, I guess, yeah."

Really, I was an accountant, a glass worker, and a tresses-challenged redhead. I was not an investigator.

She came around the desk, pointed to a visitor's chair. "Have a seat," she said on her way to the door. "You know what you're looking for or you need a copy?"

"I can have a copy?"

With an eye roll she said, "Two dollars," and disappeared.

I could have a copy? For the bargain price of two dollars?

Okay, so it was only a bargain if there was useful information in it. Trouble was, I didn't know what would be considered useful.

From somewhere beyond the doorway came the sound of drawers slamming followed by the creaking complaints of what I guessed to be a prehistoric copy machine.

While I waited, I pulled up my e-mail, scrolled through the usual morning barrage of sale notices, social media updates, and international news overnight headlines. Nothing caught my attention sufficiently to make me click open the message, which was perhaps a good thing as it left me free to answer the incoming call.

"Don't worry," I said in lieu of hello, "I'll be back in time."

Grandy's morning grumble had the sound of a car engine rumbling reluctantly to life. "Where's my car?"

"With me."

"And you are where?"

"Town Hall." It didn't occur to me to lie or to dodge. Certainly there were a lot seedier places I could have got off to.

"For Pete's sake, Georgia, what the devil are you doing there?"

"Just checking on a couple of things." I stood, somehow feeling like I needed to be on my feet to defend myself to my grandfather. "Why? Did you need something? You want me to bring something back for you?"

His sigh carried with gale force. "I need to go to the bank. I've got to pick up change for the week. This would be infinitely easier if my car was where I left it."

No, I had no idea why Grandy persisted in calling his Jeep a car. Maybe it was a generation thing. It would always be an SUV to me. "I'll be home in—" I had to pull the phone away from my ear to check the time. "Fifteen minutes, twenty tops. Plenty of time to make the bank."

"You know, it may be time for you to think about

getting your own car and stop giving me stress attacks by helping yourself to mine."

But I wouldn't need a car if I returned to the city—to most any city. I caught myself before I shared that thought with Grandy. I suspected me having his car was not really what the call was about. I suspected his world was a little upside down, and he was looking for areas in which to regain control. If I were him, I'd start with reclaiming my possessions, too.

The noise of the copy machine stopped. Leaning out the doorway, I peered down the hall. "I gotta go. I'll see you in a little while."

I ended the call before he could respond, before I could even catch the sound of his sputtering.

"Here you go." The brunette clerk handed me a stapled bundle of papers, legal-sized. No chance I could fold them down sufficiently to tuck them in my little cross-body bag. "Two bucks."

Setting the papers down on her desk so I could wrestle my wallet free, I flinched when my phone pinged another incoming call. One eye on my wallet, one eye on the phone display, I read Carrie's number while Bon Jovi played softly. "Sorry." I shot an apologetic look at the clerk, but she wasn't looking. She had gone back to pulling her purse over her shoulder and taking up her keys from her desk.

I didn't think she'd mind if I picked up the call, but she'd done me a favor getting the copies instead of insisting I come back later. Rude wasn't a fair payback.

Passing her the two bucks, I thanked her earnestly for her help and skittered out of the office before she could boot me out physically. Getting out of the office for lunch on time—or even early—was something I could whole-heartedly relate to.

Down the stairs and back out the door, I once again immersed myself in the midday heat. There was not a breeze to be had, not a wisp of a cloud in the rich blue sky. I shielded my eyes with a hand and made my way back to the Jeep, clutching keys and copies to my chest.

Inside the SUV, I started the engine and gathered the patience required to wait for the air-conditioning to kick in. While I waited, I skimmed the agreement between the Wenwood Town Council and Stone Mountain Con-struction. At second glance, the pages appeared covered with legal mumbo jumbo interspersed with English art-icles such as *the*, and *a*, with an occasional *whereupon* to make me feel like I hadn't wasted all that money on a college education.

I folded the papers in two and tucked them between my seat and the console. I needed to look at them another time, when I could focus.

It wasn't until I pulled into Grandy's driveway and tapped the horn that I placed a return call to Carrie. Chat-ting with her while waiting for Grandy to emerge from the house seemed like a good idea. As a bonus, I figured he most likely wouldn't give me too much grief about making off with his car if I was on the phone; he wouldn't want to be overheard.

"You rang?" I said when Carrie picked up the phone.

"Oh, hon," she said, "we have to talk."

Hon? Why the endearment? Tendrils of worry raised gooseflesh on my arms. I forced my voice bright. "What's up?"

"All right, listen. I'm telling you this because I think you should know, but don't shoot the messenger, okay?"

The slam of the door alerted me to Grandy's imminent arrival. I glanced up, wished away my sudden increase in anxiety as he walked, head high, down the steps. He carried a worn leather satchel in lieu of a briefcase, and his somber blue tie paired with a starched white shirt made him look like a throwback to the early sixties—proud, dignified, certain.

I prompted Carrie. "What's going on?"

"There's a letter to the editor in the *Town Crier* that came out today."

I knew the *Crier*. Grandy subscribed, kept each week's issue in the reading basket in the bathroom.

The man himself yanked open the door and climbed into the passenger seat with the verve of a man half his age. "Let's go."

I nodded, threw the Jeep into reverse. Checking over my shoulder, I eased up on the brake and let the SUV roll down the drive. "I'm guessing you're calling because you have an issue with the letter?" I said into the phone.

Grandy didn't have to raise his voice to communicate his displeasure. What he did was switch his voice from speech to growl. When he ground out "Georgia" as the tires hit the street, I knew I'd made a grave error.

"Promise you won't hold it against me?" Carrie asked.

"I'm going to have to call you back," I said. "I'm driving."

"Put me on speaker," she said.

"Georgia," Grandy grumbled.

I clenched the steering wheel tight with one hand, the phone with the other. "I have Grand—Pete with me."

"Oh, God," Carrie said. "I take it back. Don't put me on speaker. Call me back as soon as you can."

She clicked off before I could stop her. *Oh God* could in no way be construed as a positive response to Grandy's presence.

I slid my gaze to him as I lowered the silent phone to my lap. The combination of Carrie's call and Grandy's insistence on getting to the bank early made me doubly uneasy. "Everything okay, Grandy?"

"Of course everything's okay," he growled. "What could possibly be bad about my granddaughter talking on a cell phone while she's driving? Unless of course you consider my granddaughter borrowing my car, talking on the phone while she's driving it, and doing heaven knows what else."

I bit my tongue—figuratively, of course. Truly biting my tongue would have been painful, and really the guilt I felt over Grandy's perfectly well-founded complaint was pain enough. "Sorry, Grandy. I wanted to get to Town Hall early and I didn't want to wake you."

"You could have left a note, you know. I can read."

"I did leave a note. I put it . . . oh, I bet the kitten . . ."

Focusing on driving as by the book as possible, I let the soft whir of the air conditioner motor and the *shoosh* of the tires on the road fill in the blanks my cowardice left.

We were almost to the bank before I felt comfortable enough to attempt conversation. "Aside from me taking your car without permission," I began, adding a bit of teasing to my voice, hoping to avoid retreading the earlier disagreement, "did anything else happen this morning? Hear from anyone?"

He leaned into his seatback, tugged absently at the knot of his tie. "Your little flea magnet thought it important to attack my toes while I slept."

I pressed my lips tight to keep the laughter in.

"And clearly she thought hanging from the belt of my bathrobe was the best method of traveling from my room to the bathroom, where she captured and ingested a spider."

"Ew, Grandy, don't let her eat . . . wild things."

"Why not? It's protein. It's good for her."

His improved mood made me feel marginally better. And yet . . .

"That's all?" I asked. "Nothing else unusual happen?"

"Why don't you just ask the question you want to ask, Georgia? I'm not getting any younger, you know."

Stopped at a red light, left-turn indicator clicking away, I wished I could close my eyes, avoid seeing his reaction in the event the topic reawakened his ire. "Did you get this week's *Town Crier* yet?" I asked.

He folded his hands in his lap. "Let me see now. It's Monday. And the mail comes early. And the *Crier* comes by mail. So I would say yes, I've got the *Crier*."

I allowed myself a moment's gratitude that sarcasm didn't aromatically bleed through pores like sweat did. The confines of the Jeep were too small to contain the abundance of aroma Grandy's attitude would create.

Turning into the bank parking lot, I asked, "Did you read it?"

"I put it in the bathroom."

I let out a breath. "Grandy . . ."

"No, I did not read it. What's this all about anyway?"

With the Jeep tucked into a parking space near enough to the door that even Grandy couldn't complain, I threw the gear into neutral and shifted in my seat to face him. "Something Carrie said. You know, during the call you wouldn't let me take."

"It's the law, Georgia, and it's for your own safety. And mine." He released his seat belt, turned to glare at me. "What was it Carrie said?"

I shook my head. "She didn't get a chance to explain. I got the sense, though, that something in this week's *Crier* may be, um, displeasing. I'll give her a call back now and find out."

A bit of Grandy's bluster faded in on itself, as though whatever might be in the *Crier* was capable of hollowing him out. "Let me know . . ." He exhaled slowly. "Let me know what you find out. And turn off the car. Do you have any idea how expensive gasoline is?"

"Do you have any idea how hot it is? I'll melt without the air-conditioning."

He glared. I caved. But no way was baking in a Jeep part of my plan.

I locked up the SUV and trailed Grandy into the bank. He marched directly across the green-carpeted lobby to the commercial accounts queue, head up, eyes forward. Several paces back, I saw what he didn't: the abandoned tasks, the following eyes, the speculative stares. A shiver raised the gooseflesh on my arms once again. Surely not everyone in the bank was watching my grandfather. Surely the beer-bellied gent chatting with the blonde half his age wasn't whispering about my grandfather.

Rather than linger near the doorway waiting, I edged around the perimeter of the bank and slid into a scratchy fabric club chair, cell phone in hand. Keeping watch on the people watching Grandy, I redialed Carrie.

"Tell me now, tell me fast," I said when she picked up.

"Georgia?"

Even though, really, I had no reason to expect she would recognize my voice, I rolled my eyes. "Yes, it's Georgia. And before you ask, I promise not to blame you for what's in the paper."

"Okay. Let me get it. I'll read it to you."

"No, don't do that. I don't know how much time I have. Just give me the highlights." On the commercial accounts line, Grandy was next up for assistance.

"Oh. Oh." A clunk and a thud came over the line, and I pictured Carrie banging into the edge of a display table and toppling antique picture frames in her haste to get back to where she'd left the paper. "I could do that, I guess. That might even be a little bit, you know, nicer."

"Nicer?"

"Not as offensive," she half whispered. "Then again,

telling you in my own words . . . kinda makes me feel really guilty."

I put a hand to my head. "Carrie, please, just tell me, before I start imagining some really awful things about Grandy. This is about Grandy, right? About Pete?"

"Yeah," she said slowly. "About Pete, and Tony Himmel, and even about you."

"Me?"

"About how people involved in a murder investigation have no business attending the wake of the victim. How that's in really bad taste and an insult to the deceased and his family and friends and neighbors, and how—"

"Wait a second. Grandy wasn't at the wake."

"I know that, but—"

"Well, then why is he being singled out? And why me? I didn't have anything to do with . . . anything."

"No, but you're Pete's granddaughter. I guess they figure that if he's being questioned about a murder, then you must be guilty, too."

The words hit me with the force of a physical blow. My breath caught and the muscles of my stomach clenched. "Please tell me you're just speculating and you don't actually believe that."

"Oh, Georgia, of course not."

Curling over in the chair, I put my elbow on my knee and my head in my hand. I knew this would do nothing to prevent the people in the bank from seeing me—I no longer had the convictions of a three-year-old, after all— but it would prevent me from accidentally making eye contact with Grandy.

I supposed it had been only a matter of time before the whole of Wenwood and parts beyond knew about the police questioning Grandy. And yet . . .

"Is this normal?" I asked, keeping my voice low. "Do the police always disclose who they've been talking to in relation to cases?"

The jingle of the bell over the door at Carrie's shop carried clearly enough across the phone that the bell could have been at my elbow. "I don't know. I don't think it's a big secret, though."

"But it couldn't have been common knowledge, could it?"

"That's why I called," Carrie said. "If it wasn't before, it is now."

Incomplete questions and ideas swirled through my mind, none forming into coherence in time to voice them.

"I have to go," she said, "I have a customer. Call me later?"

I mumbled something sounding vaguely affirmative and disconnected the call.

The *Town Crier* couldn't possibly reach every household in Wenwood, could it? Even if it did, not everyone read it.

Did they?

How many people knew Grandy had been questioned? And Tony Himmel? How many people agreed with what was in the paper, agreed we shouldn't have been at the wake? Attending had seemed like the right thing to do, but perhaps I'd been wrong. Seriously, it wasn't like Emily Post had an official position on the matter.

Pushing to my feet, lifting my head at last, I was vaguely relieved to realize the other people in the bank had returned to their tasks. Or, at least, they had given up watching Grandy as though he was going to do something more interesting than collect a bank bag full of rolled coins and singles.

I crossed the lobby and met him beside the teller's window. On the other side of the thick Plexiglas, the bank clerk was running singles through the bill-counting machine.

"What did Carrie say?" Grandy asked.

I kept my yap shut while I searched for the right way to break the news.

"I'll put it this way," he said, voice pitched low, face turned away from the window, "what's in the paper will explain why everyone's staring, won't it?"

I answered his concern with false brightness. "What makes you think people are staring?" Tapping the window lightly with his knuckles, he nodded at the glass. "This," he said.

To understand what he was saying, I had to take a step back. It was then I spied the reflection of the bank floor and the eyes of all the employees turned our way. "Nice espionage work, Grandy." I grinned. "How long has that James Bond flick been running at the dine-in? You're picking up some good tips."

He smiled at the clerk, who slid bundled singles under the glass, but he scowled at me. "Just tell me why everyone's staring."

Sighing, I held open the burlap bag Grandy produced

from the depths of his satchel so he could slide in the bills. Already, the clerk was pushing rolled coins under the glass. "There was an editorial or letter to the editor or something in the *Town Crier* outing you and Tony Himmel as suspects in Andy Edgers's murder. And lambasting me for going to the wake."

The muscles of his jaw rolled as he clenched his teeth. He glowered down at me, exhaled volubly through his nose. "I told you not to go to that thing," he ground out.

"No, you didn't."

He straightened, standing tall enough to make me feel like a child again. "Was I at all unclear in my displeasure?"

I admitted his belief I was making a mistake had been apparent, but that was hardly the same as telling me not to go. But the teller's window at the bank was not the ideal place to conduct our disagreement. "Let's stick to the point on this one, okay? Anyone who read or is reading or is going to read the *Crier* will know the police had you in for questioning, that you're a suspect."

Nodding his thanks to the teller, Grandy reached for my elbow and turned me toward the door. "I have a feeling that's not news to a lot of people."

As we pushed through the exit doors, I glanced back at him. "What makes you say that? All those people in there staring? You don't think it's because of the article?"

"I think they were staring at you because of the article. Me, they're already suspicious of." As we crossed the parking lot, he held out his hand. "Give me the keys."

"You've lived here your whole life, Grandy. These people know you. They know you wouldn't do such a thing." I passed him the keys then waited while he unlocked the car and powered down the windows. "If they're staring, it's because they're wondering how you're handling all the attention, that's all," I said, climbing into the car.

"If that were all, they'd be coming to the dine-in to get a look at me, instead of staying away in droves."

He busied himself checking the mirrors, adjusting his seat, retuning the radio to the all-news station. To each move, he gave his full attention, ignoring me.

"You're just being paranoid, Grandy. I've been at the dine-in with you. You and double-oh-seven are pulling in a good crowd."

Backing the car out of the space, he scowled. "Not so. When we get up there, you'll see the receipts. You'll see."

I opted not to continue protesting. Grandy was right. When I saw the receipts, I would know whether his concerns were grounded in fact or paranoia. I trusted numbers. Unlike people, numbers never lied.

11

Grandy cleared his desk of the random odds and ends that had collected there, giving me space to spread out the tax withholding binders and line up the time clock punch cards. Why Grandy persisted in manually preparing payroll remained a mystery to me. Control issues? Secrecy? Frugality? Whatever the reason, on that afternoon I was pleased to be lending a hand to the task of putting pay vouchers in his employees' hands. The counting, the columns, the ten-key machine were as comforting to me as ice cream to others.

All right. That might be an extreme reaction, ice cream being the frozen miracle of deliciousness that it is, but it had been a tough seven days.

While I wrote up the vouchers, Grandy wandered off to take inventory for the kitchen and concession. This allowed me to happily change the station and turn up the volume on the little office radio. Better, it kept Grandy from pacing behind me, peeking over my shoulder to check my progress and warn me to double-check my addition.

Best yet, Grandy's absence gave me the opportunity to review his box office records without interruption. He may have been dependent on paper while the rest of the world moved on to computer records, but his organization rivaled any file management system to come out of Silicon Valley.

With payroll tidied away, I returned the withholding binders to the cabinet and took down the binders for the prior two years' receipts. Comparing week-on-week gave a narrow view of change, month-on-month a bit broader. For a true picture of trends I would need more than numbers. Honest as they were, numbers were only part of the story. Other factors played into totals: weather, feature film, current events, overall economy, and more.

Even without knowledge of all the variables, a simple eyeballing of the totals—attendance, kitchen receipts, concession receipts—revealed an insignificant deviation year on year. So Grandy was wrong. Folks weren't avoiding his theater because of his potential involvement in Andy Edgers's murder—at least not yet. Attendance wasn't a worry. But in flipping through the books, seeking the information I needed, I spotted a troubling pattern.

I dialed down the volume on the radio until the music was more of a background hum, reducing my chances of distraction. Payroll work had a strange sort of routine to it, a straightforward exercise in core mathematics. The puzzle that had caught my curiosity required a close focus.

One hand scratching notes on a scrap paper, the other flipping pages, I assembled a financial picture that left my belly leaden and my palms slick with sweat.

The dine-in had been losing money. Not a great deal, not all at once, but little by little, month by month, a steady trickle downward from slim profit to no profit to straight loss.

I sat back in my chair, let out a long breath. Why hadn't Grandy said anything?

Of course he wouldn't, would he? He wouldn't want to worry me, wouldn't want me to mention anything to my mother, wouldn't want either of us for a moment to question his ability to maintain his own business.

Thing was, I had no such doubt. In the preceding couple of weeks of being with Grandy, he'd given me no cause for worry. Though there was no argument of his age, neither did I have any doubt about his mental acuity. True, he had been shaken by the police questioning, but that sort of reaction was to be expected of anyone.

"Right, then," I told myself. Hands on the arms of the chair, I pushed myself out of my seat, resolved to find Grandy and confront him about what I'd learned.

Grabbing up the payroll vouchers, I switched off the radio. Outside the office, I crossed the back of the theater, popping open the door to the lobby and peeking out as I passed. No sign of Grandy. I kept on, through the access doors and on into the kitchen.

He was perched on the edge of a step stool, bent double

and leaning his head into the interior of a cabinet. A spike of fear shot through me. Considering his age as I had been, my first terror was of his having a heart attack while counting the jars of cooking oil.

"Grandy?" I hurried to where he sat crumpled. "Grandy!"

"For Pete's sake, Georgia, you've made me lose count." He straightened, his expression showing more exasperation than anger. "Now I'll have to start again."

I let out a sigh of relief—cranky was still alive—then I looked pointedly at the massive cans. "There can't be more than seven cans in there, Grandy. How could you lose count?"

He grimaced, pushed himself up off the stool. "Finished with the payroll, are you?"

"Never mind about payroll." Still clutching the vouchers, I crossed my arms and attempted to give Grandy back the same glare he'd been giving me for the entirety of my life whenever I displeased him. "I looked at your receipts. You're not having a significant downturn in attendance over last year."

His lips quirked to the side as though he were biting the inside of his cheek, deep in thought. The troubled furrow in his brow smoothed quickly. "That's good news, then. I was sure things were falling off."

"A little," I conceded. "But it's not a result of the Edgers thing. Grandy, when were you going to tell me the theater is in trouble?"

He straightened as though I'd slapped him, but his eyes revealed no surprise. "What are you talking about? How much *looking* did you do?"

"Enough. This place is losing money week after week, Grandy. Why didn't you—"

"You have no right to go poking into my business, Georgia." The grumble returned to his voice.

"You asked for my help. You told me you were worried about attendance. Well, now I understand why."

"Georgia."

"Why didn't you say anything, Grandy? Why do you insist on keeping things to yourself?"

"It's *my* business, not yours."

"Yes, technically, on paper, this is your business. Sole proprietor, I get it. But that doesn't make you alone in this. You have a neighborhood, you have a staff, you have family. There are other people that care about you and this theater and its success."

He shook his head, turning away from me. "You have no idea what you're talking about."

"Maybe not. Maybe it's all guessing. But I wouldn't have to guess at these things, Grandy, if you'd just be honest with me and tell me what's going on."

"There's nothing to tell," he snapped.

Leaned up against a center-aisle counter, I folded my arms and glared at him. My dear grandfather had plenty to tell. I intended to stand there waiting until he caved and spilled.

The air-conditioning kicked on with a metallic rumble. Air shooshed through vents and fluttered the edges of dish rags dangling from cabinet pulls. A black fly circled busily around the clock mounted above the grill.

At long last, Grandy huffed. "Business could be better.

It will be better. I've got a terrific schedule set up for this summer, guaranteed to put this place back in the black. There's nothing at all to worry about."

"But you're worried," I said. "You're already watching your year-on-year and you're worried the fallout from this Andy Edgers thing is going to make things worse here, not better. So what happens then? How much longer can you keep this place running at a loss?"

This was my grandfather I was talking to, the man who bought side-by-side burial plots as soon as he and Gran returned home from their honeymoon, the man who had a college fund set aside for my mother before she was born. The man who always had a long-range plan.

The man shook his head. His whole body sagged, from shoulders to elbows to knees. "I doubt I'd make it to the end of the year."

To keep from gasping my shock, I pressed my lips tightly together. He may as well have told me he was getting remarried. It took several deep breaths before I could look at him again. Funny, I expected his appearance to have altered along with my understanding of him. "Grandy," I said softly, "how did this happen?" I shook my head, disbelieving. "I don't understand how . . ."

He shoved his hands in the pockets of his trousers. "I'm not infallible, Georgia. I'm sorry if you thought I was."

"Infallible? No. Careful, smart, prepared, yes. What happened?"

"I made a mistake, all right? It happens to the best of us."

"What kind of mistake? Grandy, you're not—"

"I trusted Andy Edgers," he said. "I shouldn't have."

"What are . . . I . . ." I couldn't form a coherent thought much less give it voice.

Grandy paced the length of the double grill, fingertips trailing the edge of the counter as he walked and spoke. "A little more than two years ago, Andy and I decided to partner in a little investment opportunity."

I braced myself. *Investment opportunity* was often a polite phrase applied to pyramid schemes and condo scams. Though I didn't voice my conclusions, Grandy guessed at them.

"I know what you're thinking, and this was no scheme. It was a solid investment, a nice, diversified portfolio of stocks and properties. I did all the research, even looked things up on the computer." He flashed a grin, proud of embracing technology however briefly. "But all the research in the world isn't any help when the market goes bottoms up."

"So the money's gone."

He nodded, defeated. "It's gone. I still own my shares. Drew said I was better off waiting for a rebound than selling at a deep loss. But rebounds take time, and I'm not getting any younger. And the nest egg intended to keep this place running through the lean times . . ."

Grandy had invested in the stock market, a concept he equated to gambling. Gambling was, of course, an activity restricted for foolish, careless, and gullible people.

"And that's what you and Andy Edgers had been fighting about? This investment?"

"He blamed me," he said, "as if it had all been my idea,

as if I had some control over the stock market and had personally burst the property bubble."

In the quiet while I struggled to process all I had learned and formulate the next question, the kitchen door leading to the back of the theater rattled.

The door swung open and the cooks ambled in, laughing, calling greetings, and generally bringing high energy and smiles into the kitchen.

Grandy welcomed the intrusion with the glee of a man pardoned from his execution. I suspected the cooks were confused by Grandy's sudden and inexplicable joviality, but they rolled right along with it, joking with him as they started the task of prepping their stations. Only the grumpy head chef, brother of the assistant manager, Matthew, didn't participate in the unexpected fun, instead scowling and disappearing into the walk-in with the look of someone who had better things to do.

With kitchen prep getting under way and Grandy still with inventory to do, I surmised that was the end of the conversation and likely the last time Grandy would give up any information about the loss and his partnership with Andy Edgers. I handed off the payroll vouchers and returned to the office.

I put away the receipt books, turned up the radio, and switched on the computer.

Gone, Grandy had said. The money was gone. In reality, it was locked into a group of stocks whose value had plummeted. Time may yet restore their value. But for people who didn't have a lot of years ahead of them, or who needed the money now and not maybe some day in the distant future, *gone* was an accurate assessment.

As I leaned back in the chair, waiting for the computer to boot up, one intriguing thought paraded through my mind.

If Grandy's money was gone and his business was on shaky ground, where had the investment loss left Andy Edgers? And what might he have done to recover from that loss?

Morning came entirely too early.

I awoke to Friday sleeping draped across my neck like a living stole. She was very adorable. She was also making it very hard to breathe.

As I lifted her off my throat, she came awake with an instant alertness I envied. Eyes wide and bright, tiny tail straight up in the air, she bounced across the bed in search of trouble, or maybe a bug. We spent the time it took for me to reach a somewhat functional state playing with the tie from my bathrobe. It was a delightful way to wake up, and when I finally tumbled from my bed, I was ready to face the day with a smile.

Dressed, pressed, and ready to roll, I left fresh food and water for Friday before closing her in my room, left a note for Grandy so he didn't stress the absence of his Jeep, and left the house.

Smack in the middle of a James Bond car chase the night before, I'd snuck out of the theater and tiptoed through Grandy's Rolodex. (Yes, Rolodex—I have no idea where he got the blanks for it.) It hadn't taken much to convince Drew Able, Esquire, to meet me for breakfast at the luncheonette, just a promise to pick up the tab and treat to pastries from Rozelle's afterward.

Planning to pass through the market after breakfast to pick up some fresh fruit, I parked the Jeep behind Village Grocery, in the shade of my favorite walnut tree. I had no idea who had planted the tree on the other side of the fence—black walnuts weren't indigenous to the area—but I was happy to make use of its reliable shade.

With the sun still low in the sky, the air retained its overnight cool. Town Council agreement in hand, I walked along the access driveway that divided downtown Wenwood into two blocks, and I kept on smiling as I crossed the street and entered Grace's luncheonette.

The counter stretched to my left. Tom sat on his stool, tucked into the corner by the wall. Grace stood before him, reading aloud to him from the paper. I paused long enough to determine she was reading the horoscopes. Some lucky sun sign might meet their lifelong partner . . . if they're open to the possibility.

I continued on to one of the half-dozen tables, sliding into the booth opposite Drew Able. "Am I late?"

He grinned as he looked up from the laminated menu. "I'm early. I'm always early. My mother's influence. I can't quite shake it."

"That must be why Grandy hired you. He's big on punctual."

"I'd like to think that was the case, but I'm afraid he hired me because I'm the last lawyer left in town."

"That could be it, too. Shop local and all that."

Grace ambled by with a menu, checking to see if I wanted coffee. I requested a double. She headed off without even blinking, and I knew right then she intended to bring me a regulation-sized cup.

"So to what do I owe the pleasure?" Drew leaned back, tugged at the collar of his pale blue polo shirt.

"I wanted to ask you to look at something for me." I set the photocopies of the Town Council's agreement with Tony Himmel on the table.

"You need legal advice?"

"I need a decoder ring," I admitted. "It looks straightforward enough, but I can't help thinking I'm missing something."

Drew nodded. "We lawyers like to sneak innocuous-looking clauses into contracts that in reality demand payment in blood."

"Yes, that's my understanding as well." I slid the agreement toward him. "So if I'm reading this correctly, Stone Mountain Construction made this deal with the Wenwood Town Council promising any building or decorating materials that can be ordered through a Wenwood business would be ordered through a Wenwood business."

Without looking at the agreement, Drew nodded vigorously. "Exactly. The granting of building permits to Stone Mountain was contingent upon that proviso. I was there."

"Okaaaay. But what I can't dope out from reading this is what the penalty is if the construction company violates the terms of this agreement. What happens then?"

Coming to a stop at the end of the table, Grace plunked

down a heavy porcelain coffee mug. "Then we put 'em in the stockade and throw rotten vegetables at them."

She hooted at her own joke while I pictured Tony Himmel locked in the stocks, his broad shoulders stretched to accommodate the distance from wrist-lock to wrist-lock. I wasn't sure whether I'd be one to throw tomatoes at him, or help him escape.

"Heard you stopped by the station house yesterday," Grace said, pulling an order pad from her apron pocket.

"Umm . . . yeah . . ." was the best I could do. Diana had been less than friendly, yet she mentioned my visit to her aunt?

"You went to the station?" Drew asked.

I met Drew's gaze. "I wanted to talk to Detective Nolan, but he wasn't in. Come to think of it, I left a message at the desk asking him to call, but I haven't heard back."

"I'm sure Diana let him know." Grace's tone held a slightly defensive lilt.

"I'm sure she did," I said, "even if she wasn't thrilled to be doing something on my behalf."

The words sneaked out. I didn't mean for them to. I didn't mean for my inner insecurities to be released in the light of day, right there in the luncheonette.

Grace caught me in the crosshairs of her glare. Brow furrowed, mouth turned down, she put a fist on her hip and asked, "Did something happen between you girls again?"

"If it did, I don't know what it was," I said. A little afraid of Grace, I explained to Drew instead. "Okay, I probably screwed up by mentioning cheerleading as a poor career choice but how was I supposed to know?"

Not to be distracted, Drew asked, "Why did you go to the police station?"

"Diana doesn't like to talk about her past," Grace said. "Can we just order?"

Drew bowed his head over his menu and Grace put the tip of her pencil to the pad. "Shoot," she said.

Of course, I hadn't looked at the menu, but how tough could breakfast be? I faked my way through an order of eggs over easy then waited while Drew recited precise instructions for the preparation of his western omelet with a side of well-fried hash browns and just-this-side-of-golden toast.

Grace collected the menus and bustled off, muttering.

"The police station?" Drew prompted.

"The penalty for failing to order building supplies in Wenwood?" I shot back.

Drew lifted the photocopies as though in salute. "Let me check."

While he skimmed the pages, I tipped some cream into my coffee then pulled my smartphone from my bag. A quick review of my e-mail—or lack thereof—reminded me of what I kept trying to forget: I wasn't simply in some location where my friends couldn't reach me. I was in a life where my friends refused to follow. I was on my own.

Feeling a wee bit sorry for myself, I dumped some sugar into the coffee cup and added a little more cream, thus turning a breakfast beverage into a high-calorie comfort drink.

I waited while Drew skimmed, flipped pages, read, reread, flipped pages again. By the time he finished,

Grace had arrived with our food order and I was in need of a coffee refill. Pulling his plate close with one hand, he tapped the papers with his other. "Mind you, I'm not sure this would hold up in court," he said, as though completing a thought he'd already shared. "But it could certainly be a long and ugly fight."

"Interesting." While I tried to make sense of the implications of Drew's assessment, I centered my breakfast plate in front of me. Etiquette be damned, I broke my egg yolk with a corner of toast, held the toast in place while the yolk soaked in. "If the agreement won't hold up, why write it up in the first place?"

"Now, I only said I'm not sure it would hold up. I don't do a lot of contract law, so I can't say for sure."

"But why would the town even try?" I popped the egg-dipped toast into my mouth and savored the mixture of creamy egg and crunchy toast. "And why would Stone Mountain agree?"

He cut into his omelet with the side of his fork. "Why they would agree, I couldn't say. Why the town would try, the council's pretty vested in keeping Wenwood businesses successful. There's a lot of crossover between the Town Council and the merchants' association."

"And the politicians or whoever at Town Hall always just do whatever the Town Council asks them?"

I had to wait for an answer while Drew chased down a bit of omelet with a sip of coffee.

"Council members give a lot of money to those politicians and whoever. Grease the wheels a little and you have a say in where the car goes."

"All right, all right." The small town thing was making my brain hurt. I waved a hand as though I could brush away the detour in topic. "Let's get back to this agreement," I said, pointing with my fork at the photocopies. "Would you tell me what the penalty is for getting materials from outside of Wenwood?"

Drew swiped a napkin across his lips. "Well, it starts in Wenwood, but then moves out to nearby towns in the county and then—"

"I got that part. What happens if that chain is broken at any point?"

"Then everything is invalidated. All the deals are void, and Stone Mountain's building permits expire."

It took me a moment to remember to swallow the food I'd chewed. "All of them? So . . . construction just . . . stops?"

"Like I said, it would make a tough fight in court." He broke off a chunk of home fries that looked crunchier than my toast. "But with construction, lost time is lost money."

"And even if the company didn't argue and simply applied for new permits . . ."

Drew bobbed his head, following the thread of thought. "They'd be starting all over again, and no doubt have to agree to even more absurd terms in order to get the town's blessing."

More absurd than having to source all your materials through Wenwood and the remainder of Pace County? It struck me anew how much Tony wanted to see that marina built if he was willing to put up with the Town Council's crazy demands.

The jingle of a cell phone wrenched me away from thoughts of Tony. Drew set down his fork and shifted in his seat. The snap of a cell phone belt case was followed by Drew lifting a phone to his ear. "This is Drew Able," he said. "How can I help you?"

I hadn't intended to watch him while he took the call. There was little else to look at in the luncheonette, though. Thus, the change in his features from relaxed and somewhat happy to alert and somewhat steamed was instantly apparent. He said no more than "uh-huh . . . uh-huh" before disconnecting the call and returning the phone to his belt.

"You might want to come with me," he said quietly, sliding out of the booth. "Your grandfather's been arrested."

12

Drew drove to the police station, taking the interstate rather than the scenic river road. Though I'd already acquired a preference for the river road, on that particular ride to the station, I welcomed the speed and sameness of the interstate. It was easier to panic about Grandy when I wasn't being distracted by beautiful vistas or grand old lady houses.

When we made the turn into the lot at the station, my heart sunk. Three times in the span of a week were too many visits for someone not employed by the police department or delivering their mail. That feeling of "here I am again" weighed on my shoulders like a yoke. I didn't want to be eligible for my own parking space. At the glass shop, yes, but not at the Pace County PD.

Nonetheless, I hustled up the cement-patched steps

beside Drew and into the waiting area. Sergeant Steve stood behind his desk, phone to his ear. He looked up as we approached. Any semblance of the kitten-loving nice-guy I met earlier in the week had vanished. His hard-ass, world-weary cop mask was tightly in place.

"Steve," Drew said with a nod.

Sergeant Steve nodded in return. His eyes flicked in my direction but gave no impression of greeting.

I wrapped my arms around myself and hoped for strength.

"Got a call that Chip was bringing in Pete Keene. They here yet?"

Sergeant Steve muttered a thanks and good-bye into the phone and lowered the receiver to its cradle. Resting both hands on the edge of the counter, making him look bigger than he probably was, he grimaced. "They're processing. Have a seat. I'll let you know when you can go back."

Egg-soaked toast slid uncomfortably in my belly, but I sat in the molded plastic chair, Drew Able, Esquire, to my left, a table of outdated and careworn magazines to my right. "When will we know why he's been arrested?" I asked.

Drew picked at the crease in his khakis. "He's been arrested on suspicion of murder."

"I know that. You told me that much. When will we know why? What happened that made them arrest him? I thought after the questioning the—"

"I don't know, Georgia," Drew said. "I'll find out as soon as I get to talk to Chip."

"You said that before. Chip. Who's Chip?"

"Detective Nolan." He caught the crease in his trousers between thumbnail and forefinger, scraped back and forth as though pressing the crease with his nails. The motion created a soft whistling, sounding loud in the quiet of the waiting area. "You know," he said, "I wasn't thinking when I said you should come. They may not speak to you. You'll be stuck out here while I go in to talk—"

"I'm fine," I said. "I'll wait."

"Are you sure? Maybe you can call someone who—"

"I'll wait."

It was another half hour before Sergeant Steve told Drew he could go back and meet with Detective Nolan. He gave me a glare that said "stay put" louder than ankle shackles would have.

Alone in the waiting area, I resorted to checking my phone again. It was that or last year's *Car & Driver*, or half an issue of *Time* magazine. Looking at the display, I was surprised to find the missed-call icon illuminated. I'd have to remember to ask Carrie if there was a dead zone on the interstate.

I dialed into my voice mail and stood. I felt that picking up messages was a good excuse to pace, and I was in sore need of some pacing. Sergeant Steve had obviously decided I would behave myself and had disappeared into the little space with all the gun belts and radios.

The voice that spoke to me from my messages stopped me in place. "Georgia, I'm hoping . . . that is, if this is actually Georgia's phone, give me a call back." And then Tony Himmel rattled off his phone number.

I clicked out of my voice mail. I stared at an outdated flyer for Prescription Drug Take-Back Day. I racked my brain for a reason Tony would call me.

And then I questioned the wisdom of calling him back while waiting to talk to my grandfather's lawyer about his murder charge.

I had returned to Wenwood to start over, to find a solid base from which to relaunch my life. Wenwood was supposed to be a sleepy little town where the biggest obstacles I would face would be how to deal with Grandy's sweet tooth and where to find high-speed Internet. I was supposed to move forward from Wenwood with renewed confidence and determination. I was not supposed to run screaming from it in search of yet another place from which to relaunch my life.

Hand to my head, I resumed pacing. With each step, I focused on pushing away thoughts of my personal drama. For sure I'd hit a low in life. There was no denying that. But Grandy had been there to soften my fall, no questions, no assumptions, no judging. It was my turn to return the love. In time I would sort out my life. For the foreseeable future, I needed to put Grandy first.

Veering off my back-and-forth path, I turned for the desk and shouted for Sergeant Steve.

He stuck his head around the corner, not committing to actually coming out of the little room to talk to me.

"I need to see Detective Nolan," I announced.

Steve smirked. "He's busy."

"He's going to talk to the lawyer, Drew, and then Drew is going to go talk to my grandfather, Pete. So while Drew is talking to Pete, Detective Nolan would be free to talk to me."

He held his eyes closed for a long moment before meeting my gaze again. "That's probably right."

"Would that be now?" I asked. "Is Detective Nolan free to talk to me now?"

"I really don't know."

"Can you go find out?"

"Miss Kelly, I don't—"

"Just go find out. How long could it take? One question. Simple."

"Miss—"

"One question." I made a hurry-up motion with my hand. "Go."

Sergeant Steve did not appear pleased to have me giving orders. The aggravated sigh and the bunched jaw kinda gave away his slow-bubbling anger. But he disappeared, and his shoes scuffed along the floor as he walked away from the little room.

I sucked in a quick breath for courage and ducked behind the desk.

Sergeant Steve was the desk sergeant. The desk sergeant kept a log—at least, he did on television cop shows. That meant somewhere on the desk was a list that would tell me what had precipitated Grandy's arrest.

Careful not to disturb the stacks of paper, listening close for the sound of Sergeant Steve's return, I scanned the edges of files, the clipboards pegged to the edge of the desk, and the scratch pad beside the phone.

What the hell was I doing? If I could just be patient,

Drew would tell me everything I needed to know. But patient meant waiting. Meant doing nothing. I needed to do *something*.

A door slammed somewhere in the building, and I jumped. I was convinced in that precise moment my deodorant failed. My courage slipped several notches, and I leaned my weight toward the pass-through out from behind the desk and to the waiting area, poised to make a run for it.

It was then I realized I was a big idiot. It was then I spotted the spine of a blue binder on which an adhesive label read DUTY LOG.

Carefully, I lifted the binder toward me. Ignoring a sudden need for the ladies' room, I opened the binder. Quietly as I could, I flipped the pages until I reached a series of blanks, then worked my way back until I reached the entries for today. Again, I worked backward, learning everything that had transpired in the precinct.

Traffic accident mile marker 8, River Road. (Lucky us, taking the interstate.)

Domestic disturbance. (I didn't read on for the address.)

Suspected break in. (Some town I didn't know.)

And then came the line that left my mouth dry and my knees weak:

Anon. call: blood-soaked brick found behind the Downtown Dine-In

I found the information I was looking for . . . and understood the cat that was killed by curiosity was one lucky duck. Because sometimes, finding the answer was the worst thing that could happen.

When Drew spoke to me after his meeting with Detective Nolan, I pretended shock at the news of the discovery of a brick behind the dine-in. Shock, I figured, was a better option than distress. Distress required continued acting. For shock I could feign stunned, at which point no communication would be required.

Detective Nolan briefed me with the same information Drew had and told me I couldn't visit with Grandy until after he'd been arraigned and either relocated to the county jail or released on bail. No acting required there; the tears that filled my eyes were as real as they get.

I sat in silence while Drew drove me back to Wenwood, back to the lot behind the grocery where I'd left Grandy's Jeep. The shade of the walnut tree no longer seemed comforting. It seemed sad, the car sitting all alone away from sunshine.

Drew promised he'd call me later on and waved out the window as he left the parking lot.

For longer than perhaps I should have, I stood in the lot, watching long after he drove away. I was at a loss for what to do next. There was still the grocery store to contend with; my need for fresh produce hadn't magically vanished even though my desire for a pound of milk chocolate had appeared. And I knew it would be best to get the grocery shopping done before word of Grandy's arrest spread. Yet I found myself walking not toward the back door of the market, but toward the access driveway, intent not on buying lettuce and limes but on visiting with Carrie.

She'd been right when she said trips to the police station required a friend. I hadn't realized it before, not having made any. Now it was a lesson I would never forget.

When I turned the corner and stepped onto the sidewalk running parallel with the storefronts, I spied Carrie standing in front of her store, arms crossed as she conversed with a tall, balding man. Not until I got closer did I recognize the man to be Warren Edgers.

My pace slowed, feet clinging to the pavement longer than necessary. Indecision held me back. That, and fear. How could I face Warren Edgers knowing my grandfather had just been arrested on suspicion of murdering his father? Was Warren already aware of the arrest? Had he yet made the connection between me and Grandy?

I had just determined to be a chicken and retreat to the grocery store when Carrie spotted me. She called out a big hello, waved me over.

I considered running in the opposite direction. But already my frozen pose on the sidewalk was attracting attention. A young couple slowed as they passed me, no doubt trying to figure out what my problem was. Across the street, Rozelle watched from the doorway of the bakery. I imagined Tom and his cronies sitting at the counter in the luncheonette, gazing out the window at me standing still in the middle of the sidewalk, waiting to remember what had brought me to town. Running would only have given them more cause for gossip.

When Warren met my gaze without a hint of animosity, I figured I was safe to approach—at least for now.

Still, it took an effort for me to smile, to walk toward them as if my feet were not attached to my reluctant and guilty conscience.

"What's eating you?" Carrie asked when I was within earshot.

Great. Who knew my acting range was limited to stunned silence?

"I had a . . . um . . ." I shook my head. "Morning. Bad. Better now." I tried the smile again. "How are you?"

Carrie looked sideways at me, eyes narrowed as though peering for something hidden. "I'm fine."

She knew I was lying. I could see the knowledge in the crease beside her eye, the line of her mouth. But she smiled in return and gestured to Warren. "You remember—"

"Warren," I said, extending my hand. "Of course I do. But what are you two doing standing out here in this heat? Will there be a parade coming through that no one told me about?"

"I was just coming back from lunch," Carrie said with a nod to the luncheonette, "and Warren came out to say hi."

He shrugged. "I was trying to get a handle on the store. Got a lot of work to do in there."

A wave of guilt washed over me. "I'm so sorry about your dad."

Taking a step backward, Warren lowered his head. "Thank you. It's been . . . a lot to deal with."

"I just can't imagine . . ." Carrie said.

We stood in a silent triangle. Across the street, Rozelle went back into her bakery. People walked along the sidewalks, flip-flops slapping against their heels. Cars rolled slowly past, tires softly thumping on the cobbles. Not a breeze stirred.

"At any rate." Warren sucked in a breath. When he spoke again, his speech was halting, hesitant. "I was looking for a place to start. Trying to come up with a plan. Thought I'd start with the receipts, paperwork, that sort of thing. I noticed my dad's brick was gone and it just threw me for a loop."

My jaw worked, doing its best to aid my mouth in the formation of words. None came.

Carrie took my lack of eloquence for confusion. "We all have bricks," she said. "Original Wenwood bricks. It's a goofy thing that Bill Harper did a few years back, gave all his tenants a brick with the shop name engraved in it. Bill's the only man in town with a stash of original brick left."

I felt my brow crease with confusion. "Why Bill? Who would save bricks?"

The good-natured huff Carrie let out reminded me that I still didn't grasp the devotion to Wenwood brick. I pushed aside the niggling fear that my lack of understanding had more to do with a lack of hometown pride and a lingering longing for city life.

Warren swiped a line of perspiration from his temple. "It had something to do with his family. His father was a foreman at the brickworks, or . . ." He looked to Carrie.

Slipping her hands in the back pockets of her khakis,

she said, "Bill's family worked brick for generations. It was his first job. To hear him tell it, the Harpers built this town. I guess there were some leftovers when the brickworks closed and they went to the Harpers. Now Bill hands them out like golden trinkets," she finished on a laugh. "Only for his favorite people."

"I know, it's sentimental." Warren grimaced. "But I'd like to have it."

Still, words swirled in my mind, complicated by surprised and confused thoughts. They didn't know. The discovery of a blood-covered brick—a brick I could only surmise was the exact one Warren was looking for—was not yet common knowledge.

I had that knowledge. But how could I tell Warren the object potentially used to kill his father had been found? It wasn't the sort of news I was used to delivering. It also wasn't the sort of news I was accustomed to keeping to myself.

My internal argument over giving up the information or keeping my mouth shut created a conversational gap quickly filled by awkwardness.

Carrie looked from Warren to me and back again. "Um, we could help you look? That is, if you're okay with that? Unless Georgia has other things . . ."

"I'd be grateful for the company, and the help," Warren said, eyes on Carrie, "but I don't want to keep you from your store."

"I've already got my OUT FOR LUNCH sign up," Carrie said, a slightly higher pitch in her voice.

The tone was enough to snap me out of discordant

thoughts and into full awareness of the moment. Carrie stood with her body angled toward Warren, fingers pulling at the ends of her hair. Why, the shameless flirt!

But Carrie flirting with Warren had the potential to distract him sufficiently to allow me to look for something more than the brick I knew wasn't there.

I tried for a smile again and believed I succeeded. "I'm happy to lend a hand."

Warren inclined his head, stood back, and waved us toward the door to the hardware store.

He had no overhead lights on across the sales floor, leaving illumination to what sunlight passed through the window. A soft glow came from the back of the store, where the register was located.

"Careful," Warren said. "And just come straight back."

Carrie followed behind Warren; I followed behind Carrie. Air that had been scented with dust and must days earlier now held the remnants of an additional odor. I didn't want to examine too closely what my brain was trying to tell me about the source of the odor, no more than I wanted to examine too closely the stretch of sales floor to my right, where police tape remained in place.

I hugged myself against the sudden chill, though the feeling was more internal than external. The knowledge I was walking through a space where someone had been murdered, passing feet from the spot where a man had died, unsettled me. Too, it made me realize anew that Grandy would have had nothing to do with this. The police had the wrong person in custody. I needed to find a way to convince Detective Nolan of that fact.

We trailed behind Warren, back behind the makeshift sales counter and into the backroom-slash-office behind. The wide space, well lit, featured a full wall of filing cabinets, another wall of cubbies, and a desk opposite the filing cabinets, papers and binders strewn haphazardly across its surface. Beside the door leading to the back parking lot, a staircase led up.

"There's a second floor?" I said, because obvious things often surprise me.

"More of a loft, really." Warren rested a hand on the stair rail and gazed up into the shadowed space. "There's off-season stuff up there. Shovels and ice melt and things like that."

Edging closer to him, Carrie asked, "Do you think you'll move back here? Take over the business?"

He kept his eyes on the staircase. "I don't know. Wen-wood . . ." He shook his head, shook away whatever thoughts threatened to distract him from our purpose. Releasing the railing, he moved to the center of the small space. "I thought the brick would be back here somewhere. I don't think my father would put it out on the sales floor."

"Are you sure he kept it?" Carrie wandered to the wall of cubbies, tugged out a drawer whose contents clinked and clunked. Some type of building hardware, no doubt.

"When I came up last Christmas, he had it by the register." He headed back through the pass-way to the register.

On her way past, following Warren's path, Carrie stopped beside me. "Are you okay?" she asked, concern wrinkling her brow.

"I . . . yeah." I sighed. The tumult of the morning came crashing back. "I'll tell you after."

The sound of rustling paper and heavy items being moved carried easily to the back room. The conversation between Warren and Carrie, though, was little more than a murmur.

I dropped into the office chair in front of the desk, discovering too late that any cushioning on the seat had long since flattened to the consistency of cement. My lower spine complained of the impact, and I leaned into the desktop to relieve the compression.

Binders were stacked beside a tumble of parts catalogs. Clumps of papers covered every surface. There was no safe place for me to lower my head and feel sorry for myself. Anything could be lurking beneath the chaos.

Planning to clear a space and at least present the illusion I was looking for a brick I was relatively certain wasn't there, I grabbed a handful of papers and lifted.

The center of the stack of papers slipped out, causing a cascade of paperwork to flutter down around me like oversized confetti. Inspiration struck. If I made a thorough mess of the papers, I could focus on "putting them back in order," thus being able to quickly review the text on the pages while cleaning up my disaster and *not* looking for a brick.

Loving the idea, I reached for a couple of the catalogs and dragged them toward me. More papers floated to the floor. I voiced a mild curse in case anyone was paying attention, and stood from the chair.

I knelt on the floor and began pulling the papers

toward me, one by one, taking my time. Each paper I added to the pile at my feet I scanned as quickly as I could. There were lists that resembled part numbers—combinations of letters and numbers and slashes and dashes—and lists that looked like rough inventory. There was a notice about a holiday parade planned for July, and there was a survey from the state about the number of trees on the property.

And there were invoices marked SECOND NOTICE, and bills marked FINAL NOTICE. I thought of Grandy's confession about losing money in an investment plan with Andy Edgers, of the dust in the store, of the Town Council's requirements for Stone Mountain Construction.

No great intellectual leap was required to realize Edgers was in a financial tight spot. Was it tight enough to overcharge the construction company?

I snatched up more papers, searching for a lumber order, a wire order, anything that looked like it might have been written for Tony Himmel's marina project.

"What happened here?" Warren ambled into the room, knelt beside me, and scooped up some papers.

"Sorry," I said. "Knocked them off the desk trying to see if maybe the brick was under the catalogs. Guess I'm not a whole lot of help." I said a silent prayer my skin didn't go red from the embarrassment of being a bad liar. Though not being a lot of help—that part was true.

"My fault," Warren said, throwing the papers back onto the desk. "I'm the one that made that mess in the first place, doing the same thing—looking under the catalogs."

Oh, mercy. Guilt made my shoulders droop and my stomach ache. He was being so nice and understanding, and I was basically spying on him.

I opened my mouth to tell him the truth.

Who was I kidding? I couldn't tell him the truth. The poor guy's father was just murdered. My grandfather was arrested on suspicion. Warren was going to hate me enough when he learned that part. The last thing he needed was for me to confess I was spying on him.

Grabbing for the edge of the desk to help get to my feet, I got one foot under me before my fingers slipped. A new set of papers slicked onto the floor.

"I'm hopeless," I muttered. And I meant it wholeheartedly.

Rather than kneel, I simply bent down and shoved the papers into a rough pile. As I was handing them to Warren, my new habit made me skim the top sheet.

And damn it, that's what I was looking for. An order written out to an East Coast lumber giant whose radio commercials played more frequently than the weather report. The order was calculated in square feet, but the cost shown meant little to me; I had no knowledge of what was considered fair.

"None of this would have happened," Warren said, straightening, "if my father had put paperwork in the filing cabinets instead of plumbing supplies."

I shrugged, forced my brain to kick out an innocuous response. "Everyone has their own system."

"Yes, but it makes it a little tough on the next guy."

Crossing to the file cabinets, I slid open the middle

drawer on one. Sure enough, some sort of burnished metal thing-a-ma-whosit was nestled in the center of the drawer, with smaller, plastic-wrapped parts lining the bottom. It was the sort of filing system I was certain Grandy would approve of.

"I looked through most of those already," Warren said.

I nearly slid the drawer closed, but instead kept it open and turned to him. "Second set of eyes?" I suggested.

He didn't respond immediately, but did finally nod his assent. "Good idea."

I smiled until he left the room then slid the drawer closed and opened another. I was ninety-eight percent certain I wouldn't find a brick, but I was betting I'd find a caulking gun.

13

"**S**o dish. Tell me what's bugging you." Carrie leaned on the counter inside Rozelle's Bakery and bounced her eyebrows at me. "This morning's breakfast date with Drew Able not go well?"

Breakfast seemed a million years before. I wasn't sure what was most surprising: that I'd forgotten all about breakfast, or that Carrie thought I'd been on a date.

I kept my attention on the glass display showcasing row after row of cookies. For all Grandy's love of sweets, he never brought cookies home from Rozelle's. He did, however, refuse to buy bread at the grocery. "Drew is my grandfather's lawyer," I said firmly.

The humor left Carrie's face. "Is Pete okay?"

"He's fine." The response was a reflex, and I had to

shake my head and take back the statement. "Wait. That's not right."

"What's wrong with Pete?" Rozelle's voice was sharp with strain.

"There's nothing wrong with him." My voice betrayed my strain and frustration. In an instant all I wanted to do was go back to Grandy's house, crawl into bed, and pull the covers over my head. I had no experience trying to function in public while a member of my family sat in jail. I had no idea it caused such exhaustion.

"So you were having breakfast with his lawyer and it wasn't a date but everything's okay with Pete?" Carrie asked. "That doesn't sound, you know, right."

"What's wrong with Pete?" Rozelle asked, louder. "Is he all right?"

How was I supposed to answer that? I wasn't sure myself if Pete was all right. I hadn't seen him since the night before when we returned from the dine-in.

I met Rozelle's gaze over the counter, the question of whether she thought Grandy was guilty still coloring my opinion of her. Though this visit had not yet ended with her ushering me from her store, still I wasn't filled with fondness. "He's fine," I snapped. "Can I have a pound of these cookie cake things?"

She frowned as she pulled a waxed paper square from the container on the counter and used it to transfer the cookies from the display case into a bakery box. "You don't have to be short with me," she said, and in a flash, guilt wormed its way into my anger. "I would take it back if I could. How was I to know why the police wanted to know about Pete being at the hardware store? I was just trying to be a good citizen."

I glanced at Carrie, pulled a face to silently ask if she knew what Rozelle was referring to. In response, Carrie shrugged, the corners of her mouth turning down.

"What does this have to do with the cookies?" I asked.

"I didn't know, you see. When the police came and asked if I saw anyone coming out of the hardware store that day? Of course I told them. You can't not tell the police things. But I swear I didn't know they were going to arrest him."

A little late, no doubt, but clarity struck. Rozelle was the reason Detective Nolan had taken Grandy in for questioning the first time.

I wanted to grab her and shout, demand to know what she thought was going to happen after she told the police she saw Grandy leave the scene of a murder. But I simply lacked the energy. Worn down, I asked, "Why were you even watching?"

Eyes cast down, Rozelle hid her hands behind her apron. She took a shuffling step to the side, opened and closed her mouth a few times before the words finally escaped. "Because it was Pete," she nearly whispered. "I saw his Jeep go by, so I watched for him. Like I always do. I was hoping he'd stop in here."

Carrie made the tiniest squeaking noise ever, the sort of gleeful noise I make when Friday curls herself into some overboard adorable pose. "You're sweet on him," she said.

Rozelle fluttered her fingers behind her apron, making

her look as though she were fanning her thighs with a napkin. "You girls take the cookies and go. I have to check the . . . the . . ."

"There's nothing to be embarrassed about." Carrie reached across the counter. She would have put an arm around Rozelle if only her arms were longer.

Though I rarely saw that side of him, I knew Grandy could be a big charmer. Rozelle having a crush on him was not so far outside the realm. Nonetheless I struggled to find the right words to both apologize and reassure her while my attention lapsed. My mind was gnawing on something else entirely. It had taken an idea off into a corner to examine until my conscious was ready to learn what my subconscious had determined.

"I'm sure Pete would be flattered," I managed.

Rozelle shook her head. "Maybe he would, and maybe he wouldn't like that at all." Her eyes flashed to mine, narrowed with command. "You won't say a word about this."

Absolutely not. With Grandy's affinity for breads and cakes, the last thing his cholesterol needed was a romance with the owner of a bakery.

"Not a word." I set a ten-dollar bill on the counter and pulled the cookies toward me.

The bell over the door jingled. Both Carrie and I turned as one of Wenwood's senior citizens shuffled in. Carrie greeted the patron, exchanging small talk that showed she'd known this woman for some time. I focused on the bell hanging over the door. A classic bell and clapper hung from the ceiling at the right height so the opening door would clip it. It could have been installed yesterday; it could have been installed a hundred years ago. Like all the other shops in the village.

My brain coughed up the results of its deliberation.

Rather than shout the question down the length of the counter, I waited until Rozelle returned with my change. "Rozelle," I said, keeping my voice down. "You saw Pete leave the hardware store the day Andy Edgers was killed."

Her eyes narrowed, but not enough to hide a hint of sadness. "Don't mock me, missy."

"Not mocking you. I just want to be sure. If you saw him leave, that means he left through the front door."

"I think you're mocking me."

I scooped up my change and lifted the cookies off the counter before she decided mockery was cause for taking them away. "Was he carrying anything?"

Rozelle pursed her lips. For a moment I feared she was going to accuse me of disrespecting her. But she turned her gaze to the ceiling, tapped her fingers thoughtfully against the display case. "Nothing I saw," she said. "I imagine he had his keys in his hand."

"What's this?" Carrie asked, turning back to us.

"And if you saw him," I said, "it had to be maybe late afternoon? What time do you close up here?"

"Four thirty," Rozelle pronounced. "Unless we have a rush."

My mind ran back to its private corner with the idea of any shop in Wenwood having a rush. I would giggle at the idea later. Repeatedly. For the time being, I nodded and smiled. "Thanks," I said as brightly as I could. "I appreciate it."

"You'll give my regards to Pete?" she asked.

Around the sudden lump in my throat, I managed to assure her I would, then hurried from the shop, heedless of Carrie's progress behind me.

"Hold up," she said, bursting through the door. "What's going on?"

I strode along the sidewalk, one hand clutching the bakery box, the other hand held to my forehead, physically holding on to my thoughts.

"Georgia," Carrie called.

I stopped, turned.

"What's going on? Something's not right with you. You've been acting weird all afternoon. Now either talk to me or I'm going back to the store."

In her shorthand way, Carrie was right. She'd extended her lunch break to help Warren and kept the store closed to walk with me to the bakery. I owed her an explanation.

Checking the street, which was alive with pedestrians running afternoon errands, I walked back to Carrie and handed her the bakery box. "Take these," I said. "I'm going over to the luncheonette to get some coffee. I'll meet you back in your store. You want coffee?"

"Tea," she said. I got the feeling she was asking for tea just to be contrary, and that made perfect sense. In her shoes I would do the same thing.

On the remaining walk to the luncheonette, I decided to explain everything to Carrie. I determined to share the news of Grandy's arrest and the why, the information I'd learned from Drew about the Town Council's agreement with Stone Mountain Construction, and the puzzle Rozelle's information created.

Rozelle had told the police she saw Grandy leave the hardware store through the front door. I was no expert, but I strongly suspected crashing a brick against someone's skull would make a mess of your wardrobe. Who would be brazen enough to walk out the front door? Plus, even on the day they questioned Grandy, the police didn't have a murder weapon. It stood to reason, then, that whoever had murdered Andy Edgers had left with that weapon.

The police had to know this. They had to know Grandy left the hardware store in daylight, empty-handed, in clean clothes. They had to know finding the supposed murder weapon behind the dine-in meant anyone could have put it there.

So if they knew all those things, why was Grandy under arrest?

As expected, the bell over the door jangled when I entered the luncheonette. The scent of burgers, fried onions, and fresh coffee assailed my senses, making me wonder how such disparate aromas could smell so appealing.

I made the quick left, past the rack of dusty postcards, and walked the length of the counter. Two of the stools were occupied by people I didn't recognize hunched over white bread sandwiches. The next two stools were empty, and on the fifth, Tom sat sipping coffee and gazing out the window.

Perching on the edge of the empty stool beside Tom,

I gave him a polite hello and waited to see if he would remember me.

He lowered his coffee cup and gazed at me over the rim. "You back again?" he shouted with a grin. His pale blue eyes were bright, practically twinkling in his age-wrinkled face.

Tom hadn't been sitting in his counter seat when I'd had breakfast with Drew, leaving me to wonder whether he knew who he was talking to or if he was mistaking me for someone else. I smiled. "Just can't get enough of Grace's coffee."

"Nectar," he said at a surprisingly normal decibel, before taking another sip of his own. He set the cup down with a satisfied sigh and fixed his gaze on the window behind the counter. "Pretty day, wouldn't you say?"

I followed his line of sight out the window, knowing full well the shuttered hardware store was directly opposite but, oddly, needing to reassure myself. "We're having a nice summer so far."

"How's Pete?" Tom asked.

His question hit me like a bang on the shin in the dark—sharp, unexpected, and painful. I moved my mouth around, waiting for words to form, but all I managed in the end was to lean over the counter and call out, "Hey, Grace! Can I get some coffee to go? And a tea?"

Grace shouted back a "Sure thing, sweetie" and I settled on my stool again.

I let the noise of the luncheonette wrap the space around Tom and me. People chatted at tables, flatware clacked and clanged against stoneware, and laughter rolled out of the kitchen.

Grace would pop out at any moment. I had wasted enough time. "Tom, can I ask you something?"

He turned his merry blue eyes on me. "What can I do you for?" He was back to shouting.

"Do you, um, do you remember the other day I stopped in and asked Grace if she'd seen Pete leave the hardware store?"

He scratched at his poorly shaved chin. "What day was that?"

"Do you mean what day did I ask or what day did Grace see Pete?"

Continuing the scratching, he looked away from me, down at the counter. "I haven't had a good chin wag with Pete since, oh, couple of months now. Met him and Terry for lunch. Pete had the Reuben."

"Terry," I repeated, running the name through my memory. "I thought Terry moved."

Tom lifted his head. "Terry moved?"

In and out of coherence, Carrie had said about Tom. That seemed about right. "Yes, Terry moved. He went . . ." My memory failed, and I had a surge of sympathy for how Tom must struggle.

Grace appeared from the back, empty paper hot cups in hand. "Terry moved down to North Carolina to be with Amy, Tom. You know that."

Tom scowled. "Of course I know that," he bellowed, then repeated it softly to himself. "Of course I know that."

I wanted to put my hand on his shoulder, but wasn't sure if he would appreciate or resent the gesture.

"Same way I know Grace said she didn't see Pete leave the hardware store that day before they found Andy."

Ah ha! He was back. "What about you, Tom? Did you see anyone that day?" I asked.

Grace set the cups side by side on the counter and turned for the coffeepot.

"Nope, didn't see anyone leave," he said.

Coffee splashed into the cup, dispersing its heavenly aroma and giving me a little thrill at the idea of the caffeine-induced energy to come.

"Not leave." I leaned a little closer to Tom. "I'm not worried about anyone leaving. I'm wondering if you saw anyone go in."

"Oh, that's easy. You should have asked that in the first place. I saw Pete go in, sure enough. And Bill Harper, too. I remember because I thought he'd come over here after." Tom shook his head. "He didn't."

"Bill Harper? From the grocery?"

Settling covers over the hot cups, Grace rolled her eyes.

"How many Bill Harpers we got in Wenwood?" Tom shouted. "Of course that Bill Harper." He lifted his coffee cup, quickly lowered it before taking a sip. "But there was another guy. Didn't recognize him."

Grace rested a hand on the counter, leaned her weight in. "You probably just forgot who he was."

"No, no, this was a different guy. Tall fella, brown hair. Seemed kinda angry, walkin' all puffed up and hurried."

He waved a hand over his chin. "Had a . . . a beard you know." He shrugged. "I'd say it's too hot for a beard, but what do I know. I probably just forgot what summer feels like."

Tom glared good-naturedly at Grace, who backed away and gave me a grin. "Three dollars, sweetie."

I dug out the money and set it on the table, mind racing. Tall guy with brown hair and a beard. Angry.

It sounded like Grandy's head cook, Matthew. But it couldn't be Matthew. Could it?

Too many thoughts crowded my head: the orders at Andy's store, Rozelle's guilt, Tom's confusion, and more than anything else, worry about Grandy sitting in jail. How had life gotten so complicated so fast?

At least the entrance to the grocery store had automatic doors. In my present state, I doubted I could reliably work out whether to push or pull the door open.

I bypassed the little selection of newspapers and shopping guides decorating the store's entrance, grabbed a handbasket from the stack, and headed directly for the produce aisle. At the rate I went through fresh fruits and vegetables, it would have made sense for me to set up a vegetable garden in a corner of Grandy's yard. I wondered again if it was too late to start planting.

Turning into the aisle, I spotted Bill Harper smack in the middle, adding lemons to the citrus display. I froze. I really didn't want to talk to the man, didn't want to talk to anyone. I wanted to pick up something healthy to have in the house without having to deal with anyone else asking after Grandy.

"Well, hello again, Georgia!"

Too late to turn tail and run. I forced myself to smile. "Afternoon, Mr. Harper."

He grabbed another trio of lemons from a box on the cart he stood behind, the blue of his latex gloves against the yellow of the fruit making me think of putting flowers in the garden I could plant in Grandy's yard. The splashes of color would look nice if, you know, I planned on staying and Grandy was released from jail.

"Everything all right?" Mr. Harper was watching me from below lowered brows. I must have been lost in thoughts of gardens longer than I'd realized.

"Sorry." I shook my head and tried a little laugh and a little lie. "Forgot what I needed for a second there." I scurried to a display of honeydew. Ducking my head with embarrassment, I studied the melons.

"How's Pete doing these days? Haven't seen him around much," Mr. Harper said.

If he didn't know Grandy was in custody, I wasn't going to be the one to tell him. I could use a few moments of denial. Besides . . . "I heard you were in the hardware store with Pete last week, the day before they found Andy."

"Oh?"

At the sound of something hitting the floor, I turned. A lemon had gotten away from him and was rolling toward me. I stooped to pick it up. "I was wondering, did you happen to see anyone else in the store? Tall guy, maybe? Brown hair, beard?"

He reached a hand out for the lemon and I crossed to him, handed him the fruit so he could drop it into a little box of loose leaves and a badly bruised banana. "Sorry, I didn't notice anyone like that."

I supposed I should have tried to get some idea of time frame from Tom. When he described who he'd seen, it sounded like all the men arrived fairly close together. But time appeared to move at a unique pace for Tom. If I wanted to know whether Matthew had visited the hardware store, the only way to find out was to ask Matthew himself.

"I only stopped in long enough to remind Andy about his rent being due."

I tried for another smile. "It's okay. Thanks anyway."

I turned my attention back to the melons. If I wasn't careful, I'd end up leaving without what I came for.

"You give Pete my regards when you see him, okay?"

I assured him I would.

If only I knew when that *when you see him* would be.

M y call went straight to Drew's voice mail. Three times. I phoned the police station in hopes of learning from them the outcome of the arraignment, but they had no information and only advised I contact Drew. I tried asking directly for Detective Nolan, planning to use the laundry they were holding as an excuse, but recognizing Diana as the desk sergeant who answered the phone, I opted not to leave a message requesting a return call,

I stood in the kitchen of the quiet house, missing the

rattle and clatter of Grandy's morning routine, and listened to the ticking of the clock instead. It was the sort of sound I never noticed normally. Like the hum of the refrigerator's compressor, it stayed in the overlooked background. In the empty house, however, this simple rhythm was amplified into a disturbing noise.

Friday lay belly up in my arm, allowing me to stroke her stomach while I turned over thoughts in my mind. Mostly I needed to talk to Drew. I needed to know when bail would be set for Grandy and what to do if—or when—my depleted savings couldn't cover the cost.

Friday wriggled and let out a teeny *mew*. I ruffled her head one last time and lowered her to the floor. She bounded out of the room, tail straight up like a feline antenna. I couldn't imagine where she was going in such a hurry.

Alone in the kitchen, I sat down at the table and put my head in my hands.

Alone. I could have turned on the radio or the television, used the electronic world to keep me company. Instead, I tugged my cell phone free of my purse and opened an Internet browser. There were at least a few things I could do that were better than sitting and feeling sorry for myself. Punching the name of the East Coast lumber giant into the search bar, I realized I was going to have to return Tony Himmel's call.

Learning the price per square foot of lumber presented a steep challenge. I knew numbers. I knew glass. I was learning about kittens. I didn't know lumber. What was the difference between pine and whitewood and Douglas fir? My knowledge was limited to what would make a good Christmas tree, not what would make a good building. And the prices varied widely.

I clicked out of the browser and stared at the wallpaper on my phone. The image was of Louis Comfort Tiffany's dogwoods in stained glass. Typically, losing myself in the depth of color, the brilliant use of shape, the rich-hued background soothed and centered me, allowed me to tackle the next moments of my day with a fresh perspective.

That afternoon, gazing on a place of beauty only made me restless. Maybe it was the ticking of the clock. Maybe it was the absence of human company. Maybe it was an emotion I was too much of a wimp to attempt to identify.

One deep breath, and I tapped on the missed call icon on the phone, selected the option to return call.

Moving the phone to my ear, I gripped the device tighter than necessary while I listened to the ringing on the other end. Two cycles elapsed before Tony picked up the call, giving his name as a greeting.

"Tony. Georgia Kelly returning your call."

"Georgia, how are you?"

Yeah, I was in no shape to answer that question. "How did you get my number?"

He responded with one of those heh-heh chuckles that only men can pull off. "I took a chance that the number on the 'Found: White Kitten' flyers belonged to you."

"Are you calling to tell me it's your kitten?"

"Not a chance. I'm still recovering from puncture wounds sustained during our first meeting."

"So you called to request reimbursement for medical expenses. How much do Snoopy Band-Aids go for these days?"

"I called to ask if you would meet me for a drink, or dinner, whichever you're comfortable with. Tomorrow night? I'd like a chance to apologize for my bad behavior. Again."

A measure of unease prickled my spine. Meeting with Tony would be an ideal time for me to learn what he was being charged for lumber. It also meant I might be meeting with someone who would benefit a great deal by Andy Edgers's removal from the supply chain. But I wanted answers, and neither Detective Nolan nor Drew was around to consult with. Mostly, though, the house was too quiet. I would have gone mad there. A crowded restaurant sounded not only safe but far more pleasant than sitting in the house alone.

"Dinner sounds fine. But I'm going to need a favor."

14

Tony had graciously allowed me to select a restaurant and having been secretly harboring a craving since leaving the city, I suggested Italian food. This turned out to be a stroke of luck. Nothing was as comforting to me as a big plate of pasta, and when Drew had called the prior afternoon with the news Grandy's bail had been set at sixty thousand dollars, I developed a need for serious comfort. I neither had that kind of money nor any property to use as collateral against a bond. Grandy would be stuck in jail until his trial date, or until the police found the real killer. Any information I could gather to help the police with that was well worth the effort, and Mr. Jaguar definitely had information, if not outright guilt.

Arriving at the restaurant, I made sure to locate Tony's

car and park on the complete opposite side of the lot. This, I reasoned, would allow me to part company with him at the door, announcing, "I'm this way." And yes, I purposely arrived late to facilitate that plan.

Dressed in a summer top, narrow skirt, and flip-flops, I sidestepped the maître d' by pointing to the interior of the tiny restaurant and announcing, "I'm meeting someone."

Those damned butterflies were once again doing aerial exercises in my belly as I wove my way between tables. Tony had been easy to spot, the only table with one occupant, the only occupant who made my hopeless heart skip. Was it possible for someone to be too handsome to be a murderer? Or wait. Weren't there statistics that showed most murders were committed by family members? If that was the case, the odds of Tony having murdered Andy were slim.

But slim wasn't the same as zero. And women who have recently emerged from a heartbreaking engagement need to remain impervious to handsome men, rather the same as people just recovering from surgery need to avoid crowds because they are more susceptible to disease.

Patting my hair to be certain it remained in its loose ponytail, I gave myself the same silent pep talk I'd used when walking into a boardroom full of skeptical men. *You're every bit as smart as these guys*, I'd tell myself. *It's okay to let it show.*

As I reached his table, I announced my presence by stating, "Tony."

He glanced up from the smartphone he had set on the

table. He grinned and half stood from his chair. "Thank you for agreeing to meet me. Please, sit. I just have to finish up this message."

Regaining his seat, he focused his attention on the phone, typing madly with one finger.

On the one hand, I was put out by his dismissal. On the other, his actions proclaimed the dinner all business, no romance. The clarification put me marginally at ease. A two percent margin, I estimated.

A busboy rushed over and pulled my chair out. As I settled into the seat, he filled my glass with water and promised to send the waiter over to take my drink order.

I sipped at the water, blissfully cold after the heat of the outdoors.

Tony punched one final button on his phone. He looked up at me as he slid the phone to the far edge of the table. "My apologies." He nodded to the phone. "My sister. She's considering breaking off her engagement and was asking my advice."

My first instinct was to offer unsolicited advice based on my own experience. The second, overpowering instinct was to heed the alarm bells going off in my mind. It was mighty convenient, wasn't it? Tony Himmel just *happened* to have a sister with a troubled engagement? He just *happened* to be e-mailing or texting with her when I arrived? What were the odds?

"That's too bad," I said.

Tony nodded. "She deserves to be happy. I keep telling her if this guy isn't making her happy, it's not going to get any better. She should call it off."

I took another sip of water.

"Do you agree?" he asked.

Lifting a shoulder, I looked around the restaurant, hoping to make eye contact with a waiter. "I really couldn't say. I don't know your sister."

When I returned my gaze to Tony, I found him watching me with a speculative expression generally reserved for reviewing expense accounts. "So," he said. "Anyone contact you yet about the cat?"

"You're the only one who's called."

"What happens if you don't find the owner?"

"You mean if I don't find the person who threw her away?" I shook my head. "I don't know. I'd like to keep her, but my grandfather's not too keen."

He lifted a glass of wine, nearly empty. I wondered how long he'd been waiting while I played the *fashionably late* game. "How is he, your grandfather?" he asked.

I nodded, playing for time. As near as I could tell, Grandy's incarceration was not yet widespread knowledge. Somehow the Pace County PD had kept a lid on news of the arrest. Telling Carrie the news hadn't been easy, and I had come to consider her a friend. Was that something I wanted to share with Tony Himmel?

Then again, perhaps his reaction to the news might inform me about whether I was about to dine with a killer.

I took hold of my water glass, wished for the waiter. "The police took him in the day before yesterday," I said.

Tony's brow furrowed. "More questioning?"

"They believe they've found—" I couldn't say it. I

couldn't put a murder weapon in the same context as Grandy. "Further evidence."

He knocked back the rest of his wine, which did nothing to clear the furrow. "In the Andy Edgers case?"

Was there more than one case he thought Grandy should be implicated in? "That would be the one."

Resting both elbows on the table, he leaned a little weight upon his forearms. I had to wonder if the pose, with its resultant emphasis on his shoulders, chest, and biceps, was an intentional move to distract me. He had to know he was handsome, right? He had to know he had a decent physique and these two things combined had a tendency to turn a girl's head.

"That just doesn't make sense. What kind of evidence would they need to find to link Pete with that crime?"

I locked my eyes with his. "They think they have something." I didn't want to give anything away, and didn't want to miss any hint of reaction he might show.

He turned away from my gaze. "Must be pretty convincing." After a moment's scanning the restaurant, he lifted an arm ever so slightly. "I'm sorry he's caught up in all this," he said an instant before a waiter appeared at our table.

"Something from the bar?" the waiter asked.

Something strong would have been wonderful. But I was driving. Moreover, I needed to stay alert, needed to be able to observe Mr. Himmel with my mind clear. I ordered a dry white wine on the grounds I didn't really care for it and so would sip it slowly while still appearing social.

When the waiter departed, Tony resumed the conversation as though there had been no interruption. "What sort of evidence did the police find? Fingerprints? DNA?"

"No, it was nothing quite so definitive." I drew out the statement, all the time watching for a reaction.

He shook his head slightly, shook his concerned expression into a neutral one. "It's a shame they're holding him, then. He has a lawyer?"

I nodded while mentally counting the hours since I had last left a message for Drew asking if Grandy was willing for me to visit. "I'm waiting to hear back."

"Is he local, the lawyer?"

Again, I nodded, and Tony nodded in return. He was mirroring my movements, a classic method for putting the person you are talking with at ease. "Why do you ask?" I shifted in my chair, leaning one elbow and my upper body weight on the left armrest.

He echoed my action by leaning to the right. I wondered why he felt he needed to win me to his side . . . in the split second before the waiter placed our wine upon the table. "If he didn't have anyone, I could give you a couple of names," he said, lifting one shoulder dismissively.

"No, I mean, why does it matter that he's local?"

"The lawyers I could recommend wouldn't be, that's all." He glanced at his phone, glanced back at me. "I'm starved. You ready to order?"

We reviewed the menu, selected entrées, both of us agreeing to take a pass on the appetizer and go straight to the main course. With the order placed, it was an easy enough matter to get Tony talking about his marina project.

As he spoke to me of slips and repair docks, tackle shop and restaurant, he sat straight, his eyes brightened, he smiled around every word, every gesture. Even when our food arrived, his posture didn't change. He talked intensely of the years of planning, of seeing the old brick-works falling into ruin while taking vacation trips as a child with his family and dreaming of one day making something of the wreckage. When at last his management group had earned sufficient respect, he'd been able to attract investors, which put him on the path to achieving his dream.

"I can't tell you what it felt like," he said, taking a break to gather some spaghetti on his fork. "The day they told me I had the financing was probably the best day of my life thus far."

The glow on his face told me he was reliving the moment a bit, once again feeling that combination of relief and euphoria present when a goal is achieved. I almost hated to bring him back to the present reality. Almost.

"And then you had to face the Wenwood Town Council," I said.

He rested the fork on his plate. Sitting back in his seat, he shook his head while chewing. He turned his gaze to the window. "What a mess," he said, reaching blindly for his wine.

I knew the mess. I had a lawyer explain it to me. What I wanted was Tony's opinion of it. "How so?" I asked.

He nearly snorted on his way to a wry laugh. "You'd

think the town would be happy to have a new business come in. Without something new, Wenwood is destined to become a ghost town." He peered into his wineglass then set it away from him and reached for the water instead. "The marina will bring a whole new revenue stream to the town. New visitors. New residents. New life. And me . . . I should have known better."

The manicotti was the best I'd had in months, but I swallowed down the mouthful after barely a taste. I needed to keep him talking. "What do you mean?"

He took a long drink of water. "Look, I knew the agreement was restrictive and basically over the top."

"The agreement?"

Tony's gaze bore into me as if he knew, as if someone had told him I'd visited Town Hall and gotten a copy of the agreement. "The list of requirements set down by the Town Council to ensure my project failed. Your friend Carrie brought it up the other night at the funeral parlor, in fact."

"Wait," I said, "you think the town . . . what? Rigged the deal so you—"

"So the marina would fail, yes."

"Well, that's just crazy. Why would they do that?"

He stabbed a fork into the spaghetti. "You tell me. You're a resident. Or at least, related to one. You can probably explain the mentality better than I could. That crazy attachment to the brickworks, to the past. The resistance to moving forward. They'd rather let the town fade away than see it thrive again."

"I don't think that's so," I said. "I think folks genuinely love the town and want to see it survive. The fact they granted you the right to rebuild the brickworks is a perfect example of that. They could have just refused your request or application or whatever it is you had to submit. But the Council came up with an agreement to help everyone benefit now instead of waiting any longer than it had to for your project to help local businesses get back on their feet, or stay on their feet."

Setting his fork down carefully, he leaned back and stroked a hand across his chin. "Maybe you're right. I can't think clearly about any of this anymore. Too involved. Too emotionally attached."

I sensed that was not the moment to push. I took a tiny bite of pasta, drawing out the quiet moment by chewing slowly. The busboy refilled the water glasses. The table of four beside us pushed back their chairs and departed.

At length, Tony met my gaze again. "I'm an outsider here in Wenwood. My family comes from Connecticut, not Pace County. I went to college in Boston. That makes me the next best thing to a terrorist. I can't even get served a decent cup of coffee in Wenwood."

"Oh, I don't think that's you." I smiled. "I think that's the water."

He smiled back, reluctantly it seemed. "That may be so, but it doesn't negate the rest of it. The stares. The odd looks."

"Geez. You're as paranoid as a teenage girl. You're nothing special, Himmel. They look at everyone like that. Small town. Low on trust."

"I could handle all of that, okay? I've had tougher gauntlets to run. But Andy Edgers constantly hiking the lumber costs, that was the pinnacle. That's where I drew the line."

Belatedly I recalled this was the information I wanted to ask him about. This was why I agreed to meet him. But . . . "What do you mean, *constantly hiking*?"

"On an escalating basis." He reached into the pocket of his suit jacket hanging over the back of his chair. Handing me a collection of folded papers, he said, "I brought these, just like you asked. You'll see, the first order was slightly above market. The next slightly more so, and the one after that more so again."

"How much are we talking? What's above market?" I riffled through the papers, Tony's copy of the orders Andy sent to the national lumber giant. The numbers on Tony's orders clearly did not match those on Andy's.

"Lumber is sold by piece or by square foot, that's how the price is derived, right?"

I nodded as if this was knowledge I had possessed my whole life.

"I'm ordering by square foot. The first order goes in, Edgers is charging twenty cents above average. Okay, that's maybe a variance in who he's using to fill the order. But the next order is thirty-five cents above, and then sixty cents above. I don't need to tell you that sixty cents is one thing if you're looking at replacing a few beams and another if you're rebuilding something the size of a factory."

"No, you don't," I put in.

"That's what led to the argument you witnessed at the hardware store."

"And did not tell the police about."

He flashed a quick grin. "And did not tell the police about. I couldn't have Andy Edgers overcharging me anymore. If it was a matter of finding another supplier, he'd have to find one. He said that the price he was giving me was the best price he could get. That's a crock. I could pick up the phone now and call six guys that will give me a better price."

"How did that argument end anyway? The one you were having that day?"

"You mean after I told him he ought to treat his customers better?" He winked.

Holy crap, he actually winked! How was I supposed to focus on price gouging when Mr. Blue Eyes and Broad Shoulders winked at me? I distracted myself by folding up the order sheets and passing them back. He set them underneath the phone, still on the table.

"I left the store," Tony said. "I got back in my car and put in a call to the Town Council's emergency number."

"What did they say?"

He lifted his water glass, swirled the contents until the ice cubes clinked against the glass. "Please leave a message." After a healthy swallow he set the glass down. "I never got a call back. But I figured with Andy's passing, the timing wasn't right to pursue a complaint or suggest renegotiating the agreement."

"And now it doesn't matter, right? You can order your supplies from anywhere."

A tip of his head showed his agreement. "The hardware and lumber, yes. Please don't mistake me. I'm sorry about what happened to Andy. And I'm trying to balance that regret with the relief that I can resume construction. It's tough."

He didn't deny what he couldn't. He was free to purchase hardware from any source he chose. Tragic as Andy Edgers's death was, it was also a boon for Tony Himmel.

Watching him as our dinner plates were cleared away, his easy posture, his half smile, I tried on the idea that in his determination to get his project back on track, he had killed Andy Edgers. It didn't fit comfortably.

But what did I know, really, about reading men? The man I had once planned to share the rest of my life with had turned out to be a man I would not want to share my Tic Tacs with. Who was to say I couldn't sit across a table from a murderer and think him a gentleman?

Because the fact remained, *someone* in Wenwood had murdered Andy Edgers. The polite little town was home to a killer. He—or she—could be anyone.

Anyone.

I pulled the Jeep into the closest parking spot I could find. The lot in front of the dine-in was reassuringly full. At least for one night it looked like people weren't opposed to patronizing Grandy's place of business.

Flip-flops scuffing against blacktop as I walked, I tucked the keys in my purse and crossed the lot. With each step I tried to force down the recent memory of dinner with Tony and the uncomfortable questions it raised. I couldn't believe he had killed Andy Edgers. Or did I not want to believe it because a little tingle of attraction raced through my veins at the remembrance of his smile? But certainly I wasn't the best judge of a man's character . . . except for Grandy. I had no doubt about the quality of Grandy's character. Some other folks appeared to need convincing.

On the sidewalk in front of the entrance, I paused. The lobby doors would rattle in their frame when I tugged one open. Staff members would know I'd arrived. Not that my presence was a secret. More that, having arrived at my destination, I worried about the wisdom of my plan. Sure it all sounded good in my head after I'd said good night to Tony—and tried to identify whether I was relieved or disappointed there was no parting kiss—but now that the moment was upon me . . .

Drat it. Grandy, who had never denied me love and support and desserts, was sitting in jail, and I doubted the decision to try and find out why his head cook just happened to visit Edgers Hardware.

With a disgusted huff at my own spineless streak, I yanked open the lobby door and tried not to wince at the rattle of the glass in its frame.

I bypassed the empty ticket booth and was halfway to the refreshment counter before the clerk behind it turned and saw me.

"The movie's already started," she said, sliding open the front of a napkin dispenser. She had a paper-wrapped package of napkins within reach, ready to refill the dispenser so the next night's clerk was ready for an opening rush. Grandy had trained her well. Or someone had.

I continued toward her. "I'm here to see Matthew," I said. "Is he still in the back?"

Her eye roll would have put a varsity cheerleader to shame. "You can check."

She could also have poked her head through the door at the back of the counter and looked for herself, but I let that one slide, fairly certain I was better with an element of surprise. But as I continued through the lobby then through the doors to the theater proper, I revised my opinion of her being well trained and determined someone other than Grandy had taught her.

Through the doors and along the short hallway to the kitchen, the swelling sound of James Bond's theme music expanding behind me from the theater alerted the previously quiet butterflies residing in my stomach that something dangerous was afoot.

I stopped at the swinging door to the kitchen and peered through the circular inset window. As I'd hoped, Matthew had yet to go home. Once again, though, I wasn't sure whether to be relieved or disappointed.

Shoulder to the door, I pushed into the kitchen. A unique aroma wafted on the air, putting me slightly off balance mentally. Where the scent of fried onions and grilled burgers should fill the room, instead the fragrance was a mix of something sweet and savory, something familiar. Despite my recent meal, my mouth watered. And my eyes locked on to the plate Matthew held.

He stood at the aluminum prep table in the center of the kitchen. His brother—Grandy's assistant manager, Craig—stood beside him, chewing . . . until he spotted me. A mix of annoyance, and curiosity, created wrinkles in his forehead.

"I'm Georgia Kelly," I said. "We've spoken on the phone."

Understanding lit his eyes. He nodded and resumed rapid chewing, while checking the integrity of the knot of his tie. Moving toward me, hand outstretched so I could shake it, he swallowed loudly. "Craig Meadows. How's Pete?"

I shook his hand, cut my gaze to his brother. "Stubborn as ever," I said.

Matthew lifted the plate from the prep table and turned his back on me, but not before I caught the scowl that creased his face.

"What have you got there?" I asked. "Smells good." I hoped the complimentary-acting-friendly approach would keep things low-key. If Matthew really had been the one to kill Andy Edgers, probably best not to get him riled up.

"Mud pies," he growled over his shoulder, "from my own garden."

Craig grinned, clueless. "He's kidding. That was a little pulled pork. We served mac and cheese wedges earlier."

"Craig," Matthew snapped.

I didn't know which required explanation first, what a mac and cheese wedge was or . . . "What do you mean, *served*? Does that mean you were off menu?"

Matthew huffed and turned to face us. "No, served as in handed legal papers. What do you think it means?"

The first question that sprang to mind was the next thing to fall out of my mouth. "Does Pete know about this?"

"See? I told you," Matthew snapped, eyes on Craig.

"No way can I change so much as a pinch of salt without Pete Keene's approval. And no way is that approval ever going to come. As long as he runs this place—"

"Now, now, now . . ." Craig held up a hand.

Matthew turned his anger on me. "What, did someone call you? Do you have spies? Or are you psychic or something?" He moved to step toward me, but banged a hip against the prep table, setting the aluminum clattering. I flinched at the noise, jumped back, hopefully out of his reach.

"Look, I only came by to ask, um, by any chance . . ."

Matthew opened his eyes wide, inclined his head toward me as though impatient to hear what I had to say.

"Did you, um, happen to be in Wenwood the other day? I thought I saw you—"

"Saw me . . ."

I tried to swallow down my nervousness. "Going into the hardware store."

The wide-eyed look remained. "And you came all the way up here to ask me that?"

"Well, no. I came to see how everything was going, what with Pete not around, just in case there was anything I could do, but it seems like everything is okay." I knew I was babbling but couldn't stop. Must have been the wine. "And I figured as long as I was here, I would ask about, you know, the hardware store."

"Since you explained so nice, no." Matthew smirked. "I didn't go to the hardware store. Is that what you wanted to hear?"

The tiny bit of courage I screwed up outside the dine-in shriveled to nothingness.

"You know, everything is fine here, just fine." Craig grinned. "Good-size crowd tonight. Nothing to worry about. Next time you see Pete, you can let him know that everything's fine. Fine. Good really."

Reluctantly I turned to face Craig. "Good. Good to know." I didn't want to put my back to Matthew, especially when he was within an arm's reach of an impressive variety of knives. "I'll just—I just wanted to say thanks, Craig, for handling things here while Pete is . . ." Still I couldn't bring myself to say the words. "Thanks."

Then I turned and walked away as fast as my flip-flops allowed, frightened and humiliated and wishing I'd stayed and had one more drink with Tony Himmel and not gone to the dine-in at all.

Friday had a way of sleeping so deeply, so completely, I could lift her from where she slept and she would drape over my hand like a wet T-shirt. In the middle of the night, following my disastrous attempt at getting information out of Matthew, I lifted the wet T-shirt/sleeping kitten off my chest and deposited her at the foot of the bed. I padded into the hallway and down the stairs into the workshop. After switching on all the lights, I rolled back the sheet covering my stained glass worktable.

The oblongs of glass I had left the day before remained at the center of the table. I took a moment to switch on the old radio Grandy kept by the stairs. Classic rock filled the corners of the room while I unpacked my tools and laid out all my supplies.

With plans to keep my hand steady and my mind focused, I laid my metal, cork-backed ruler against the glass, its edge less than a quarter inch from my earlier botched break. Using the ruler to brace my cutter against, I took a breath and scored the glass. To be doubly sure I didn't blow this second attempt, I took my line-run pliers from my tool box. Pliers aligned precisely along the score line, I applied the gentlest of pressure, and the square of glass snapped cleanly in two.

Feeling a million times better about my ability, I lay the glass pieces down, switched the pliers for the glass cutter, and scored the next line, halving the sheet again. Again I switched cutting tool for pliers and snapped the glass.

With the glass in workable sizes, I began to cut the pattern pieces. Nature doesn't draw in a straight line. Each piece required combinations of inside and outside curves. Outside curves at the top of petals broke clean with the help of a break plier. Inside curves took a combination of tapping the glass into breakage for some. Grozing—snicking away unwanted pieces bit by bit with the pliers—was needed for others. Free of the square, the resulting pattern pieces were little bigger than the length of my thumb. Lavender teardrops and rich blue half ovals collected on the table like a trove of jewels.

Double-checking my work, I slid the pieces into place on the pattern copied onto the heavy paper. Each piece nestled into its intended place. So simple. So obvious. The teardrops laid flat snuggled neatly beside the ovals. Soft-cornered trapezoids accommodated free-form shapes. Matching one against the other, cutting and adding more pieces, the picture began to emerge.

Satisfied to have cut a good number of pieces, I picked up a handful and carried them to the glass grinder I had set up in the corner. One at a time I stroked each piece along the grinder bit, water sluicing across the surface and washing away the sand-sized bits of glass the grinding created. Applying careful pressure allowed me to smooth down the edges of the glass, grinding away sharp ridges, without reducing the size of the piece. It was an important but time-consuming process.

Working with the glass, letting my mind wander on its own, I realized what troubled me about the things I'd learned was the missing piece. In the story of Andy Edgers's charging practices, Tony had presented the picture of a man manipulating prices to increase his profit margin. From the volume of business the marina project brought in, that margin was poised to shift from the thousands into the tens of thousands.

Yet the paperwork on Andy's desk consisted almost exclusively of unpaid bills, some of which appeared to have gone unpaid for longer than generally accepted. The hardware store itself featured nothing out of the ordinary, no new developments. Even the register resembled something I'd find at Carrie's antiques store.

What had prompted Andy to overcharge the way he had?

What had become of the money?

Realizing the question of the money was what was troubling me allowed the troubled part of me to relax. All at once I was overcome with profound fatigue. I did not hesitate to pack up my tools, store the liquids, and replace the sheet over the worktable.

When my head hit the pillow again, I slept as deeply as Friday, waking midmorning in the precise position in which I'd fallen asleep. For a few moments I entertained the thought of rolling over and hiding from the day, but my mind was eager to remind me of the questions that needed answers, the phone calls unreturned, and Grandy's detainment.

I threw the covers off and tumbled out of bed. I had a killer to find.

Wenwood does not have a large population, so I was stunned to find a line stretching out the door of the bakery. Where had all those people come from? Was there some sort of Friday morning special I was unaware of? Had they driven in from neighboring towns to pick up a pound of Rozelle's Linzer tarts?

Wishing I'd thought to bring a travel mug of coffee, I took my place in line among a couple dozen people I'd never met before. I kept an eye on people joining the end of the line, and people exiting the bakery. I couldn't shake the feeling they were watching me, whispering about me, but neither could I catch them in the act.

Rozelle had a couple of extra helpers in the store, rushing back and forth behind the counter. High school girls, I guessed. I had no real need for bakery goods, having binged on three-layer pastries the day before. In hopes the police would release Grandy, I ordered his favorite. "Loaf of rye bread, no seeds," I called across the counter.

The fresh-faced high school kid nodded and bustled off before I could tell her not to slice the loaf.

Pushing up on to tiptoe, I tried to spot the clerk. I opened my mouth to shout for her at the precise moment my phone vibrated to life. The humiliating Bon Jovi ringtone followed. I tugged the device from my bag, prepared to hit *Ignore call*. But the caller ID read PACE CNTY PD.

Maybe Grandy was miraculously being released. How did police departments work? Did they function the same way as hospitals, calling the next of kin to let them know their loved ones could go home? Or even the other end of the extreme—which I really didn't want to think about.

Either way, I couldn't ignore the call. Etiquette violation be damned, I tapped the green button and hello'ed into the phone.

Such a simple motion earned me scowls and cross looks from the patrons surrounding me. I mouthed "Sorry" and attempted to remove myself to a quiet corner of the bakery. Still I needed to hold my other hand over my ear to hear. "Sorry, Detective, can you repeat that?"

Detective Nolan spoke up. "Your grandfather wanted me to call you."

"How is he? Is he okay? Does he need anything?"

Several patrons, so recently annoyed, now looked at me with concern.

"I'm sure he's fine," Nolan grumbled, and I relaxed and angled my body away from the onlookers. "To tell the truth, it's your call I'm returning," he admitted. "But I've got less than five minutes so talk fast."

"How can you be returning my call? I—"

"You called the station looking for me. You want to take up the little time I have for this conversation with me explaining how caller ID works?"

Rats. That meant Diana was fully aware I was the one who'd called and chickened out of leaving a message. "I wanted to know what happened to my laundry," I said.

"That's it? That's why you called?"

"Well, I'd wanted to know what happened at Grandy's arraignment." I spoke as quietly as I dared. "But I figured I'd start with something I had a chance of you answering."

He exhaled; the noise came through like static on the line. "I would have to confirm with evidence but I believe your clothing can be returned. Pete's has gone on to the state crime lab."

Warm fuzzy thoughts of getting back my Pink Panther bra vanished at the mention of the crime lab. "Why would—why is that necessary? What's going on?"

"Look, Georgia, let me just say that this is all pretty routine, all right? Pete's shirt and pants had blood on them so—"

"But they were washed," I blurted out. *Then* I wanted to kick myself. More so when Detective Nolan let a measurable amount of silence elapse.

"Bloodstains. A couple of washings in standard detergent aren't going to have much effect. Ten aren't going to have much effect. Blood is pretty tough stuff."

All I could manage to say was, "Oh." Which was probably best. I wasn't doing a stellar job of keeping the light of innocence on Grandy. "But if you don't know yet whose blood you found, how can you keep Grandy in jail?"

"He's been charged with voluntary manslaughter. He hasn't been convicted. And let's just say the town would prefer to show its diligence in a murder case. You can pick up your belongings any time you're ready."

"What about Grandy? When can . . . can I see him?"

"It's up to him. He needs to get your name on the approved visitors list. You might want to remind his lawyer."

He sounded regretful when he said he had to go, and I faltered through polite thanks and good-bye.

I stood so long motionless in the corner, it took an alert suburban-mom type to reach out and grab me by the forearm and tell me my bread was ready.

Of course, I wouldn't need the bread, but I could hardly tell this woman that. I had a vague recollection of my mother saying you could freeze bread. Or was that you shouldn't freeze bread?

I stumbled over to the counter, where the clerk patted a white-paper-wrapped package. "You wanted that sliced, right?"

"Oh, no. Oh, beans. Did you slice it?" Grandy had his preferences in how thick the bread should be sliced, and the automatic slicers at the bakery did not meet his specifications.

But then, would it matter?

"You know what, that's fine. It's fine. What do I owe you?"

She gave me a price and scuttled away with the money as though afraid I'd change my mind about the slicing, or about the bread entirely.

With the loaf tucked under my arm and my mind gone to panicked silence over the prospect of coming up with bail money, I elbowed my way out of the crowded bakery and onto the sidewalk.

Drew. I needed to speak to Drew. I could reach him by phone—potentially. At the very least I could leave more messages, asking him to call me, asking him to convince Grandy to allow me to visit. In the mean time, I would have to test the freezing bread theory.

13

Laying down the loaf of bread on the luncheonette counter, I climbed up on the vacant stool next to Tom.

"You brought your own food," he shouted in my ear. "Smart."

As I winced away from his surprising decibel level, I figured out why the stool had been empty in the otherwise crowded restaurant. I leaned as far to my left as I could reasonably get away with without offending. "Service that slow?" I asked.

Tom nodded, raising a corner of toast to his mouth. "Hope you're not hungry."

"Don't listen to him," Grace said. She strode through the doorway connecting the kitchen to the counter, pot of coffee in hand. Without question, she banged a porcelain mug down on the counter in front of me and poured. "It's always busy at breakfast but no one ever goes home hungry." She slid a sour glance at Tom.

"Good to know," I said. Not that I had much of an appetite anyway, despite the inviting aroma of fried eggs and bacon filling the air. All I really wanted was a cup of hot coffee and a place to sit down and work up the fortitude to call my mother.

Grace stowed the coffee carafe below the counter. Setting both hands on the counter's edge, she leaned close to me. "Diana told me about Pete," she said in the voice of a conspirator. "If my own niece wasn't one of 'em, I'd have plenty of bad to say about that police department."

I struggled to find the appropriate response, but the realization that a member of the "general public" knew of Grandy's predicament slowed my mental processes.

"I want you to know, I know and the folks in this place know"—she tipped her head to indicate the restaurant area behind me—"Pete would never do . . . what they say he did. He's a good man, your grandfather. Don't forget that."

The lump in my throat formed long before I could get a swallow of coffee down to prevent it. "Thanks, Grace."

She nodded firmly, certain and reassuring. "Now what can I get you, sweetie?"

I hadn't even checked the menu. But then, I would no doubt be unable to make a selection before the luncheonette closed at the end of the day. "Just some pancakes, maybe? Side of bacon?"

As Grace disappeared through the doorway, my cell phone jangled. I wrestled it from the narrow confines of my purse, one wary eye on Tom. If anyone in the place were to make a "darn kids and their phones" outburst, I figured him to be the one.

He dropped the last nibble of toast onto his plate. "Must be for you," he said.

Caught off guard, I picked up the call without checking the incoming caller information.

"I'm calling about the kitten," the voice on the other end announced.

All I registered was a female voice and the feeling of being wrapped in defeat. Because the day wasn't going bad enough, someone was going to claim Friday to make it really abysmal.

I pulled in a resigned breath. "Are you the owner?"

"Me? So not. I gave the kitten to my boyfriend. When we broke up, he *swore* he would take care of it. Swore. I knew he was lying. I never should have believed him."

"Wait." I needed to get a word in; I had a suspicion there was a tirade in the works. "Are you sure we're talking about the same kitten? Maybe—"

"White. Female. Fluffy. Spot of gray on her head that looks like someone dropped cigarette ashes on her."

Gross, but accurate. My heart sank a little more. "So you think it got out on him?"

"I wish. I think he let it out and locked the door. The jerk."

She sounded young. But even given our age difference, I felt a twinge of kinship for her. She had a boyfriend who was a jerk. I had a former fiancé who was . . . worse words. I wondered for a moment if jerk boys were supposed to prepare us for jerk men, then I refocused on the issue at hand. "And you want the kitten back?"

"I can't. My mom's allergic. Like, violently allergic."

"So . . ."

"You should totally call the police and have the jerk arrested for animal cruelty."

Oh, yes, because the police were so eager to be of service to me. Then again, when it came to Friday, I was fairly certain I had an ally in Sergeant Steve. Still . . . "I'd like to check with your ex-boyfriend first before I call the police. Pets have been known to wander off on their own."

The girlfriend sighed forcefully, but gave me the phone number and address of her ex-boyfriend, Scott Corrigan— which I cleverly wrote down on the paper wrapping my loaf of rye.

Once the call with the girlfriend concluded, I punched in Scott's number. I sipped coffee while I listened to the line ring. The strong java didn't mix well with the anxiety and upset churning through my stomach. If this guy wanted Friday back, would I be able to return her? Would she fare better than she had in the past?

On the other hand, if it turned out the guy had discarded Friday, then what? The good news was, I got to keep her. The bad news was, the guy was guilty of . . . something. Sergeant Steve would know the precise name of the crime. Maybe the girlfriend was right and it was animal cruelty.

With no answer on the phone, I ended the connection and set the phone down on the counter. I hated myself a little bit for getting worked up over the kitten when Grandy was sitting behind bars in the county jail. Thing was, Grandy had a lot of years behind him, years which gave him enough fortitude to withstand a night or two in lockup. He was a veteran, for heaven's sake. But the kitten— harmless, helpless—she needed someone else to look out for her. Teeny sharp claws were only so much protection.

Grace reappeared with a plate of pancakes and a tea saucer piled with bacon. "There you go, sweetie. On the house."

"What about me?" Tom shouted, drowning out my meek *thank you*.

"You pay double," Grace said cheerfully.

I passed him a piece of bacon.

His smile, his genuine appreciation of such a small gesture, eased away the prickliest edges of my anxiety.

"Don't spoil him," Grace said. "He's got to watch his cholesterol."

"Since Andy stopped coming, no one shares their bacon with me." Tom took a bite off the end of his slice and grinned.

Something in his choice of words struck me as peculiar. But that was Tom. He confused his meanings. I wondered if that was an effect of age. Or maybe it was his cholesterol. The possibility reinforced my choice of fruit over cake and vegetables over pasta. Sadly, neither of those choices qualified as comfort food to me.

I poured a double dollop of syrup over my pancakes and gazed out the window while I sliced into the short stack and forked a bite into my mouth.

Not surprisingly, I thought of Andy Edgers as I

chewed. Not surprisingly, because his hardware store was visible from where I sat. Plus, he'd found a way to earn extra money by the expedient method of overcharging Tony Himmel.

Covered in syrup though they were, the pancakes went dry in my mouth. I could have kicked myself—you know, if I wasn't sitting on a lunch stool, thereby making kicking my own butt physically impossible.

Andy had invested in property and stocks with Grandy. Grandy had had savings to invest, a successful business to fall back on, as it were. The hardware store, though, its shelves coated with dust, spare parts rusting in filing cabinets in the back, the collection of unpaid bills was not the model of a thriving business. What if Andy had borrowed the money to invest?

I grabbed my phone and punched in the number for Drew Able, Esquire. This time, I was going to get in touch with the man, or hunt him down like a dog.

Okay, not like a dog. But the hunting part, definitely.

"It's a Friday afternoon in June, Georgia." Drew made a noise somewhere between a groan and a whine. "The workday's over."

"The law doesn't take afternoons off, Drew." I was relatively sure that wasn't true, but thought it sounded good. The automated doors to the grocery store swung open, and alluring clouds of cool, air-conditioned air billowed out. Between the moment I sat down at the luncheonette and the time I left, the temperature must have climbed fifteen degrees.

"The law might not, but lawyers do," Drew said.

"What were you going to do today? Mow the lawn?" I lifted a handbasket from the stack by the door and proceeded directly toward the produce aisle. Pitching my voice slightly lower and shifting the phone so the receiver was two millimeters nearer to my mouth, I said, "My grandfather stuck in jail is way more important than the curb appeal of your house."

"What do you want me to do? Pete's in police custody. Until his trial, I'm sorry, but unless you can come up with bail, there's nothing you or I can do for him."

"Not unless we find the person who really killed Andy Edgers."

Drew made no response. I let the idea of taking an active role in investigating the case sink in with him while I reviewed the selection of romaine lettuce.

By the time I reached the tomatoes and Drew still hadn't made a sound, I thought it best to press onward. "Listen, I have a theory that Andy owed money to someone. And maybe it's that someone who was the one who really killed him."

"Have you been staying up late watching bad cop movies?" he asked with that same hint of whining.

"The only way to find that person is to review the finances. Money leaves a trail," I insisted. "If we can follow the trail, we can get Grandy out of jail."

"What's this *we*?"

I selected a pint container of tasty-looking cherry tomatoes and dropped it in my basket. "Fine, the police. Would you just, please, make an exception to your 'summer Friday' rule and call them or go down there or whatever it is you lawyer folks do? Isn't Grandy paying you to do these things?"

"And what am I supposed to tell them?"

Another customer approached from the opposite end of the aisle. I backtracked to the lettuce, putting enough distance between us that I thought my phone call would remain fairly private. As quickly as I could, I told Drew about the overcharges to Tony Himmel, the abundance of overdue notices on Andy's desk, and the investment loss Andy suffered.

When I'd finished, Drew sounded as though he were sucking moisture from between his teeth. I took that as a sign he was considering all I'd said. "Well?" I prompted.

"Even if they find something, Georgia, it's not likely to get Pete released. Not with the evidence they have."

"One brick? That someone claims is covered in blood?" I huffed out a breath, tried to push a hand through my hair, but as always, got tangled in my own curls. "Think about it, Drew. How can anyone possibly look at a red brick and *see* blood?"

"Admittedly, they may be mistaken. We won't know with any certainty until the results come back from the lab. Until then—"

"What about the witnesses? Rozelle told me when she saw Grandy leave the shop that he came out the front door empty-handed. She told the police that."

"Georgia, you're not going around playing Jessica Fletcher, are you?"

"I did consider breaking into the hardware store and helping myself to whatever I could find, but I'm having enough trouble coming up with bail money for Grandy without trying to do it from the cell next to his. So the police need to do it, but someone needs to encourage them. They can collect the paperwork at the hardware store and take it into evidence—it won't hurt if it's not needed, right? But I believe the answer is there somewhere. If you wanted to find the root of the crime, follow the money. Nine out of ten times, it will lead you straight to the source."

"Nine out of ten?"

"Maybe eight out of ten. I'm making this up."

He sighed, but there was more energy in the sigh than there had been in his earlier *hello*. "I'll see what I can do."

"That's all?" I asked. "That won't work. I need you to be confident in this."

His voice conveyed the determination I wanted to hear when he said, "I'm on it."

Back home with the produce stored in the refrigerator, I tucked the loaf of rye into a plastic storage bag and slid the bread into the freezer. It either would or wouldn't keep; I considered the action an experiment to determine which.

Friday was doing her comatose sleep routine on the back of Grandy's favorite chair. Though I ruffled her fur, she didn't stir. With one had resting on her warm little body, feeling the rise and fall of her breathing, my heart melted a little. Sadness overwhelmed me. If it turned out she had escaped Scott's house, would I be able to give her back? And if he had tossed her out like so much waste?

I grabbed my phone and headed down to the work-room. Why I didn't have the police on speed dial was a mystery. I punched in the numbers for the Pace County precinct one by one and listened to the line ring.

When finally someone picked up the phone, that someone was female. I clicked the disconnect button as quick as a teenager hanging up on her crush. Too late I remembered Detective Nolan reminding me the police used caller ID. Oh well, so Diana knew I was hanging up on her. She would no doubt add that to the list of my transgressions.

Leaving the lights off, I opened all the window shades, letting in the day's bright sun. I resumed work on the lamp, losing myself for a time in the comfort of following a pattern, focusing my mind on the work at hand rather than allowing it to wander to questions and problems I could not solve.

Now and again I paused to place a phone call to Scott. No one ever picked up the phone. Friday wandered into the room, far more alert than I ever was after a nap. I found a triangle of glass in a mottled green and held it to the light. The glass created a prism that cast a dancing light across the floor, in turn creating endless amusement for Friday, who chased the bright green spot from one side of the room to another.

Her eagerness, determination, curiosity—heck, even the way her little tail stood straight up like she was receiving signals from her feline home planet—made me happy. One little kitten, amid all the bad luck, bad choices, and bad times, made me happy, acted as a balm for all the wounds life had dealt. How could I let her go?

When at last she lay down in a patch of sunlight, I knew I had to resolve the question of her ownership as soon as possible. I tried once more to reach Scott by phone, allowing the line to ring and ring while I covered the pieces of cut glass. All that remained in repairing the lamp was to reassemble the shade; the tricky work of cutting all the pieces in all the proper sizes was done. In the morning I would begin the work of wrapping the edges of each piece with copper foil, then follow the pattern to tack together the bits of glass and leaves and background with solder, setting them carefully to create the curve required for the lampshade.

Having had the same experience all day, I was unsurprised when again no one answered Scott's phone. But I was determined to speak with him, and I was in possession of his address and a GPS application on my phone. For the moment, that was all I needed.

I washed my face and hands and pulled my hair into a loose ponytail. Friday didn't put up a struggle when I moved her from the workroom into the safety of my bedroom. She had a litter box and enough food and water

Jennifer McAndrews

there to keep her satisfied, and I closed the door to keep her from getting into unsupervised mischief.

Grabbing my phone, my purse, and the keys to Grandy's Jeep, I tugged open the front door.

Diana Davis stood on the porch, finger pointed at the doorbell.

"Diana?" I asked, by which I meant more "What the devil are you doing here?" than "Is that your name?"

Dressed in street clothes of jeans and a plain red T-shirt, she ducked her head, hid her hands behind her back. She looked like any woman you'd meet on the street, not someone tough enough to survive the police academy.

Apparently, I had to be more precise in my questioning. "What are you doing here?" And then it hit me: What if calling the station and hanging up was illegal?

"Look, I . . ." She sighed, a defeated sound that lowered her shoulders and softened her spine. Her gaze met mine. "I came by to apologize."

I stepped onto the porch, pulling the door shut behind me. "Apologize? To me?"

She brought her hands forward, one on her hip, one a little lower, where the butt of her gun would be were she still in uniform. "Why do you sound shocked? You don't believe I—" Stopping herself midsentence, she held a hand up, pressed her lips tight. "I, um, I have a little problem misreading people and, you know, jumping to conclusions."

My brow wrinkled. "Isn't that kind of a problem in your line of work?"

She huffed and nodded. "Hence the desk assignment."
I bit back a grin.

"And the other day when you came in, I just . . .
assumed you knew all about how my life turned out and
were, you know, trying to hide your glee."

Shaking my head, I said, "I don't know anything about
your life."

"I know that now." She stepped backward, keeping her
eyes on me, and perched on the porch rail. "I just figured
Aunt Grace had told you everything. She said you were
in the luncheonette."

"I was hoping for a blueberry muffin," I said, then
shook my head again and waved a dismissive hand. "At
the luncheonette, I mean. Grace didn't say anything about
you except that you help out waiting tables sometimes
when the restaurant's crowded."

"Yeah, well, I thought you knew everything."

I chuckled ruefully. "You'd be surprised how much I
don't know."

"It's just . . . I had big plans, you know? Yeah, cheering
professionally might sound lame, but c'mon. It would
have gotten me out of Pace County."

"I'm sorry about that," I said. "Really. I shouldn't have
laughed. I didn't give it enough thought."

But she held up a hand again to forestall me. "I realize
that. I do. I just never realize it in the moment. Anyway,
I just wanted to apologize. So." She stood away from the
railing. "I'm sorry."

"Apology accepted," I said, because it seemed to be
important to her.

She turned to face the steps, looked back over her shoulder at me. "And hey, next time you call the station house and I answer, say something, okay? You don't have to hang up."

My cheeks tingled, warning me of an impending blush. "I won't, thanks."

She was down the steps before I thought to call her back.

"Hey, Diana, can I ask you a question?"

She turned back to me, eyes narrowed, lips pursed.

I flinched backward. "Never mind. It's nothing." I deeply wanted to retreat into the house, but that would look really weak. Better to linger on the porch until she was gone.

Again she held up a hand, palm out. Closed her eyes and visibly took a deep breath before returning her gaze to me. "Sorry," she said. "I promise, I'm working through my aggression issues. I am. What's the question?"

I slid to my right, putting the porch railing between me and her, just in case. "What, uh, what kind of crime is it to abandon an animal? Like, say, a kitten?"

"That's cruelty to animals."

"And that's a crime, right?"

"Misdemeanor." Her eyes narrowed again. "Why?"

The question popped out of my mouth before I could think better of it. "You wanna take a ride?"

16

We took the Jeep. No offense to Diana. I'm sure she was a fine, though aggressive, driver. But I would be no good to Grandy, or Friday, if I landed in the hospital following a motor vehicle accident. Besides, Diana had been on her way home when she stopped by to apologize, so it wasn't like she had a nice, intimidating, steel-reinforced patrol car in which to roll up to Scott Corrigan's house.

On the drive over, with the anonymous voice on the GPS calling out the turns, I explained to Diana about finding Friday, about putting up the flyers, and finally hearing from Scott's girlfriend.

"Could just be this girl wants to make her ex-boyfriend sweat," she said. "He may have nothing to do with the discarded cat."

"Will you stop calling her that? Her name is Friday." I turned right as commanded by the disembodied voice. "Besides, the girlfriend described the kitten."

"She may have discarded the cat with plans to blame it on the boyfriend."

"Beans. I never thought of that."

"You got her name? Her number?"

"No. She called me. So her number will be in my phone."

Diana flicked down the visor, blocking the sun streaking through the windshield following our last change of direction. "If she called from her phone."

It was my turn to sigh. "Okay. Let's start with the boyfriend and go from there."

I glanced at the GPS display, unconvinced the voice was giving the right directions.

"By the way," Diana said, "your granddad . . ."

My stomach instantly knotted. "Yeah?"

"He's doing okay."

"Yeah?"

"Yeah. He's, you know, not happy. But he's doing all right. I got a friend over in county keeping an eye on him. Says Pete spent most of the day working on the crossword and conning the guard into bringing him tea."

"Thank you," I said. "I appreciate you telling me." I had to smile. The image of Grandy spending his morning much the same as he would have at home comforted me—right up until I mentally drew in the bare mattress and steel bars. "Do you know if his lawyer spoke with Detective Nolan?"

"If he did, the call didn't come to the station. Chip's off today."

Chip. Detective Nolan. It was strange trying to envision the same official-looking man who'd questioned me and arrested Grandy as the sort of man who had a nickname, probably a family, maybe a dog.

I made a mental note to give Drew another call and stored it in my mind conveniently ahead of the mental note to call Mom. If I could avoid calling and explaining to her the entirety of the situation and begging for help coming up with bail money, I would, without question. Making the final turn to Scott's house, I was still holding out hope the police would uncover a new lead in Andy Edgers's office. A scary, cartoonish loan shark would be ideal.

The voice on the GPS advised me I'd reached my destination, but the voice didn't see the cars lining the road in front of the house. I hung a U-turn and parked the car across the street from the faded blue in-line ranch.

Diana was out of the Jeep before I pulled the key from the ignition. "Let me ask the questions, okay?"

"Why you? It's my cat. I mean, it's my problem."

She offered a grim smile and whipped a badge out of her back pocket. "We'll get to the truth a lot faster if he knows he's talking to the police."

"Fair enough." I mean really, what was I going to do? Flash my library card?

At least Diana let me ring the bell. We stood side by side on the plain cement step, waiting for someone to answer the bell.

As I reached to ring again, the door opened inward, revealing a cheery, heavyset woman with short hair and an impressive array of freckles. "Can I help you ladies?" she asked, squinting a bit, as if she was trying to place our faces.

"We're here to see Scott. Is he home?" Diana kept her badge concealed, kind of like a secret weapon.

"Big Scott or little Scott?"

Diana looked to me. I shrugged. "Little Scott, I guess."

Nodding, the woman turned away. She called for Scott, telling him someone was at the door for him.

While we waited, I admired a basket of fuchsia hanging beside the door. In the light of the lowering sun, the pinks and purples of the blossoms shined like gems. If I could find glass to replicate those colors, the leaves and flowers of the fuchsia plant would make a lovely night table lamp. Maybe online—

"What's up?" A string bean of a teen sporting red hair and freckles clearly inherited from his mother's side lounged inside the door.

"Scott Corrigan, we need to ask you a couple of questions." Diana flashed her badge.

Scott's eyes popped wide. The relaxed lounging posture vanished. He stood straight, tense. "What? I . . ."

"Where were you last Tuesday night?"

Scott looked from Diana to me and back again. "I, um . . ."

"Tuesday night. Wasn't that long ago."

"Yeah. I—"

And then he turned his back on us and bolted.

"Where's he going?" I asked Diana.

"Back door." She dashed down the steps and disappeared around the side of the house before I recovered sufficiently to consider following her. But what if it was a trick? What if the kid planned to backtrack and escape out the front?

One thing was clear: This was our culprit in the discarded cat case.

When a door in the near distance screeched open, followed by a loud *oof*, I figured Diana had been right. I double-timed it down the steps and jogged around the side of the house.

Diana had Scott pressed up against the aluminum siding, one hand pulled up behind his back in a classic half nelson. "Now we can do this the easy way, or we can do it the hard way," she snarled.

Uh-oh. Aggression issues. "Wait, wait, wait!" I called.

Scott's mom burst through the side door, all her cheer gone. "What's going on out here?"

Keeping a grip on the kid, Diana looked to his mother. "We need some information from your son."

"Let go of him." Mrs. Corrigan said. "Who are you?"

"Pace County Police." Diana released her grip on Scott but remained close enough to grab him again if he tried to run.

Mrs. Corrigan's look of surprise shifted to one of anger. She narrowed her eyes at her son. "Scott, what's going on?"

"Nothing," Scott said. "Nothing, I swear. I didn't see anything."

If we weren't standing on soft ground, we could have heard a pin drop. If someone were in possession of pins.

"What are you talking about?" I asked.

"Nothing," Scott said.

His mom folded her arms and glared. "Scott."

Scott clenched his jaw, lifted his chin in a show of defiance. But his eyes shifted from face to face to house to ground, and he held himself too still to be anything but afraid.

"Maybe we can start at the beginning," I suggested. With no one objecting, I continued. "Did you leave a white kitten in the parking lot behind Edgers Hardware last Tuesday night?"

"Yes. No." He glanced between me and Diana again, avoiding his mother's glare entirely. That part I could relate to.

"Which is it?" I asked.

Diana pulled a face. "You're supposed to let me ask the questions." She looked to Scott. "Well?"

"I, uh, I lost the kitten. She got out." Sweat gathered on his brow, glistened across his freckled nose. "And I tried to catch her but she went behind the stores and I lost her."

"Last Monday night," Diana said.

"Yes. It was Tuesday night. Definitely Tuesday."

Mrs. Corrigan planted her fists on her wide hips. "Scott Michael Corrigan Junior, don't you dare lie to these police officers."

"Oh, no. Not me," I said. "I'm not an officer. I'm just

the one who found the kitten." I glared at Scott. "On Wednesday morning. In a box."

"Scott," his mother said in that warning voice moms do so well. "You were home all day Tuesday playing that cod game."

"All right fine." Scott put his hands on either side of his head. "It was Monday. And it's C-O-D, Mom, not cod."

Moving her hands to her back pockets, Diana skewered Scott with the kind of suspicious glare all police officers learn to master. "Why lie about the day?" she asked.

"I didn't lie." He shifted his weight from one foot to the next. "I just lost track of the days."

"Scott," his mother warned.

"What is it you saw when you discarded the kitten in the parking lot Monday night?" Diana asked.

"I told you. The kitten got away. I was just chasing her, trying to get her back."

I folded my arms. "And yet, in all the time I spent putting up found kitten flyers, I never came across a single notice for a lost kitten."

Diana held up a hand to hush me, then shook her head and changed the full-stop motion to a single-fingered *give me a minute*. "Scott, are you aware that intentionally setting loose a domestic pet is considered animal cruelty?"

"N-No?"

"Are you aware that animal cruelty is a crime punishable by up to a year in jail?"

Scott looked at his mother. "Mom?"

Mrs. Corrigan sprang into action. "Inside, everyone.

Inside." She waved to the side door. "No need to put on a show for the neighbors."

We filed into the house, the side door entrance leading directly into the kitchen. I caught the edge of Diana's sleeve, slowing her sufficiently so I could say, "I just want to know if I can keep the kitten, really. Is all of this necessary?"

"There's something more going on here," she murmured.

Scott's mother settled us around a kitchen table with an artificial African violet plant at its center. Scott slumped into a chair, hands folded loosely in front of him.

"I want to know what you saw," Diana said to Scott.

"I didn't see anything."

Resting her forearms on the table, she leaned forward. The aggression she was reputedly dealing with held her spine rigid. "I can arrest you right now, Scott, and have you brought into the station on charges of animal cruelty."

"I didn't—"

"Or you can tell me what you saw that night and we can let my friend here keep the kitten and you can get back to *Call of Duty* instead of having your fingerprints and mug shot taken." She glanced up as Mrs. Corrigan set a glass of iced tea in front of her. "Thank you."

On her way to her chair, Mrs. Corrigan smacked the back of her son's head. "Tell the officer what she needs to know."

I lifted the glass of tea Mrs. Corrigan had given me and took a long drink. The motion gave me something to do with my hands, some way to distract myself from an uncomfortable situation.

"But if I tell you what I saw," Scott said, "you're going to arrest me anyway."

Mrs. Corrigan gasped. "What are you saying? What did you do?"

Both Diana and Scott ignored her. Scott stared unwaveringly at his hands; Diana stared at Scott. "Why do you think I would do that?" she asked.

"I dunno, like, obstruction of justice or something," Scott mumbled.

"You tell me what you saw, and I promise *I* won't arrest you."

He looked at his mother, whose slight nod conveyed support and encouragement. "When I was . . ." He paused, sighed, and began again. "I liked the kitten, okay? But every time I looked at it, it reminded me of Phoebe."

"Who's Phoebe?" I asked Mrs. Corrigan in a whisper.

The distasteful turn of her lips spoke volumes. "The ex-girlfriend."

"So you let the cat loose?" Diana suggested.

"I brought her out to Griffin Park. I wanted to drop her in the lot behind the stores, but I didn't want anyone to see me, so I went through Griffin, over to the back fence." He shrugged halfheartedly. "I just kinda dropped her over the fence."

I clenched my teeth, held my jaw tight to keep from calling him a careless jerk. The look on his mother's face told me he'd be getting in enough trouble for that later.

"Right away I felt bad. It was a stupid thing to do. I was just so mad at Phoebe." He removed his hands from the table. "I figured the best thing to do was climb over the fence and get her back. And that's when I . . . saw . . ."

Though the room was nicely air-conditioned, Scott's tone seemed to pull the air from the room. I don't believe any of us breathed while we waited for him to finish his thought.

"I saw Bill Harper coming out the back door of the hardware store."

My voice rang with disbelief. "Bill Harper? The grocer?"

Scott nodded. His mother gasped and put a hand over her mouth.

"And?" Diana prompted Scott gently.

"And he was carrying a brick. And his pants were . . . they were messed up, like he'd spilled something on them, you know?"

"Spilled coffee maybe?" his mother asked.

He turned to face her, his tough teen exterior slipping away and leaving a little boy behind. "No, Ma. I think it was blood."

Afraid of calling attention to himself, Scott had left the kitten where she was and scampered. His guilt over abandoning the kitten paled in comparison over his fear for his life.

Back in the Jeep, Diana called Detective Nolan at home while I reset the GPS to direct us to downtown

Wenwood. It wouldn't have done to allow me to remain at the Corrigan house, where I was furious at Scott both for dropping a kitten over a fence and for withholding information from the police that might have kept my grandfather out of police custody. I might have channeled some of Diana's aggression issues.

Behind the grocery store, I headed for my usual parking spot beneath the walnut tree.

"What are you doing?" Diana asked.

"Parking the car. And beginning to see why you're not a detective yet."

She shook her head. "Nope. You're dropping me here and heading home. This is police business."

I shifted the Jeep into park and pulled the key from the ignition. "This is about my grandfather. I'm not leaving."

"You are. This could get dangerous."

"You're not going to say something clichéd like, 'We already have one murder on our hands,' are you?"

Diana sighed. "Not saying it doesn't make it any less true."

"Well, I'm not leaving. If what Scott said is true and Bill Harper came back here after . . . visiting Andy"—I let out a breath—"then there's evidence in there that could lead to my grandfather's release. I'm going to be here when it's found."

"Suit yourself. But once Chip and his guys get here, you're staying in the car. You can't tag along on police business."

I said nothing, allowing her to decide for herself what

she thought my silence meant. Of course, I had no intention of staying in the car.

"What do you think?" she asked. "You think Bill Harper is inside the store?"

As if I could see through walls, I turned to face the back of Village Grocery. Lights remained on inside, though the store had been closed for going on an hour. No shadows passed within to give a clue to the building's occupancy.

"I don't know," I muttered. "But I know someone who might."

I grabbed my phone from its temporary storage space in the center console of the car and punched in Carrie's number.

"Who are you calling?" Diana asked. "You're not going to say anything about what we're doing, are you?"

I shook my head as Carrie picked up the call. "Hey, it's Georgia. Quick question for you. Does Bill Harper work late on Fridays?"

"I'm not sure. Probably," Carrie responded. "Why?"

"No reason. Thanks." I ended the call and passed on the information to Diana.

"Maybe we should send a car to his house," Diana said, her tone more thinking out loud than inviting input.

"What are we waiting for anyway?" I asked.

She leaned forward, peering around me to the back of the store. "Chip has to get a warrant. That means tracking down a judge. At home. On a Friday night." She shook her head and leaned back. "Better him than me."

"A judge," I repeated. Something was tugging at my memory. Something I'd seen.

Then it hit me. "The courtroom," I said. If I closed my eyes, I could see in my memory with absolute clarity the patchwork below the window of Town Hall. Brand-new Wenwood bricks used to patch the building where Wenwood held court, where Wenwood's judges worked. "The judge . . . I don't think he'll sign the warrant."

"What are you talking about? Of course he will. Mind you, he'll probably make Chip sweat for a while."

"No," I said. "I don't think so. The judge won't sign it because Bill Harper has his fingers in . . ." In what? What did a few bricks prove? But the police station was crumbling, while Town Hall stood as pristine as ever. Those bricks could only have come from one place: the last man in town with a stash of Wenwood bricks.

What sort of deal had Harper made with the town elders? With the politicians and the judges—the elected officials—and the rest of the Town Council? If he provided those bricks, what kind of favors was he owed in return?

In half sentences and incomplete thoughts, I explained my concern to Diana. "What if the judge won't sign the warrant? What if he insists on, I dunno, more information or some kind of sworn statement from Scott Corrigan?" I asked when I'd finished. "Then Grandy will spend even more time in prison and . . . And what if the judge calls Bill Harper and warns him the police are closing in?" I was nearly shrieking by the time I accused the unknown judge of being a little bit crooked.

Diana laid a hand on my arm. "Hey, relax. Take a breath, okay?"

"Easy for you to say. Your grandfather is—" I cut myself off. In fact, I had no real way of knowing if her grandfather was or wasn't incarcerated, or was or wasn't alive even, and I didn't want to risk accidentally offending her again. "What if the only thing that will get Grandy out of jail is in that store and Bill Harper gets rid of it before Detective Nolan can secure a warrant?"

She took her hand back, sat still in her seat while chewing on the inside of her lip.

I gripped the steering wheel hard enough I was surprised it didn't crack. Minutes ticked away on the dashboard clock. A breeze ruffled the tree above, and a single green leaf fluttered down onto the windshield. At last I couldn't take it anymore. "Well?" I demanded.

Pursing her lips, Diana nodded once, firmly. "Okay," she said. "Let's check it out."

Before the import of her statement registered, she was out of the Jeep.

I scrambled to follow, cursing the tangle my seat belt caught me in when I tried to exit the vehicle without first unlatching.

She circled around to my side of the Jeep, tipped her head in the direction of the shop. "We're just going to go see if there's anyone in there, okay? If no one's in there, there's no worry of anyone moving or removing anything without us seeing them arrive. Right?"

I nodded. "Right. Wait." I looked her over head to foot. "Where is your gun anyway?"

Cutting me a hard glance, she said, "Aggression issues." She rolled a shoulder. "I'm required to leave my weapon in the station house when I'm not on duty. It's temporary."

"Oh. Okay. Night stick?"

"Same."

"Oh. Okay." So basically we were headed for a building in which a killer may be lurking and all we had to defend ourselves was our charm. And frankly, I feared Diana didn't have a whole lot of that.

There had to be something we could use as a substitute. I glanced back at the Jeep, considered its contents: jumper cables, ice scraper, windshield wiper fluid. Would it be possible to use jumper cables as bolas?

"What's the holdup?" Diana asked.

"Trying to think of something . . ." And then I saw the bigger picture. The walnut tree.

I retreated to the Jeep, pulled open the door, and grabbed one of my reusable shopping bags—the small one, the one suited for fresh produce or cosmetics. With silent apologies to Grandy, I climbed up onto the hood of the Jeep, draped the tote bag from its handles along my forearm. Reaching carefully, I tugged a branch low. It took more force than it would have later in the season when the fruit was ready to drop on its own, but I ripped several clusters of walnut fruit from the branch and dropped them into the tote. At the center of each piece of fruit resided the walnut that made for tasty salads and healthy snacks. Its outermost shell, though, the protective outer fruit, was hard as a baseball. As weapons went, walnut fruit was on the puny side. Still, I wouldn't want to be hit by one.

"What do you plan on doing with those?" Diana asked as I rejoined her.

I pulled a fruit from its cluster and handed it over. "Aim for the head."

"*Niiice*," she said.

Once again we headed for the market. I kept my attention on the back door, where the lights inside continued to illuminate the back end of the produce aisle, the very spot where I had encountered Bill Harper just two weeks earlier and had forgotten his name. I knew without a doubt I would never forget it again.

"You stay here," Diana said, indicating the back with the slightest gesture. "I'm going around the front."

"Why? Why do you get to go around the front?" The front offered the potential of other people passing by, the potential of witnesses, the potential of help coming quickly should it become necessary to start pitching walnuts.

"Just wait here. If you see him, shout."

She hurried up the narrow access driveway and disappeared around the front of the store.

Left on my own, I turned a small circle, taking in my surroundings. The Jeep we'd arrived in was one of only two vehicles present in the lot behind the market. The other was a smallish sedan the make and model of which I was unfamiliar with. There was no other sign of life. Friday night in a small town; everyone had gone home.

In a matter of seconds, the restlessness took me. Diana

meant for me to stay put and give a holler if Bill Harper appeared. Standing still didn't suit me.

I approached the door, intending to peer through the window. But the motion sensor remained engaged. The door swung open.

Surprised, I hurried backward and watched as the door closed. Door opening and car in lot proved to me someone was in the store.

Giving wide berth to the door's sensors, I headed into the access driveway, doing my best to shout in a whisper for Diana. For several moments I stood at the mouth of the access driveway, rocking back and forth from foot to foot, struggling to decide whether to go to the front and retrieve Diana or stay where I was, where I could see if anyone left the store.

Once more I called her name, letting my voice come slightly above that whisper. She poked her head around the corner and I waved her close. "The back door is open," I whispered.

"So someone's in there."

I nodded, not trusting myself to keep a sarcastic tone from my voice.

"I'll call Chip and see where he is with the warrant."

"He's nowhere with the warrant. I'm telling you, the judge is never going to sign it. Or sign it in time at any rate. Let's just sneak in there, check out the . . . I don't know, the locker room or the storage room or whatever kind of place a supermarket has where people would keep a change of clothes."

"We can't go in there," Diana said. "Any evidence recovered without a warrant is inadmissible."

Who knew that being embroiled in a scandal at Washington Heritage Financial would provide useful?

I smiled at Diana. "Any evidence *you* recover is inadmissible. You're a police officer. I'm a civilian. I can poke around public spaces all I want. I'm going in."

She grabbed my arm and spun me toward her. "You are not going in there alone."

"*Ow.*" I pried myself out of her grip, certain I would find bruises on my bicep come morning. "I'm going. You call for backup or whatever it is you have to do. I have to get my grandfather out of jail."

"Georgia," she snarled.

I ducked away before she could grab me again. I didn't want to test the boundaries of her aggression issues.

She called my name again, her voice making me consider the possibility that I was far safer inside the market than outside with Diana.

The door opened at my hurried approach and I ducked inside, shifting immediately to my left, using an endcap to keep me out of sight—I hoped—of the manager's office at the front of the store. Edging sideways, I peered up and around the display of crackers on the endcap. The forward corner of the store appeared dark, with only the overhead light illuminating the area.

I recalled, then, talking to Bill Harper in his office, the stack of papers held down by a bright, new Wenwood brick. The walls behind him had been hung with clipboards and notices and what was no doubt the weekly staff schedule. If that was the case, and the office no doubt a high-traffic area, I suspected it would not be the ideal place to stash evidence from a crime scene.

Where in a market would be a good place? The brick allegedly used to kill Andy Edgers was in the evidence locker at the Pace County PD. But it had to have been hidden somewhere, tucked away out of sight in the days between Andy's death and the recovery of the brick behind the dine-in.

From somewhere in the building, a *thunk* reached my ears. I froze, holding even my breath still. The *thunk* came again, as though someone were dropping large cartons to the ground. Its muffled sound coupled with the lack of vibration beneath my feet made me suspect there was some activity taking place in basement storage . . . meaning somewhere in the store was basement access.

For the number of times I'd been in the store, I had failed to notice any doorways not leading to the outside. But they had to be there. If there were doors somewhere in the middle of an aisle, certainly that I would have noticed. Therefore, logic dictated the doors were somewhere on the perimeter.

I resettled the tote on my arm then belatedly withdrew a walnut fruit. Keeping it at the ready in my hand, I crept slowly away from my place of concealment.

I moved along the back of the store, where shelves of cookies, breads, and muffins ran the length of the wall. At the very end, bins for fresh-baked breads nestled into the corner, guiding shoppers into the turn for the far wall.

There had been only one more *thunk* as I crept along.

Just as well. The proper sound effect for the view after the turn would have needed to be tense violins.

"Damn," I said on a breath. There before me were the meat cases. Plastic-wrapped packages of steaks, chops, thighs, breasts, filets. Roughly twenty feet down, the cases were interrupted by a pair of swinging doors of dull aluminum. The cases on the opposite side of the doors, I knew, contained milk and cheese and other dairy products that were of no concern. It was the space behind the meat cases that held the answers. Because behind those fresh cuts of raw meat stretched an open window onto the butcher's workspace. Visible in the half-light spilling in from the store, a steel table gleamed at the center of the butcher's area. And on its opposite side, another windowed door provided a view to the next room. There, hung from a series of pegs set into the wall, were coats and trousers stained with blood.

Continuing on in stealth mode, I crept to the double doors and carefully pushed one open. Laws of evidence aside, I really had no intention of removing anything from the store. But if I found among the clothing in that back room trousers resembling those Bill Harper had been wearing on Monday, well I might have to make an exception.

Once through the doors, I paused. I'd gone from illuminated sales floor to darkened butcher's shop. Not only did I need time for my eyes to adjust, but the awareness of where I was struck me as just plain creepy. Worse, I knew somewhere in that space lurked an impressive array of knives. I had no wish to stumble into the wrong end of any of them.

Though I waited for my eyes to sufficiently dilate, still I could not make out much more than shadows.

Skimming the wall beside the door, I found a switch and flipped it to the on position. An overhead fluorescent light hummed and flickered and I dropped the walnut I held back into my tote. Straight ahead the meat prep area. To my right, the other door. I dashed through the door, arms outstretched, reaching for the coat pegs while holding open the door with one foot.

My fingers touched twill as the light behind me warmed to full brightness and spilled into the smaller area. Three white coats with varying intensity of faded yet visible stains hung atop trousers—two pairs white, one pair khaki. Carefully I lifted the lower hem of the coat covering the khakis and peered beneath. Pale spots speckled the legs of the trousers. Was I looking at residue from someone's weekend barbecue order? Or residue from a murder?

"Hello there, Georgia."

17

I wished the voice belonged to Detective Chip
Nolan. But even before I turned, I knew I wasn't that
lucky. I knew I was about to come face-to-face with the
man who killed Andy Edgers.

Moving my hands behind my back, I turned. "Bill
Harper," I said.

His smile was just as open and charming as ever. "You
remembered my name."

I tipped my head.

"You realize the store is closed, don't you?"

Carefully, so as not to reveal any movement, I caught
the handle of the tote bag in my opposite hand and began
inching the fabric upward. "Really? You're going to pretend there's something remotely normal about this?"

"Well, I admit it's unusual to have a customer get this

far into the store after hours, but strange things happen all the time."

I nodded—if it's possible to nod sarcastically. "So you're just going to let me leave."

That smile remained in place. The longer it hung there, the less natural it looked. "Why not?"

"What are you going to do? Burn the evidence or something?" I almost had it. An inch, maybe a little more, and I'd have the tote bag hitched high enough I could grab a walnut fruit.

"There's no need to burn anything, Georgia. What strange ideas you have."

The potential I was wrong flittered through my mind. What if there was no evidence there? What if the spots on the trousers truly were occupational hazards for a butcher? What if Scott Corrigan had lied about seeing Bill Harper just so he could avoid animal cruelty charges?

"No." He took a step to his left and straightened the knives adhering to a wall-mounted magnetic strip. "Thanks to Pete and Andy having such a long and recently ugly history, there's no need for me to do anything more than escort you out."

"You think I won't talk?" I said. "You think I won't tell the police—"

"Tell them what?" He ran his finger along the grip of a meat cleaver. "They won't believe a word you say. You're an outsider. Nothing you can say will stop my plan to lead Wenwood into a new prosperity. Besides, you'll be leaving town as soon as Pete is convicted."

Prosperity . . .

My mind, its habits so ingrained, followed the money to put the pieces together. "You want that marina to be built just as badly as Tony Himmel," I said, unable to keep the amazement and disgust from my voice. "These are your properties."

I couldn't believe I hadn't seen it all before. A thriving Wenwood would make Bill Harper a wealthy man. Andy Edgers spoiling the deal, threatening the construction . . .

"That's why you killed him," I said. "And you intended to let my grandfather go to prison."

He sighed. "Pete *has* gone to prison where he will stay and you will leave my store now."

"You're wrong. Pete's not going to stay in prison. Because those are your trousers." I lifted my chin in the direction of the wall pegs. "And that's Andy Edgers's blood on them."

Bill Harper chuckled. "You'll never prove that. There's blood on all those clothes. And they're washed routinely."

In my mind all I could hear was Detective Nolan's voice. It was my turn to smile. "A couple of washings in store-bought detergent aren't going to remove the evidence."

His wicked grin faltered, and I pushed the moment. "The police labs can isolate blood evidence after up to a dozen washings," I announced. "I looked it up."

I was proud of myself.

I was foolish.

"Well, then," he said. "I guess we'll have to make sure the police never know about those pants." He grabbed a meat cleaver from the wall-mounted magnetic strip. "How convenient we're in a room designed to be washed of blood."

Oh, crap.

I took a step backward, bumped into the line of butcher coats. Bill Harper stood between me and any possible exit.

He took a step closer, testing the heft of the blade in his hand. I glanced at the window above the meat case. I could make a dive for it, but if I fell, I would be wholly at his mercy.

He took another step, grinning, lifting the cleaver. I whipped my hand around from behind my back and sent a walnut screaming for his head. The baseball-hard fruit impacted the side of his head, eliciting an angry roar.

I screamed in return and dived for the steel table. Summoning all my strength, I lifted and pushed and the table crashed to its side. I didn't wait for the table to settle, but pulled another cluster of walnuts from my tote and let the whole bunch fly before ducking behind the steel barrier. "Help!"

Bill Harper covered his face with his forearm. The walnuts impacted his skull with an audible *thwack*. He cursed and staggered backward.

"Get away!" I shouted. "Help! Help me!"

"Georgia, where are you?"

Clearly it wasn't Harper asking; he knew right where I was and had no intention of allowing me to leave. Neither did the voice belong to Diana.

"Carrie! Call the police! Get help!" I popped my head up above the table while digging into the tote for another walnut. Bill Harper wiped at his balding head, checked his fingertips as though looking for blood. When his gaze again fell on me, the fury in his eyes made liquid of my insides.

"Georgia, where are you?" Carrie was somewhere in the store. Near? Far? I had no way of knowing.

"Bill Harper is trying to kill me. Get help!" I threw another cluster of walnut fruits, but the bunch was heavier than the last and fell short of my mark.

He growled and started toward me.

Oh crap, oh crap, oh God. I gathered the tote bag. I could use the weight of the walnuts, swing the bag, knock the cleaver from his hands.

I said a quick prayer, clutched the tote, and stood . . .

. . . in the same moment Carrie burst through the double doors.

I swung the tote bag forward. Carrie swung at Harper's shoulder with the business end of a steel roller sponge mop. Our makeshift weapons impacted in the span of a breath. Harper shouted and dropped the knife. Carrie and I struck again and he fell to the floor. I scrambled out from behind the overturned table and kicked the cleaver clear. We were both wound up to hit again, Harper crouched in a fetal position on the floor, when a chorus of shouts and a swarm of motion in my peripheral vision penetrated my panicked haze.

Sergeant Steve crashed through the swinging doors, revolver trained on the sprawled, cowering form of Bill Harper. "Freeze! Pace County PD!" Two more uniformed officers hurried in behind him. It wasn't SWAT, but it was all the cavalry I needed.

I dropped my shopping bag of unripe walnuts and staggered toward Carrie. "What are you doing here?"

"Stayed late to do inventory and then saw Diana lurking around the back lot. She explained what you were doing and I just . . ." She shrugged. "Thought I could help."

"Thank you. Thank you, thank you, thank you." I threw my arms around her and hugged her hard.

"Hey," she said, hugging me back, "what are friends for?"

In an ideal world, Grandy would have been released the moment Bill Harper was taken into custody. Unfortunately, the real world of Wenwood, the heart of Pace County, did not qualify as ideal. It qualified as small and self-interested and populated by people who—with the exception of a small, murderous percentage—truly cared for one another.

While the police went through the routine of bringing Bill Harper in and charging him with suspicion of murder, I accepted a ride home from Carrie, Diana following behind in Grandy's Jeep. For some reason, they didn't want me to drive. I was in no position to argue.

At the start of the ride I planned to invite them both in for a soothing cup of tea, or a measure of something stronger. But in the brief distance between the village and Grandy's house, the adrenaline drained away, taking all of my energy with it. I thanked Carrie and Diana equally and profusely, apologized for my lack of good manners, and dragged myself up the steps to the front door.

I swung the door open and took a step inside, the sound of Diana starting her car and pulling away disturbing the quiet of the neighborhood. In moments, the headlights of Carrie's car flashed across the house as she U-turned to head home, exposing the living room for what it was: an empty room filled with empty furniture, not a hint of a sound in the still air.

Reaching to flip on the light, I felt the same emptiness yawn within me. All the little sorrows I'd managed to forget in my worry over Grandy reminded me of their painful presence . . . or maybe . . .

Friday bounded up the stairs from the studio. Eyes wide, stopping just out of reach, she gave me a friendly "mew" and raced across the living room, under the polished wood coffee table. And I smiled a little, and realized the sorrows weren't as painful as they had been, and I would only be alone in the house until Grandy was released—hopefully in the early morning. Until then, I had Friday to keep me company, and a pillow to lay my head on, and that was enough for one night.

In the morning I woke early and drove past the old brickworks on the way to the county jail. The construction site buzzed with activity, heavy machinery rolling across the weed-infested parking lot, and excavators digging into the ground. And there was Tony Himmel, striding across the site in a pair of blue jeans and a heather gray T-shirt. He looked happy.

At the jail I brought in a clean change of clothes for Grandy. I handed them off to the sergeant on duty and sat down for the final wait.

Grandy emerged nearly a half an hour later, in need of a shave but standing tall as always. I hugged him tight, held on long enough to show him I loved him. He wasn't the mushy type who liked to hear the words.

When I stepped back and looked up at him, I caught him blinking away tears. "How did you get here?" he asked.

I pointed in the general direction of the parking lot. "I brought the Jeep."

He huffed. "You took my car again without asking."

"Yeah, sorry," I said with absolutely no remorse. I took hold of his arm. "C'mon. Let's go."

Halfway to the door, he asked, "Anything else you need to tell me about?"

I thought for a moment. "Yeah, you're out of Devil Dogs." We reached the doorway. "Oh, and one more thing."

"What's that?"

"You need to call Mom."

As I drove down the cobbled main road of Wenwood village, I stuck my hand out the window and waved at Rozelle, sitting on a patio chair in front of the bakery enjoying the sun. I parked the Jeep in front of the vacant shop that used to be Andy Edgers's hardware store and tried to guess who might rent the space next. But I was afraid no matter how deep my cravings, Wenwood just wasn't the sort of town for a sushi restaurant.

I climbed out of the SUV and into the enveloping heat of an early July morning. I squinted across the road but the glare against the luncheonette window prevented me from seeing inside. Nonetheless, I waved, just in case Tom was at the counter gazing out.

After a little effort, I had the fully repaired and protectively bubble-wrapped stained glass lamp out of the back of the vehicle and safe in my arms.

Rather than put the lamp down, I used my elbow to knock on the door of Aggie's Gifts and Antiques. I waited only moments until Carrie pulled the door open.

"Is that it?" she asked. "Is that the lamp? Get in here. Get in."

"Sure, easy for you to say," I said, backing into the shop. "You have no idea how heavy this thing is."

I glanced over my shoulder, making sure I had room to turn around without knocking down some display of very old, very fragile things.

"Just put it right on the counter," Carrie said. "I can't wait to see this."

She rushed ahead of me to the sales wrap counter. Smile splitting her face, she clapped her hands a bit when I set the lamp down.

"Sheesh." I huffed. "You could have helped me carry it."

"Sorry. Sorry. Can I open it? I want to see."

I gave her the go-ahead and assisted in the removal of

the wrappings and bits of cardboard I had used to secure the lamp for transport.

Though the light from the front window didn't reach as far back as the counter, the glass in the lampshade glittered and sparkled with color. Carrie let out an appreciative sigh.

"You did it," she said reverently. "This is . . . amazing."

She moved this way and that, watching the light play on the glass. Coming out from behind the counter to see the other side, she swore she could no longer tell where the damage had been. I could find it with embarrassing accuracy, but Carrie declared the new work flawless. She gushed and complimented and I blushed and pushed her praise aside until finally she stopped and rested her hands on the counter. "Georgia . . ."

Something in her tone, in the solemn look in her eye, made me take a step back and put a hand to my head. "Is it my hair?" I asked. "Again?"

She ignored my paranoia. "How many stained glass pieces do you have?"

Lowering my hand, I pictured the workspace at Grandy's—the few pieces I'd used to brighten the room, the boxes with works still packed. "I dunno." I hadn't left any behind for fear my idiot ex-fiancé would try to sell them at the flea market. "A bunch, I guess."

"What would you think about letting me sell some of them?"

"Sell?" I repeated. Did I look as dumbstruck as I felt?

Carrie waved toward the window. "We're in full-on summer here and the tourist traffic has started. I bet your work would get snapped right up. Antiques hunters come through here all the time and you know there's my online shop, too."

Sell my work. Part of me thought Carrie was crazy. Who would spend money on my little therapy projects? But the other part of me, the confident part that had risen to the challenge of repairing a Tiffany-style lamp, knew it was possible.

"This way," Carrie continued, "you could be making a little money while you look for work here."

I blinked away my momentary fog and gaped at her. "Look for work here?"

"Well, not *here*, here. But somewhere in Pace County. Nothing's really that far away. I mean, that is the plan, isn't it?"

Stay in Wenwood. Find work. Make (more) friends. Put down roots?

I turned to the side and leaned back a tad, enough to see out the shop window. Cobbled road, faded awnings, trees so heavy with summer leaves their branches ought to have brushed the sidewalk. Wenwood was nothing like the city I had left behind, the city that I loved, the city that had spat me out. I'd thought Wenwood was just the place I was raised to return to when life went sour, but maybe that had been a rationalization. Maybe there was a shy piece of my heart that had loved this place all along—this place that never spat me out, and always welcomed me home.

I took a deep breath and faced Carrie. "How many pieces do you want?"

Amateur sleuth and bookstore owner Tricia Miles gets caught up in a local election that turns lethal...

FROM *NEW YORK TIMES* BESTSELLING AUTHOR
LORNA BARRETT

NOT THE KILLING TYPE
➤ A BOOKTOWN MYSTERY ◄

It's November in Stoneham, New Hampshire, and that means it's time for the Chamber of Commerce elections. The race is already a bit heated, as the long-standing Chamber president is being challenged by a former lover—Tricia's own sister, Angelica. Then local small business owner Stan Berry throws his hat in the ring.

Unfortunately, it's not there for long when he's found murdered in the Brookview Inn. The murder weapon is a brass letter opener belonging to the inn's receptionist. Tricia knows there's no way the receptionist is a killer. And when Angelica asks Tricia to help clear her name and win the election, she sees little choice except to start snooping.

She soon uncovers a ballot box full of lies and betrayals, and a chamber full of people who had grudges against the victim. But were they serious enough to lead to murder? Tricia will have to do some serious sleuthing before she pulls the lever on a killer.

INCLUDES RECIPES

facebook.com/LornaBarrett.Author
facebook.com/TheCrimeSceneBooks
penguin.com

M1265T0213

Penguin Group (USA) Online

What will you be reading tomorrow?

Patricia Cornwell, Nora Roberts, Catherine Coulter,
Ken Follett, John Sandford, Clive Cussler,
Tom Clancy, Laurell K. Hamilton, Charlaine Harris,
J. R. Ward, W.E.B. Griffin, William Gibson,
Robin Cook, Brian Jacques, Stephen King,
Dean Koontz, Eric Jerome Dickey, Terry McMillan,
Sue Monk Kidd, Amy Tan, Jayne Ann Krentz,
Daniel Silva, Kate Jacobs...

You'll find them all at
penguin.com

*Read excerpts and newsletters,
find tour schedules and reading group guides,
and enter contests.*

Subscribe to Penguin Group (USA) newsletters
and get an exclusive inside look
at exciting new titles and the authors you love
long before everyone else does.

PENGUIN GROUP (USA)
penguin.com